THE 7TH ASTRONAUT

a novel

Skip Della Maggiore

ARCHWAY
PUBLISHING

Cover Images Courtesy Of Nasa: Chosen by Don Brown
Lawrence Livermore Laboratories References by Permission
Edited By Sandra Farrin and Will Della Maggiore

Archway Publishing books may be ordered through booksellers or by contacting:

Archway Publishing
1663 Liberty Drive
Bloomington, IN 47403
www.archwaypublishing.com
1 (888) 242-5904

ISBN: 978-1-4808-2429-4 (sc)
ISBN: 978-1-4808-2430-0 (e)

Library of Congress Control Number: 2015918337

Print information available on the last page.

Archway Publishing rev. date: 11/19/2015

THE HAPPENINGS PORTRAYED IN THIS
NOVEL COULD NOT HAPPEN,

OR COULD THEY?

THIS BOOK IS DEDICATED TO THE MEN AND
WOMEN OF THE UNITED STATES ARMED FORCES
WHO HAVE FOUGHT IN MEANINGFUL AND
NON- MEANINGFUL WARS. WARS THAT
HAVE MADE AMERICA THE WAY IT IS.

THEY ARE AND WERE ALL HEROES,
NO MATTER WHAT THE WAR.

THIS BOOK IS ESPECIALLY DEDICATED TO THE
MEN AND WOMEN WHOSE PURPOSE IN LIFE IN
THESE TIMES IS TO ROOT OUT, AND FIND THE
ENEMIES AND TERRORISTS THAT ARE AMONG US

Prologue

"**W**atch it! You're going to crash too!" Yelled the exasperated, and frustrated flight instructors. The space shuttle was tilted to the left thirty degrees as it approached the landing. Its wing tip was about to scrape the ground. The instructors looked at each other and cringed. This would be another failed correction and crash. Then suddenly, Falcon fired the left thrusters to full power and pulled the control stick to the right. The shuttle wings leveled out and the shuttle settled to a smooth landing. A two-second delay would have resulted in another crash.

As astronaut James Falcon, and the two flight instructors emerged from the space shuttle flight simulator, the other NASA astronauts, engineers, and scientists who were observing sat in silent astonishment.

NASA Deputy Director Jay Hart stood and addressed the seated group. "Okay," he stated, "Sixteen of you hotshot astronauts crashed the shuttle in this simulated exercise. We have a lot more work to do."

He then looked at two of the astronauts and spoke directly to them. "Irving and Falcon, I am satisfied with your performances today. Out of eighteen astronauts, only you two landed the shuttle simulator without crashing. Tomorrow we will have a sit-down session, and you can tell us all how you managed to land safely despite the flight problems thrown at you by your instructors.

Chapter 1

The Lawrence Livermore National Laboratory is internationally known as one of the major testing facilities for the United States Department of Defense. Because of the caliber of educated personnel and scientists that work there, it has an earned reputation as "the smartest square mile in the world." Its location is in the mountains surrounding Livermore, California. It is approximately twelve miles from the city limits, and forty-five miles east of San Francisco.

At the time the complex was planned and constructed, it was isolated and far from any population centers. Now, the pressure of California's people influx has caused the areas surrounding the complex to endure a population increase requiring the complex to increase its perimeter security. This was the situation the morning of the test.

Test Site 4 was well known to the crew assigned to the early morning test. The test site equaled the square area of four football fields and was fenced in by a ten foot-high cyclone fence. Coiled razor wire covered the top of the fence. At the far end of the test site were three six-story concrete buildings. They had been built several years ago as auxiliary office buildings. The buildings were grey and unpainted, and they were never occupied due to budget cuts by Congress. They were still empty on this particular morning.

At the other end of the test area, opposite from the three concrete buildings, and near the vehicle entrance, was a reinforced concrete control bunker. The bunker itself was fifteen feet long and ten feet wide, and it was dug into the ground eight feet. The walls were two feet thick. The ceiling and roof were also reinforced concrete. The bunker was configured so a six inch wide observation opening ran its full length. The observation opening was one foot above ground level so the entire test area could be seen. This morning there were six men inside the bunker to observe and record the test.

Test Site 4 was chosen because it was two miles from the main laboratory complex. It was connected by a single lane road. A heavy steel gate guarded the entrance to the road. On the gate was the warning sign: *"AUTHORIZED PERSONNEL ONLY BEYOND THIS GATE"* The test site itself was hidden in a small plateau surrounded by small, rough mountains. A thick growth of trees surrounded the test site. The trees were old, fully grown, and a lush part of the forest that covered the entire laboratory property, and ended at the boundaries of the city of Livermore. Test Site 4 was deep inside the depths of the laboratory complex.

The test was classified "Top Secret." A force of one hundred and ninety-eight U.S. Army military police was deployed to patrol the outer perimeter of the test site and the surrounding area. They were fully armed. The patrols started six days in advance of the test. They were continuous, twenty-four hours a day. Their orders were to be sure that no one, and no equipment, were set up to observe the test. The patrols were relieved and removed from the area thirty minutes before the test was scheduled to commence. The secrecy of the test was intact.

Dawn was just breaking when the button was pushed and the weapon fired. Sudden tremendous, and violent explosions erupted immediately, shaking the entire test site.

"Alert Central Security! Tell them to call the fire department and sound the general alarm!" Jeff Hansen, in a panicked voice, yelled at the communications officer when he was able to stand and speak. The blinding flash, and resulting concussion from the explosions that had just occurred, knocked Jeff and the entire crew to the floor of the bunker. The unexpected intense heat from the test firing of the weapon had immediately set the trees and forest surrounding the test site on fire. The fire was burning intensely, spreading rapidly and completely out of control.

Then, as Jeff began to regain his wits and composure, he commanded in a calmer and more authoritative voice, "Tell them if they don't stop this fire now it will threaten the Lab's main complex and burn to downtown Livermore!"

As Jeff took a good look at the test site through the bunker observation slit, he involuntarily lost his breath and gasped at what he saw. "This can't be happening," he said out loud.

Jeff, and the other men in the bunker, saw that the three concrete buildings at the far end of the test site were no more. They existed now as a large heap and pile of fiercely burning rubble. In the middle of the site, where a specially constructed target building had been erected, there was a jagged thirty foot circular hole, with smoke and flames spewing from it. The building no longer existed. Next to the bunker, three trucks with the logo, "Lawrence Livermore Labs" on their doors, were completely enveloped in flames.

"What the hell happened?" Jeff implored of his assistant.

"I don't know for sure," replied his assistant Joseph, as he picked himself up from the floor of the bunker, "We set the range and spread to hit the target building in the middle of the test site. Those other buildings and this bunker were well out of the range of the target building."

"We're lucky those buildings were not occupied. Hell, for that matter we're lucky we didn't burn ourselves up along with those buildings," Jeff stated in a shaking, non commanding tone of voice, "Make sure everyone in here is ok, then have those weapon settings checked and recorded. The way I see it the weapon is at least ten to twenty times more powerful than we calculated. Based on what just happened there is a lot of work to be done on the control and range settings. All the calculations will need to be reworked and refined."

"I agree," added Joseph, "Except, it may be a hundred times more powerful than we first thought. We know the weapon works, now we have to make sure we can control its aim and destructive range. We know for sure it will destroy whatever it's aimed at."

Jeff Hansen began to regret his enthusiastic volunteering to be in charge of testing the potential and readiness of the laser weapon. He looked around the bunker, to assure himself the men picking themselves up from the floor were ok. Then he looked directly at Joseph, "Looks like the senior scientists were right in not wanting to be involved with this project."

Joseph nodded his head in agreement. "The chief scientists took advantage of your eagerness. Now they can say, 'I told you so,' and put the blame for this failure directly on you."

As he observed the destruction and fires in and around Test Site 4, Jeff recalled the final meeting concerning the laser weapon. The meeting had taken place in the administration conference room. He had not given it a second thought when placed in charge of the laser weapon project. Now he remembered the meeting, and that the chief scientist had been adamant in not wanting to be involved with the laser project. The other senior scientists had agreed as the chief scientist spoke his mind about the laser project.

"This project is not feasible," the chief scientist stated, "It will be hard to control and end up being a waste of time and talent. There are other projects pressing that have a better chance of being successful and more useful. I don't want to be involved when this project blows up in our faces and is abandoned."

It hit Jeff like a ton of bricks. The realization suddenly dawned on him that as a junior scientist he was assigned this project because no one else wanted it. His eagerness in volunteering to take this project reflected back to his younger years and his attitude during his entire adult life. He had always given in to his enthusiasm and eagerness in exploring the scientific interests of his world. This enthusiasm resulted in Jeff Hansen receiving many science scholarship awards, culminating in a doctorate of physics upon graduating from two of the nation's elite universities. This same enthusiasm and eagerness were part of the driving force behind Jeff accepting to be in charge of preparing and testing the laser weapon.

"This laser test was from a tower one hundred and fifty feet above the ground," mused Jeff,

"The laser was set at its lowest power setting. What if it was set at its highest power range and fired from 10,000 feet, or 50,000 feet, or from space. The resulting destruction would be unimaginable."

Joseph looked directly at Jeff and stated flatly, "Boss, this weapon will change the world."

"Yes," Jeff replied to his assistant, "That is the same thought Openheimer expressed when he witnessed the first atomic bomb test. But it will take years to perfect the laser weapon's aiming control and its destructive range capability. I have the feeling that this test disaster will end our careers here, and we won't be involved in any further activities at this lab. Maybe it's just as well. We won't be responsible for developing the most powerful weapon ever known to man."

During the months they worked on preparing the laser for its initial test, Jeff and Joseph had come to know each other pretty well. When they were first assigned to the project of using laser technology as a military weapon, both men gave very little thought or discussion to anything that did not pertain to making the weapon work.

Taking a break in one of their late night work sessions, Joseph let out a deep sigh and absentmindedly thought out loud in front of Jeff, "This weapon, if it works, could kill more people at one time than the atomic bombs did at Hiroshima and Nagasaki combined."

This verbal thought momentarily stunned Jeff. He had never until that moment given any thought to the consequences of developing the laser weapon. Now, out of nowhere, Joseph had laid this moral comment in front of him. Immediately in his mind, he saw his pretty wife of eleven years and his two beautiful and innocent young daughters. He thought of the many good human and family times they enjoyed together. What would his daughters think of their father being responsible for a weapon that could destroy families and kill millions of people?

Joseph noticed Jeff's reaction to his remark. He asked Jeff, "What are you thinking boss?"

"You bring up a disturbing thought," Jeff replied, "Here is what I think off the top of my head, without giving the thought the intense study it deserves. Yes, this weapon could kill millions of people. But, sooner or later someone will develop this weapon. It would be better if the United States developed this weapon as opposed to any other nation in the world. Also, I believe that America having this weapon may be the deterrent that saves millions of lives. So, as I said, right off the top of my head, without thinking any deeper, I am content to make this weapon work."

With the end of their conversation that night the moral question of the weapon was never brought up again.

Jeff shook his head as he dismissed these thoughts and brought himself back to the present and the reality of Test Site 4. He watched the fire engines roll in, and the devastation inside and outside of the site. He admitted to himself that he better be prepared, as this test disaster might end his career at the Lab. As Jeff left the area, he and Joseph took a final look at the tower and the laser weapon on it. They watched the first responders start the job of controlling and cleaning up the mess that had been caused by the out of control laser test. He also saw his bosses standing at the entrance to the site. The Directors of the Lawrence Livermore Lab had left their offices and were observing the results of what was supposed to have been a routine test of the new and experimental laser weapon.

Chapter 2

It was the third morning after the disastrous laser test. Jeff and Joseph arrived together at the front of the Lawrence Livermore Laboratories administration building. They both had been summoned to an 8 A. M. meeting. As they walked across the circular driveway towards the front entrance the American flag was being raised. They paused and watched as the flag reached its highest point. Several other people were also watching the flag being raised, including a couple of security guards, who looked away from Jeff and Joseph as if embarrassed to look at two men who were probably seeing their last day of work at the lab.

The meeting was being held in the secure conference room of the administration building. Jeff and Joseph arrived early. As they waited to be called into the meeting the two men spoke softly. Jeff looked at Joseph, hesitated and said, "I'm very sorry that you have to suffer because of my mistake. I should have researched and reviewed the workup of the calculations for the weapon more thoroughly. I obviously missed something."

Joseph looked Jeff directly eye to eye. "I was proud to work for you, no matter what happens. Remember, your team, and myself also signed off on the weapon's readiness. This was the initial testing and not one of us had any indication that its destructive power was so much greater than we calculated."

Jeff tried to finish the conversation. "I was in charge, the complete responsibility for the result is mine alone. I will make sure our bosses know that."

Joseph, however, would not let their little talk end on Jeff's remark, "You are a brilliant scientist and led our team and the laser project from its inception. The test and the result are just a step in the process of the weapon's development."

Jeff did end the conversation with a hard look at Joseph. "Unfortunately, I think this is the end for us at the lab. It will probably put the project on hold until it can be determined how to control its development."

Unknown to Jeff and Joseph, the meeting had commenced at six o'clock that morning. In the meeting were the Director of Lawrence Livermore, Fred Townsend, and his entire administrative staff. The United States Air Force was also represented at the meeting by General Allen Sharp and his staff officers. General Sharp was in over-all command of the laser weapon project. A two hour discussion had taken place. The Director initially wanted to fire the two scientists outright. The discussion, and debate, amongst the Lawrence Livermore staff and the Air Force officers, centered around what would be best for the successful completion of the laser weapon project; to form a new scientific team, with new leaders to take over the project, or keep the existing team leaders.

Half of the Laboratory staff and two Air Force staff officers agreed with the Director, the two scientists should be fired and a new team formed. They argued that a new team could be headed by any number of brilliant scientists already employed at the Lab. The new team could examine what had been done with the weapon so far and continue its development. The assistant director of the lab was adamant in his summation of the weapon development so far. "These two scientists should have been more prudent in preparing the weapon for the test firing. They are responsible for the destruction of site 4 and the millions of dollars wasted on the weapon's development to date."

The remaining Air Force officers and several staff members argued that any new team would have to start over from scratch. This would leave them vulnerable to repeat the same mistakes already displayed at Test Site 4. An Air Force officer summed up their position. "The existing team is headed by two highly educated and knowledgeable scientists. They have accumulated more knowledge about the laser weapon system than anyone else. They would be able to correct the problems and make the weapon operational, in spite of the disastrous failure at Test Site 4."

A Laboratory staff member who wanted to keep the same team leaders added his opinion to the discussion, "The happenings at the test site were not due to negligence or incompetence, but to the unknown real power of the weapon."

At the end of the intense discussion the Director stated, "Well, General, you have heard both opinions concerning the laser development team. It is your decision as to the final make-up of the team."

General Sharp stood and eyed everyone seated at the conference table. His staff officers, who had worked for him through war and peace, knew he was a tough and capable leader. They sat silent and in awe at his demeanor, as did the others seated at the table. They watched him intently as he contemplated his decision.

"Ladies and gentlemen," the General began, "I appreciate the input from each of you. My staff and I have reviewed and are familiar with the history and records of the existing team. My decision is that the existing team will continue to be in charge of the project. This project is high priority to the Air Force and therefore my decision is not made lightly. From this moment on, I am ordering that the project, and the chosen team, be given one-hundred percent backup in doing whatever is necessary to bring this project to success."

The room was quiet as the Director summoned Jeff and Joseph into the room. Jeff and Joseph stood in the doorway feeling the eyes of the room upon them, scrutinizing them.

"Be seated gentlemen," ordered one of the Director's assistants.

Jeff and Joseph seated themselves. A quick glance between them conveyed the anticipated doom that awaited them.

"Gentlemen," the Director began as he stood up from his chair. He did not introduce anyone seated around the table. "I'll be blunt. I was set to fire both of you immediately. However, after conferring with the military and my staff, we have concluded that the test result three days ago at Test Site 4 could not have been anticipated by anyone." The Director paused, looked around the table and stated, "There is limited knowledge of the laser weapon at this point in time." He then looked at General Sharp and seated himself.

General Sharp did not stand. He spoke in a firm and authoritarian tone. "Just to be sure every person involved with this project is clear, I am in command. This lab and the team leaders will keep me informed as to the progress of the project. I will assign a detail of Air Force officers who will record the daily activity of the project and act as my liaison to the project."

General Sharp stopped talking and stood up from his chair. Standing he was over six feet tall. He was muscular and physically fit. His uniform was perfectly tailored, and his decorations were exact in their placement. His authority was evident and unquestionable as he looked directly at Jeff and Joseph and continued.

"The people at this table, and I, have concluded it would be counter-productive to replace you two as the lead scientists in making this weapon operational. There will be no reprimands or any disciplinarian action taken against you."

Jeff and Joseph exchanged a glance, not quite believing what was just said.

General Sharp hesitated just for a moment to insure everyone was paying absolute attention to what he was saying. "You have more first-hand knowledge about the weapon than anyone else. The pentagon wants this weapon ready to deploy in three years. Therefore, you will remain in charge of this project. You will retain the responsibility and authority for this project. You will have the full backing of the Air Force and this laboratory. Anything you need to get this program completed is at your disposal. So, without further bullshit, get out of here and go to work."

As the two scientists left the building they had cause to pause as the American flag was whipping wildly from a strong wind. They both looked at the flag for a moment, and eyed each other. No words were spoken between them as there was no need to speak. Each knew they had been given the chance to prove themselves and each knew the other was silently vowing success at whatever cost.

Chapter 3

The next day Jeff called his scientists, engineers and support personnel to an organizational meeting that was to last the entire day. The Air Force liaison team was also present. Jeff opened the meeting addressing his entire team. "Each of you has been selected or retained on my team because of your ability and commitment to the success of this project. So far in the development of the laser we have failed to control it. Most of you are aware of the disastrous results at Test Site 4. I want to emphasize to each of you that working on this project means long hours of hard work. I will not accept complaining or anything less than the best effort from each of you. This is your chance to resign from the project. Let's take an hour break. Decide if you want to commit to the all-out effort it is going to take for this project. There will be no negative consequences for anyone who resigns."

As the meeting room began to clear Joseph whispered something to Jeff. Jeff immediately called for everyone's attention. "There is one other important matter for you to consider in making a decision to stay, or not stay, with the project. We are going to succeed, and this will be the deadliest weapon ever known to man. If it is ever used, it could kill more people in one strike than the atomic bombs of Hiroshima and Nagasaki. To my way of thinking the world will be safer if the United States has this weapon as opposed to any other country. If you have any qualms or moral issues about helping to build this weapon, don't come back after the break."

For the next hour the luncheon room was filled with the hum of conversations as people discussed and decided their participation in the project. When the hour break was ended over half a dozen people did not return to the meeting.

When the work commenced on the project, Jeff and Joseph worked long hours with only occasional days off. They had been smart in requesting and hiring scientists and technicians who were willing to commit to the long hours and diligent work to bring the weapon project to fruition. They requested and were given the biggest building the lab had to offer. The project was a tightly kept secret. All work was within the confines of the building and on secured Test Site 3. It was on the opposite side of the hill from Test Site 4. Test Site 4 was unusable for secure testing. The fire had destroyed the surrounding forest and trees making it open to observation from surrounding areas.

Toward the end of the third year the work of perfecting the weapon was completed. Jeff and Joseph had it ready to be certified as operational for deployment. It had taken many ground level tests and thousands of adjustments and refinements to reach this point. The final test was to demonstrate the accuracy of the weapon when fired from an aircraft at high altitude. To accomplish this, one of the weapons would have to be transported and mounted on an Aircraft.

Transporting the weapon presented its own serious problem. The weapon had to be transferred from Livermore to Travis Air Force Base in secret, a trip of about fifty miles. Then it had to be mounted onto a B-52 Air Force Bomber, also in secret.

General Sharp himself called Jeff, "I want to emphasize to you the security of this weapon is a serious concern of mine. I believe the secrecy of this weapon is intact. However, it is imperative that this weapon be protected. Use extreme measures to insure its safe arrival at Travis. If this weapon were to be taken, and used by the wrong people, the result would be the worst man caused mass killing in our history. Take no chances!"

Jeff ended up working out the transfer plan himself. He wanted the lowest possible profile for the trip to Travis. The Air Force wanted an armed convoy, consisting of one hundred heavily armed Air Force Security personnel, along with six U.S. Army Apache helicopters flying protective cover directly overhead. Jeff went straight to the commanding general of Travis Air Force Base, and as the person responsible for the entire project, nixed the Air Force plan. He told the General, "What the Air Force wants to do will bring too much attention. We will use my plan. It will both insure the safety of the weapon and cause the least amount of disruption and interest from anyone."

The transfer was accomplished by loading the weapon and its components into two enclosed civilian race car trailers. It was a tight fit. The trailers were towed by heavy duty civilian pickup trucks. A secret trial run timed the trip at one hour and 40 minutes. The real trip started at 2:30 A.M. from Livermore. The security consisted of the California Highway Patrol running the route ahead of the convoy with orders to not allow any semi trucks to be stopped on the side of the freeway, and to disperse any activity that was out of the ordinary. At intervals along the roadway, heavily-armed Air Force Police dressed as Cal-Trans highway workers and deployed as road repair crews. At each five-mile interval, a team of Air Force police with armored vehicles were stationed out of sight, but as close to the freeway as possible. Two U.S. Marine Corps Huey Helicopters, each with 20 Marines, trailed the weapon at two thousand feet, just in case they might be needed. In addition, six U.S. Army Apache Helicopters flew on each side of the freeway, keeping pace with the weapon and staying a half mile from the freeway. The entire force had orders to be prepared to defend the two specially marked trailers they had been given pictures of in the mission briefings. The Air Force officer responsible for the safety of the trailers, and in command of the security reaction force, chose to be in a command helicopter trailing behind the two trailer convoy. Jeff, Joseph, and six heavily armed Lab security officers rode in the pickup trucks towing the enclosed trailers.

Jeff and the Air Force were satisfied and confident that any action against the trailers carrying the laser weapon system would be repelled and crushed by the security reaction force.

As the two pickups and trailers entered the freeway on-ramp to interstate 80 from highway 13, the secrecy and the security of the weapon suddenly became questionable. Jeff, riding in the lead pickup tensed as he saw a large semi-truck and trailer cut in front of the two pickup convoy and begin to slow down. Jeff immediately notified the Air Force security commander, "We may have a problem down here," Jeff reported over the radio net.

"I have already seen the truck pull in front of you," Came the immediate reply from the security commander. "Slow down a little and get some distance between you and the truck, two Apaches are getting into position and will blow that truck away if it makes a move on you!" After a short pause he added, "The marines are moving closer just in case. Two Highway Patrol cruisers are passing you right now to pull the truck over and get it out of your way."

Jeff, and the men in the pickups breathed easier as the semi was pulled over and they passed without incident.

None of the extensive security was needed as the transfer was accomplished without any further problems. The secrecy of the weapon was secure. The Highway patrol, the Air Force Police, the Marines, and the Army helicopter pilots all returned to their bases wondering what the hell that mission was all about. The laser weapon was now safe, and secured, at Travis Air Force Base. The job now was to mount the weapon into a B-52 bomber in order to accomplish its final test.

The Air Force mechanics were curious as they were sworn to secrecy and ordered to make room for and mount a strange looking piece of equipment to the fuselage outer wall. They ended their work by mounting the laser control console on the inside right wall of the fuselage ten feet from the cockpit. The actual barrel or laser firing tube protruded through the fuselage. This required expert work to insure it was attached securely and the aircraft remained "airtight." It took three weeks of intensive re-configuration of the B-52 to install the laser control console and the laser itself. When it was ready, Jeff called General Sharp, "Sir, we're ready to go with the certification test."

"Schedule it immediately, I'll call the commanding general at Travis to put all other operations on hold until you have completed this mission."

It was 4 A.M., Jeff and Joseph were seated next to the laser firing control console as the huge airplane rumbled down the runway and became airborne. It was an approximate two hour "bomb" run to the target. Jeff and Joseph drank coffee, and talked low, as the pilots and flight crew went about their business of putting the aircraft over the target. Jeff was relaxed, confident, but anxious as the huge bomber approached the target area.

As Jeff sat at the control console his mind suddenly flashed back to the disaster at Test Site 4. He recalled the miscalculations and lack of knowledge that allowed it to happen. He shrugged off the thought as he knew this time the weapon was ready to be tested, certified, and deployed. The bugs in the weapon had been conquered. The expense and work the United States Air Force had put into the laser project showed how important this weapon was to them. Jeff was sure he was about to deliver exactly what they wanted.

"Tell the pilot to let us know when we're in range and we'll warm this thing up." Jeff instructed.

"OK," responded Joseph, as he crawled and stuck his head into the cockpit.

The co-pilot saw Joseph and took his ear phones off. Joseph gave him the message to let them know when they were approaching the target area. The co-pilot acknowledged the message and Joseph returned to the laser console. Jeff had already commenced checking the instruments. The two scientists along with the flight crew went down the checklist a second time just to be sure no steps in the firing of the laser were overlooked. Jeff pronounced the laser was ready, "This thing is about to show us some real fireworks!"

The flight crew chief and the airman sat back looking at the laser control console. The crew chief said to Joseph, "The word is this weapon can destroy entire cities, is that true?"

Jeff and Joseph gave each other a severe look. Then Joseph answered the young crew chief harshly, "Son, you have been sworn to secrecy for a reason. I strongly suggest you take your oath seriously concerning what you are about to see today!"

The crew chief stiffened and responded sternly, "No worries sir, we know the seriousness of our oath. We are just excited to be a part of this." That ended any further questions.

On schedule, about two hours into the flight the co-pilot motioned to Joseph, "We're over the target range at 20,000 feet. We have the target buildings on our radar. Fire the laser at your discretion."

Joseph looked at Jeff to be sure he had also heard the co-pilot and then gave the thumbs up
signal and a nervous smile to Jeff. The target was a specially built concrete block building with two foot thick walls and ten stories in height. The building blocks were filled solid with concrete. Several wood buildings had been constructed around the

target building. They were to be untouched by the laser strike. Only the target building was to be struck.

Jeff studied the instruments and scopes on the laser control panel. Suddenly, he exclaimed, "Fire in the hole!"

He then uncovered and hit the laser fire button. In an instant a red beam of light shot from the B-52 bomber. The beam struck the target building about fifty feet from the ground. Air Force and government observers on the ground reported to the B-52 crew that the building disintegrated into a pile of boiling liquid and dust when struck by the laser beam. The surrounding buildings were untouched.

With the aircraft crew congratulating them, Jeff and Joseph shook hands.

"Our work is done," Remarked Jeff.

Both men felt a great relief as they started to relax and enjoy the ride back to the air base. The Air Force had its weapon and the secrecy of it was still intact.

Joseph remarked to Jeff as the B-52 touched down, "I'm looking forward to a long, relaxing vacation."

"Me too, and amen to that!" Replied Jeff.

Chapter 4

It was approximately one month since the laser deployment certification test. The Director of NASA, Terry Walsh, and the Deputy Director, Jay Hart, were walking toward the Oval Office. The President had summoned them.

"I hope he's decided to abandon the laser installation. Our share of the space station budget is over the initial cost estimate as it is," remarked Jay.

The NASA Director responded, "From the first moment I heard there was talk of deploying a

military weapon on the space station I have adamantly opposed it. We have fought hard to keep the laser weapon off the Space Station, almost to the point of crossing the line and defying him. He knows NASA's position is to keep the station one hundred percent civilian. That's probably why he called us in from Houston."

The two NASA Directors greeted the outer office secretary and were immediately escorted into the Oval office. The President of the United States was seated behind his desk. The two men stood before him. An Air Force General was standing in the back of the room. The President looked at the Directors of NASA but did not get up or offer to shake hands. He directed his comments to the two men.

"Terry, Jay, as the Directors of NASA you both serve at my pleasure. I respect your opinion and position to keep the manned space station civilian, and your strong resistance to placing the laser weapon system on it. However, that resistance stops now."

Both Terry and Jay visibly shifted their posture and became more attentive to the President.

The President continued, "As of now you will give your full effort and cooperation to the Air Force in seeing that the laser weapon system is installed secretly into the American section of the manned space station."

Then he addressed the Air Force officer," General Sharp, is there anything you would like to add?"

The General stepped forward and shook hands with Terry and Jay, saying to them, "The Air Force is looking forward to working with NASA on this project. I want to assure you that the main purpose of this weapon is to protect the station from space junk. It can destroy the junk before it can collide with, and damage the station. An additional threat to the station in the future is the potential of attacks by missiles and rockets. The laser will negate this threat as well."

Terry Walsh could not restrain himself. "With all due respect sir," Terry confronted the General, "What about the potential horror if the laser is ever aimed and fired at the Earth?"

The General took Terry Walsh's attitude and question as disrespectful to him and the President. His posture stiffened. He glanced at the President to see if there would be any response. When none came he glared at the two NASA men.

"The only time the laser would ever be fired at the Earth," the General responded sharply, "Would be to protect the United States and the North American continent from an enemy attack, and then only as a last resort. Only the President could order the laser fired at the surface of the

Earth. Now please excuse me I have a meeting to attend."

The General came to attention, saluted the President and departed the Oval office with no further acknowledgement of the two NASA Directors.

The President looked at the two NASA Directors, sighed and said to them, "Look you guys, this weapon will be secure on the space station. It's in outer space, Damn it! The chances of it ever being used against an earth target are infinitesimal. But I believe as does our military leadership, that it's good to have it as a backup for the future. With all the terrorist bullshit going on it may be needed to protect the station from some kind of rocket attack years from now. I hope the next president agrees. If he doesn't, that will be his problem to deal with. Now, that is all gentlemen, go back to work."

With that said the two NASA Directors departed the White House. Unknown to them, the meeting General Sharp had referred to directly concerned the laser weapon system and the International Space Station.

Chapter 5

In the basement of the White House the meeting was just beginning. Paul Macal and Michael Heilman approached the double doors to the meeting room. They showed their ID's and entered the room. They were among the first people to arrive and proceeded to the seats in the back of the room. The room itself was very austere. It was approximately the size of a tennis court. It had a low ceiling with flush light fixtures. The walls were bare and painted non-glossy white. No pictures, no decorations of any kind. The chairs were in military straight rows from one side of the room to the other. There was a walking aisle in the middle of the chairs and on both sides of the room, next to the walls. There was a podium in front facing the chairs. There were no windows and the only way in, and out, were the heavy double doors; guarded by U.S. Marines. A lone American flag stood in one of the front corners.

The security was tight, as it was at the similar meeting held the previous day. Two armed Marines stood on either side of the double doors checking people's identification against the names in the meeting record book. Four additional armed Marines were lined up against the wall. They were armed with M16 rifles, and 45 automatics as side arms.

Several late comers entered the room. There were now about thirty people in the room. An audible click was heard as the

Marines closed the doors from the outside. Paul Macal looked around the room and then at Michael Heilman. He spoke in a low voice, "I hope this meeting isn't as boring as yesterday's. I got real tired of those NASA engineers describing parts of the space station and how they worked. It was like they were begging congress and the budget control guys for money."

Heilman replied in an equally low voice, "The space station is a multi-billion dollar program. Congress and the budget guys wanted to at least hear what their money is buying."

Paul Macal continued, "Yesterday, over a hundred people were in here, reporters, congressmen, federal auditors, and even private citizens. Today there are only military officers and government people with security clearances like ours. Why aren't there any reporters or congressmen here today, what the hell is going on?"

"I see what you're saying," whispered Heilman in response, "But look who is here. There's the Joint Chiefs of Staff of the Army, Navy, Air Force and Marines, and their staffs. The Secretary of Defense is here, and our boss, the National Security Advisor. You're right, what the hell is this all about?"

Suddenly the people seated in the front row stood up. The Vice President of the United States walked to the podium at the front of the room. As he is recognized all the people in the room stand. The Vice President faces the people in the room.

"Please be seated," directed the Vice President. He stood quietly as people seated themselves.

"I won't be but a couple of minutes. I am here at the direct order of the President to announce to this room that he has ordered the secret installation of a laser weapon system into the American module of the manned space station. I will tell you that NASA wanted to keep the space station one hundred percent civilian, so there would be no chance of the weapon ever being fired at the Earth's surface. That debate is over. The weapon system is to be installed. General Sharp, please take it from here."

The Vice President and two suited Secret Service agents left the room. Another audible click was heard as the Marines reclose the doors from the outside.

The Air Force officer identified as General Sharp stands in front of the room. "This is a secure room. Nothing can be heard outside this room. What you are about to hear is top secret. Each of you has the highest security clearance. Do not take any notes and nothing from this meeting is to be recorded. The laser weapon being installed into the American module is capable of pinpoint accuracy to destroy, actually disintegrate any object threatening to collide with the International Space Station. This includes missiles that may be fired at the station in the future. The weapon can cause mass destruction over large areas if aimed and fired at the Earth. It will burn and disintegrate whatever it is aimed at. It will be used, if necessary, to defend the North American continent against any attack, no matter if on the ground or in the air. Our astronauts will be trained to use the laser weapon system. Once fired, there is no defense against this weapon."

The General paused for a full minute to let the room absorb what he just said. Then he continued, "One of the main reasons for this meeting is so those of you who handle the budget and money in your agencies will know why you are being contacted and instructed as to how you will funnel money to the Air Force to pay for this project."

There was absolute silence in the room as people digested what was just said. Paul Macal and Michael Heilman exchanged surprised and excited looks. No one moved, the silence was intense.

A fleeting, vivid thought flashed through Paul's mind. He remembered his visit to the Carlsbad Caverns. When the lights in the depths of caverns were turned off, the silence and darkness were severe and absolute. You could not see your own hands in front of your face. The silence in the room was as intense as the silence and darkness of those caverns. This was serious business. A second thought struck Paul; "These stupid Americans, they have a weapon that could destroy their enemies and they have debated deploying it. If al Qaeda had this weapon or access to it there would be no debate or hesitation in using it."

Michael turns to Paul and whispers lowly, "Abreu will want to know about this right away!"

Paul gives Michael a hard and stern look and orders in a low voice, "Quiet, someone might hear you!"

General Sharp continued from the front of the room. "That is all. This meeting is over. Let me remind you that this information is top secret. If our enemies or even our allies were to find out this weapon is going to exist on the manned space station, there would be hell to pay."

As Paul and Michael hurried from the meeting, Michael blurted to Paul, "We have to get this information to Abreu right away. He'll want to know about this."

"I told you to be quiet! I've warned you many times," Paul retorted, "Your mouth is going to get us in trouble yet. If the wrong person hears you mentioning the meeting we will spend the rest of our lives in an American prison. Anyway, as soon as we get to our apartment we will transmit the information, and don't say that name out loud again! If he ever finds out we were mentioning his name out loud in public, it would cost us our lives!"

Michael insisted on having the last word. "We have worked in the National Security Office for over two years. No one has even a hint of suspicion."

Chapter 6

Paul Macal and Michael Heilman were spies, spies for the world wide terrorist organization known as al Qaeda. They were excited about this piece of information because in their two years working in the National Security office they had not been able to supply any important secret information to al Qaeda. This report of the laser installation onto the manned space station was a chance to redeem themselves. It would gain them a degree of credibility in the eyes of their superiors at al Qaeda.

Michael Heilman was born an American in Kansas City. Al Qaeda had recruited him after he was already working for a government agency in Washington, DC. Al Qaeda recruiters had tracked Michael Heilman and discovered that he was more interested in money than patriotism. They used a pretty woman to get close to him. In a lounge bar late one night she innocently flirted with him. Michael asked her to dance, and that's all it took for him to be seduced by her. After several weeks of constant and heavy dating, the bait invited Michael to her apartment. To his surprise two men were there. Along with the woman the two men carefully explained that they represented al Qaeda and had a proposition to present to him. Michael did not know it but he would disappear forever if he refused their proposition. The al Qaeda men and the woman were fairly sure they had picked the right man, and they were right on. Michael Heilman had jumped at the amount of money they offered and started supplying low level information to them. He then worked his way to an aide position in the National Security Council. He was a home grown spy.

Paul Macal, however, whose real name was Mohamed Akeim had been born and grew up in Homs, Syria. At seventeen years old Paul had found himself with no money and no prospect of earning any. His father had been killed in the war with Israel. This left Paul, or at the time Mohamed Akeim, and his mother, to fend for themselves. His mother became ill and was sick for over two months. Paul cared for her every day and was with her when she took her last breath. After his mother died he had no ties to his home, no family, no food; no money. He was starving more each day, and since he had no money to buy food, he decided to steal it. Paul was very intelligent and planned his robberies carefully. In a slum area around 2 A.M. one night he carefully picked the lock on the back door of a small store. He entered the store, and using a small flashlight in the darkened store, filled his backpack with fresh and dried fruit. Unknown to Paul two men in the alley had watched him pick the lock and enter the store. They were armed with hand guns and confronted Paul when he exited the store. In the very dim light of the alley Paul could see the weapons pointed at his stomach.

In fear for his life Paul blurted out, "Please, don't kill me, I took only food because I'm starving, I took no money!"

"Put the food back where you found it," commanded the bigger of the two men. "Our friend owns this store. We're not going to let you steal from him!"

Paul again picked the lock. He was terrified so it took him several minutes to get the door open. He could make out the two men talking in the alley behind him. He thought he heard low laughter. Paul rushed into the store, and panicking, he threw the food onto the shelves. He excited the door into the alley and vomited in front of the two men. As he was bent over unable to speak, he heard one man laughing quietly as the bigger man spoke, "Maybe I was wrong. We may be the laughing stock of the camp if we take him with us."

The second man just shrugged and stopped his quiet laughter. Then he said to Paul, "We can take you with us, or we can leave you here and our friend who owns the store can deal with you. You look like you could use food and clothes and perhaps a place to stay. If we take you with us though, you cannot be vomiting every time you get scared!"

Both men looked at each other and roared with laughter.

The two men were recruiters for al Qaeda. They had just fed and put their twenty-two young recruits to bed in the secure building next to the store. Their two previous weeks had been spent searching, finding, convincing; and preparing these recruits for the trip to the training camp in Libya. They were having a last cigarette before going to bed. That is when they had spotted Paul breaking into the store. They gave Paul meat and potatoes from the meal they had fed the other recruits, and put him in the building for the night's sleep. With that, Paul ended up in an al Qaeda training camp in the desert of Libya. The two recruiters took Paul and the other twenty-two young men to the camp. This camp was one of the first permanent training camps established by the al Qaeda leader, Usama Bin Ladin. Since it was one of the first organized camps no expense had been spared to make sure it was well equipped and stocked. What al Qaeda needed now was more young men and women to man the camp and start jihad training against the western world, especially America. The store that Paul Macal had chosen to rob that night was a recruiting center for al Qaeda.

Paul was given new clothes, good food, and most of all a place to belong. He liked the activity of the camp. He met and acquired many friends. Paul Macal, then Mohamed Akeim, was well liked both by the young men of the camp and the older teachers.

Paul was not caught up in the hatred of the western world, and America, which was being preached and taught in the classrooms of the camp. He went along with it, but deep down in his feelings he really did not care one way or another. He found the teachers and leaders of the camp well educated and knowledgeable in the subjects they were teaching. Living among the men, and the few women in the camp, he became aware of the reasons people ended up there. The reasons varied from lack of jobs, not enough food, or no home or place to live. Generally, it was just the lack of another place to be and simple unhappiness. It was interesting to Paul that one of the main themes being professed by the teachers in the camp was that America was responsible for the plight which brought people to the camp. When he got to know them he discovered there was a mixture of educated, uneducated, smart, ignorant; and stupid people within the population of the training camp. The uneducated and ignorant ones were encouraged and led by their teachers and became too enthusiastic and stupid about killing westerners and Americans. Even to the point of killing themselves to do so. Paul was receiving an al Qaeda education in the camp, and he still could not explain to himself the ignorance that led people to kill themselves in order to kill others. He concluded that these people who were willing to kill themselves did not really know who or what they hated, or why. Paul also believed the idea that 72 virgins awaiting the suicide bombers in heaven was the epitome of bullshit, and no one ever said what awaited the female suicide bombers.

Paul contemplated the al Qaeda organization. It was clear to him that its goal, realistic or not, was the destruction of America. He found there were different stratas which the members fit into. The ignorant and uneducated would potentially become the suicide bombers. The next level would be al Qaeda's soldiers in its ranks around the world. He also found there was a higher level of students at the camp. These men were being trained to be either leaders of al Qaeda's cells and soldiers, or to become spies, throughout the western world. Paul recognized there were also many very intelligent and well educated individuals in the al Qaeda organization. The one thing al Qaeda members had in common, regardless of their status, was the sincere belief that America was their enemy. Paul had no real feeling for al Qaeda's teachings or goals, and felt no loyalty to them. He made up his mind that he would take advantage of the education in the camp. Then leave the camp and find a good life for himself.

Al Qaeda itself would give Paul the chance for a good life.

Jamal Ayan was the leader of the training camp. Along with several of his seconds in command and many of the instructors, Jamal became aware of Mohamed Aikeim's intelligence and ability to get along with all types of people. Mohamed Aikeim would become Paul Macal.

The al Qaeda leadership was seeking young men to be trained as spies and moles to be placed in the new cells forming in America, and throughout the western world. They had put out a memorandum to all camp leaders that they were to be informed of any potential candidates for this training. Mohamed was suited for this training. He could almost pass as American as he had light skin and light black hair. He was tall, slender, and in good physical shape.

Jamal and several camp instructors summoned Mohamed to the command tent. They informed him of the opportunity to be trained and the potential of living in America. Without a hesitant thought, Mohamed told the leadership he would be willing to try this training. To himself he said, "I could make and live a good life in America. If I get there I can keep a low profile, and as al Qaeda is supplying the money, I know I can do whatever is necessary to placate and even satisfy them."

It took three years before the newly named Paul Macal was ready to be sent to the United States. He arrived with little or no accent. Paul Macal could speak and write English just as if it was his native language. He had a forged student visa and was already set up and enrolled in the University of California at Berkeley. This was courtesy of a group of al Qaeda operatives who had been sent to America years before.

He proved his camp leaders correct in choosing him. He graduated with honors and a degree in government administration. He applied for citizenship during his years at the university. With the recommendation of many of his instructors he became a citizen by the time he graduated. Upon graduation Paul was instructed by his al Qaeda controller to move to Washington DC and get a job at any level of the federal government.

This is where Paul and al Qaeda got lucky. Several newly elected congressmen were looking for and hiring their staff members. Due to his college resume, and recommendations from his professors, Paul was successful at being hired as an aide to a United States Congressman. After two years of successful work in this position, along with his personality and ability to get along with people, he became a trusted congressional aide. During this time the National Security Council was seeking young qualified people to fill its ranks. Paul applied for one of these positions. Through congressional recommendations Paul was hired onto the staff of the National Security Council.

Michael Heilman had been in the council several years before Paul showed up. Michael had proved successful at supplying al Qaeda with low security information. None of this information was substantial enough for al Qaeda to plan or mount attacks either in America or other countries. It was intended, now that Paul was in the same office with Michael, that together they could recognize and transmit useful information to al Qaeda, which could potentially lead to al Qaeda terrorist operations and actions against the United States. Their standing orders were to keep their al Qaeda controller informed of happenings which may be of interest to al Qaeda.

Paul and Michael had been dispatched to the NASA meetings in order to keep the National Security Council informed as to what the meetings were about. When they were leaving the room as the meeting ended, James Harden, the National Security Advisor called them aside.

He addressed the two men, "Go ahead and make a complete report on yesterday's meeting. Incorporate today's meeting into the report but make it so that none of the information from today is mentioned. I didn't know what this meeting consisted of until General Sharp's announcement. The content of today's meeting stays between the three of us. Understood?"

Both Paul and Michael acknowledged their boss's order.

Paul and Michael left the meeting and hustled to their apartment in downtown Washington DC. Once inside Paul told Michael, "Set up the computer. Make sure the encoder is hooked up, I want this message to be completely accurate."

As Michael hooked up the computer and encoder he said boastfully to Paul, "I'd give a month's al Qaeda pay to see the look on Abreu's face when he gets this message!"

Paul admonished Michael, "You are really pissing me off. You're too loose with your tongue my friend. You are going to slip up one time, and then we'll spend the rest of our lives in an American prison. Stop mentioning al Qaeda! We have to be careful, if it's discovered we leaked this information we'd have to leave fast and run for our lives. Every fed and cop in the country would be hunting us."

Paul opens the hidden wall safe and brings out a little black code book. As he sits at the computer and begins to transmit his report he feels a shudder of fear throughout his body. All the previous information and reports were routine compared to this one. For some reason the information about the laser in this report scared him.

Chapter 7

IN THE CITY OF TEHRAN, IRAN

On the top floor of a modern nine story building, a handsome young man was sitting at his desk. It was a large corner office. He was looking out the eight foot high windows at the panoramic view of the city. His name was Abreu. On his desk were reports from al Qaeda cells and spies throughout the world. He had no thought or concern that his security in the building would be threatened. At the entrance to the building was a concrete counter six foot thick. It was designed to withstand any intrusion. The counter was decorated and looked like any business entrance counter. It was manned twenty four hours a day by at least two men. Behind the counter were uzis, heavy machine guns, and anti tank weapons to greet any unwanted intruders. The ground floor was a maze of corridors which led to elevators and stairs connecting the upper floors. The layout was designed to confuse and delay anyone not familiar with floor layout. The entire second floor was a defensive position. Heavy machine guns, grenade launchers and clamor mines lined the wall perimeters. The third floor was a kitchen and restaurant. The fourth floor was a gym with all the modern workout equipment money could buy. On the fifth floor were individual rooms for the 30 guards who lived in the building and stood duty watches to keep the building secure. The guards could come and go as they chose except when on duty. Access into the building was restricted to a dozen office workers and cooks, who worked on the upper floors and were al Qaeda members. The building avoided suspicion because it looked just like the many other buildings near it. The building sign stated it was a private gym for members only. There were enough people coming and going that it seemed a normal business building.

The building was a communication center and control point for al Qaeda. Abreu was in charge of the building and its activities.

He was 30 years old. He was only known as Abreu. His name was given to him after he was found wondering the streets of Tehran as a small child. Recruiters for al Qaeda had been instructed to bring young people, and children such as Abreu, to the training camps in Libya. There, Abreu was given his name and assigned a mentor. This created a comfort zone which allowed him to grow and mature and eventually develop into an al Qaeda leader.

Abreu spent a lot of time looking out the large windows and enjoying his view of Tehran. He reminded himself that he was very satisfied to have his position in al Qaeda. He was frustrated though, because he knew that if he was not stuck in his office, he could do a better job of attacking American targets that was currently being accomplished throughout the world.

He often thought of his years growing up in the training camps. Although called a training camp, it was more like a school. It had athletic fields, training fields, and classrooms where the many young people going through the camp learned the skills necessary to become al Qaeda cell members. Experts and learned people taught in these classrooms. These teachers, and the leaders of the camp had a common theme and goal in mind, and they passed it on to the young people in the camp. That common theme was hatred toward the western world. The goal was the destruction of that world, especially America. The athletic fields were used for physical fitness, and training in the use of many types of weapons. One area separated from the main camp had specific classrooms for teaching the techniques of bomb making. This area was away from the main camp in case accidental explosions occurred. There were very few accidents as the instructors were expert in their teachings. Abreu's training from a young age included this, as well as the indoctrination against the evils of the western world. The decadence of America, and the actions taken by America against the Arab world, were emphasized in every aspect of the training in the camp.

Abreu stood out from the young people being trained in the camp. As Abreu matured through his training, he became well known for his organizational skills and leadership ability. He became friends and known to hundreds of people in the camp who were later dispatched as spies and cell members throughout the world.

During his adolescence he was escorted many times to America. He thought of the conversation that initiated his trips to America. The camp commander, Ramji Salim, asked him in front of a full classroom, "What is your feeling toward America?"

"America is our main enemy. They have proven this by their actions against our world. In my lifetime I want to attack them and find a way to bring them to their knees." Abreu's words drew a rousing response from the class. Ramji nodded his approval. Then he dismissed the class and asked Abreu to remain. Abreu was never to forget the next words spoken to him by the camp commander. "You are going to America my young friend!"

It took several seconds for Abreu to be able to react. "Why?"

"Because you have demonstrated the potential to be a leader in al Qaeda," Ramji responded. "Myself, and your many teachers believe you will be a tremendous asset in the jihad against America. We are sending you there so you learn and become familiar with the ways of your enemy."

By the time he was twenty five years old he had traveled to

and spent an accumulated total of eight years in America, and was fully capable of passing as an American.

The day before he was to leave the camp he received his assignment and a surprise audience with the leader of al Qaeda, Usama bin Ladin himself, and several other al Qaeda leaders.

Bin Ladin spoke directly to Abreu, "Our biggest problem is communication to and from our operatives throughout the world. We also need to establish ways to keep tract of our cell locations and be able to communicate with them when the need arises. We have selected you to be the person in charge of addressing these problems. From what myself, and the other leaders have been told about you, we have every confidence that the jihad will be more effective with you overseeing the co-ordination and communication problem."

Abreu sat for a moment, then demonstrated his confidence and leadership ability. He stood and faced bin Ladin and the other al Qaeda leaders and responded, "With all due respect, I am honored that you chose me to hold this position. However, the only way I will accept this responsibility is if I have the authority to do the job without interference. Also, whenever I see the opportunity to attack America, I will do so without seeking permission."

There was silence among the al Qaeda members. No one had ever spoken so bluntly to Usama bin Ladin. Usama's assistants and the other men did not know how he would react to what they considered a challenge from a very junior member of al Qaeda.

Usama bin Ladin hesitated, taken aback by Abreu's pronouncement. He was silent for several minutes, then spoke, "I agree, you have just shown the reason you were chosen to do this job."

Abreu left the camp as a member of al Qaeda's inner circle, and a trusted operative with world-wide al Qaeda connections. One result of Abreu taking over as the coordinator of al Qaeda information and operations was the nine story building. The building had a security system built-in to protect al Qaeda's information. The security system was contained on the top floors. A self destruct system of explosives and fire bombs was built into the two upper floors. It would be used, and set off from outside the building, should the building ever be overtaken by any anti al Qaeda force. The destruct system, if it ever had to be used, was designed to destroy all information in the upper floors.

As Abreu sat looking out the window he contemplated how much he loved being in the center of al Qaeda. He was single as were his hand- picked guards for the building. As a handsome and fit man he had no trouble satisfying his desire for women and parties. In Tehran the nightlife thrived even though it had to stay under the legal radar. It never occurred to Abreu that while he hated America and the western world he was living their life style.

Abreu's day dreaming and thoughts were interrupted by the computer next to the wall. It buzzed as a message was coming in through on a secure and encoded channel. His contemplations ended as he walked to the computer to read its message.

The message Paul Macal and Michael Heilman sent to Abreu describing the potential of the laser weapon, and its deployment to the space station, was to set in motion a plan that would take years to reach fruition. The plan, if it reached fruition, would threaten the safety and stability of the United States of America, and the North American continent.

Abreu printed out the report. He read it again and studied it for many minutes. He then set the report on his desk and left for the day. He had a dinner date with Sherhri, a beautiful young woman he had known for several months. She was a student at the university. He had been introduced to her by a close friend at a luncheon and liked her immediately. He particularly liked that she presented a challenge to him. She was not the kind of woman he was used to. It took a real effort, but after many phone calls and dates he finally was able to seduce her. They became friends and spent many nights together. They had great sex. But, unknown to Sherhri, Abreu did not allow himself the luxury any emotional involvement. Sherhri had no clue as to Abreu's real occupation. He had led her to believe he was a low level clerk in the local government office. He protected her by being very careful to make sure she never knew his real position. As he enjoyed dinner with his beautiful friend, he could not get the report out of his mind. When he returned to his suite on the sixth floor he was intoxicated, both by the wine consumed at dinner and the woman consumed after dinner. The sex with Sherhri added to his intoxication. Sleep came easy as he turned the lights out and rolled onto his bed.

Suddenly he awakened. He did not know how long he had slept. His head was clear, a tremendous idea formed concerning the report he received that afternoon. He quickly made some notes on the pad next to his bed. The next morning Abreu pulled a secure and encrypted satellite phone from his desk drawer. When the phone on the other end was answered Abreu spoke as calm as he could, "This is Abreu, two of our Washington spies in the White House have reported a significant happening. I think we should meet with the entire council and Usama should be involved."

There was silence on the other end of the phone for several seconds. Then a voice said, "The council is meeting tonight at the compound. Can you make there by tonight? Usama was not planning to be there. He has other matters to attend to. I'll tell him you requested his presence. Are you sure this is important?"

"It is important, I can be there tonight by ten," Abreu replied. Abreu disconnected the call and intently studied the message his two Washington spies had sent. After several minutes he pulled out his directory and looked up a phone number he had not used for a long time. He dialed the number of the training camp in

Libya. It took several minutes to make the connection on the encrypted channel. As he waited he again studied the report.

When the call was answered he spoke in a commanding voice, "Zakar, the twin boys you spoke to me about several months ago, the ones you are preparing for America, keep them in the camp until you hear from me. I hope they are as brilliant and athletic as I have been told."

As soon as Zakar, the camp commander acknowledged Abreu's order the call was disconnected.

Chapter 8

At 7 P.M. that night Abreu and two heavily armed body guards waited in a parking garage several blocks from the al Qaeda building. The guards were assigned to this detail by Abreu. One guard was very tall and large. His name was Sumid. He was known for his fierce loyalty and extreme toughness. The second guard was Abreu's personal assistant, Kallad. At exactly 7:15 P.M. a non- descript light grey limousine rounded the corner and stopped. The three men climbed into the limo. The tough guard, Sumid, sat in the front with the driver, Mahed. Abreu and Kallad sat in the rear seat. Abreu commanded Mahed, "Take us to the compound. Make sure we are not followed."As the limousine turned onto the main street two cars pulled away from their parking places several hundred feet to the rear.

"I think we are being followed by two cars," Mahed said to Abreu, "They are the same cars I reported to your office. They have been following me in this limo off and on for several days now. I did not see them following tonight until just now."

"It's either the CIA or the Israelis," Abreu said, "It's good that we did not get picked up at our building. Lose them before we get out of the city. I don't even want them to know in which direction we are heading!"

The limousine speeded up drastically as Mahed attempted to lose his pursuers. The two cars following speed up to keep pace. The limo makes a last second and sudden turn onto a busy main thoroughfare. The two following cars are able to make the turn. One of them careens onto the sidewalk scattering people and tables in front of a restaurant. Both cars are able to continue following the limo. The limo makes a high speed right turn onto a business street. The two cars are still able to keep pace. Other cars are forced to the sidewalk and several collisions occur.

Sumid, the tough guard in the front seat tells the driver, "I know the next street. Turn right and let me out. I'll stop the cars and kill them all!"

The driver turns right onto the next street and stops. Sumid gets out fast.

As he does he tells the driver, "I'm taking the AK-47!"

Abreu yells at Sumid, "Allah be with you!"

The limo speeds away. Sumid kneels in the street. People sitting at a sidewalk café are stunned, as they don't know what to make of this. A uniformed Iranian soldier sitting at one of the tables recognizes the AK-47 and realizes some kind of gun battle is about to take place. He grabs the woman sitting at his table and runs into the café. Several other people see this and follow the soldier.

As the two cars turn the corner Sumid opens fire on them. The men in the first car are caught by surprise. They are hit by the powerful gunfire from the AK-47. As they die their violent death, the car careens into the sidewalk cafe. The people still sitting on the sidewalk, who did not react as the soldier did, die a violent death along with them. The men in the second car see what is happening, and before Sumid can react they run into and over Sumid. As Sumid is killed he fires the rifle as his last conscious act, spraying the car with gun fire. The second car crashes into the side of the next building and bursts into flames.

Mahed stopped to be sure he would not continue to be followed. He witnesses Sumid's action through his mirror and reports to Abreu, "Both cars are destroyed, Sumid is dead, we're in the clear. Sumid died as tough as he lived."

Abreu looked out the back window of the limousine, "Sumid will be missed, he was a great soldier for al Qaeda. He taught our young men how to fight and set an example for them to follow. May Allah take care of him."

Mahed cruises the limousine through a dozen city streets to assure they are not being followed. Once certain no one else is following them, Abreu tells Mahed to proceed out of the city, and head for the compound. Fifty miles later on a dark desert road the limousine enters through the gates of a large compound. The gates close quickly. The compound is ten acres, and has a perimeter wall eight feet high completely enclosing the compound. There are many heavily armed guards on the grounds of the compound and stationed at guard posts spaced along the walls. The contents of the compound are secret and secure. It is surrounded by flat desert. The only vegetation is an age old natural stand of trees and bushes across the road from the gates of the compound. The trees and bushes are the remains of an oasis, of which, the old people of the area say dates back a thousand years. The people responsible for the security of the compound attempted to have the bushes cut down many times. The effort was abandoned because the bushes grew back as fast as they were cut down. This was the only spot for miles in all directions that supported any vegetation. The area of the trees and bushes was approximately five hundred feet long and fifty feet wide. The residents of the compound figure the spring that feeds their well is connected to the 'oasis' across the road.

The limo stops in the middle of the parking area. Abreu exits and is immediately confronted by a burly, bearded man wearing a turban and a dirty white robe. He is carrying an AK-47.

"Are you sure you were not followed, Abreu?" The bearded man said roughly.

"We were not followed, I'm sure of it," Replied Abreu, "We

had some trouble leaving the city. Two cars tried to follow us, but Sumid took care of it. It cost him his life."

The announcement of Sumid's death brought a dumfounded look of surprise from the burly man. He gasped, "What! Sumid is dead?"

"Yes," replied Abreu.

"He was one of our best teachers and fighters. I hope your coming here tonight was worth it!"

With that said the burly guard rushed off, announcing the death of Sumid to his fellow guards throughout the compound.

"I hope there are no repercussions because of Sumid's death," Said Abreu's assistant Kallad.

"There will be no problem," Abreu responded, "I was in command of Sumid, he did what was necessary. Now, order Mahed to destroy the limo right away when we return toTehran. Tell him to get another car and change the location where he lives and stores it. That, along with Sumid's actions today, will send a message to whoever is trying to follow Mahed."

An old two story house stands in the middle of the compound. Abreu is escorted through a rear door and into a large dimly lit room. There are rugs hanging on three walls and several pictures, including one of Usama Bin Ladin on the fourth wall.

There were twelve men seated on pillows on the floor. They were in a semi circle around several low tables. One of the men stood and addressed Abreu.

"This had better be important Abreu. Especially since our leader accepted your last minute invitation and is here at your request."

Abreu sees Usama Bin Ladin dressed in a white robe and turban. He bows to him and says, "I am honored that you have blessed us with your presence."

Usama acknowledges Abreu's show of respect, "I have known you since you were a young boy. You have served us well.

Communications with our cells and spy networks have never been better since you took charge. I have confidence in you. That is why I chose to be here. What have you brought us?"

Abreu proceeds by giving the group the information of the report. "Two of our Washington operatives have reported that the United States is secretly installing a laser weapon system in the American module of manned space station."

The same man that addressed Abreu before interrupts him now, "This is interesting, but this information could have been transmitted through regular channels. Why come to our meeting and ask our leader to be here?"

"I wanted to deliver this personally," responded Abreu, "Among its capabilities this weapon can deliver mass destruction to any surface on Earth. A most important point is that there is no defense against this weapon." Abreu hesitated, took a deep breath and continued. "I have a proposal for your consideration."

Usama Bin Ladin peers at Abreu and says, "What kind of proposal?"

Abreu responds, "Allow me a free hand in finding a way to use this weapon against America. I will need a considerable amount of money and authority over several al Qaeda cells for this plan. It will take years, perhaps many years, but if this plan I am proposing succeeds it would do great harm to America."

Usama interjects, "What is this plan?"

Abreu faces Usama Bin Ladin and replies, "Get one of our men into NASA as an astronaut. Get him on the space station. From there he can use the laser to attack and devastate large land masses in America, destroying whole cities and potentially killing millions of Americans."

The men in the room react to what Abreu just said. They all start talking loudly and excitedly among themselves. Usama holds up his hands. The men quiet except for Mamou Satim, second in command of al Qaeda, and the one man who addressed Abreu previously.

"This plan is a hallucination and ridiculous. It could never succeed!" He exclaims.

The room again erupts in an uproar of voices from the council members. Usama holds up his hands and the room quiets in several minutes. He studies Abreu then addresses the room.

"This goes way beyond the several other plans we have been formulating. The chance of it succeeding does seem slim. However, if Abreu's plan were to succeed America would never recover. It would be a death blow. We must confer on this as it is a major decision for our cause and jihad against America. Abreu, wait outside while the council confers on your proposal."

Abreu musters his courage to have a final word promoting his plan, "My plan is brash and bold, and it will require time, exact planning; and cunning. However, if it does succeed, and with the right leadership it has a chance; all other al Qaeda acts of jihad will be as mosquito bites compared to the resulting carnage of this plan."

All eyes were on Abreu as he retreats outside to the compound parking area. Mahed and his assistant Kallad, were smoking next to the limousine. Other drivers were milling around their cars. The many armed guards looked intent as they continued their patrols of the compound. It was very late and very dark. As he stood in the darkness with these men he began to have doubts about proposing his idea to the council. Most of the council members were of the same caliber as the guards walking around the compound. They were ignorant, and probably could not understand, or deal with the fact that results from the plan would not be seen for years to come. They would probably zero in on the fact that the success of the plan was dubious and would reject it outright. Abreu admitted to himself that the plan seemed dubious at this point. The details were not even worked out yet. But, he believed the plan was worth the try. Abreu decided he needed a cigarette and gestured to his driver who lit one for him.

Inside the house a debate is raging amongst the council members. Momou Satim, the council member who referred to the plan as a hallucination speaks loudly, "We cannot commit unlimited funds to a plan that is questionable at the least. No plan that is to take years to complete can be kept secret for that amount of time. This plan is doomed from the start. There would simply be too many details involved to get one of our men into NASA. any one of these details, either not accurate or discovered as false, would cause failure to this scheme."

A second council member stands and adds his opposition to the plan. "The American security agencies involved would surely uncover this plan. It would be a waste of a lot of money and threaten imbedded cells and many human resources. We should concentrate on the attacks and plans we have in process, and not engage a long range plan of doubtful result."

One of the youngest member of the council, and the member in charge of al Qaeda money operations, Ahmed uban Ali, voices his take on the proposal, "We should not be short sighted on this. In our history, and our training, we know the Americans think in terms of years. We think in terms of hundreds of years. Our ultimate goal is the downfall of America. If the weapon involved in this plan can kill thousands, and perhaps millions of Americans in a single attack, it should not matter that the plan is long term. I have confidence that Abreu would be able to control the plan and maintain its secrecy. If it does succeed it would be our greatest victory yet. I urge that we back this plan with whatever money and assets are needed."

Usama ended the debate, "The money and assets are readily available. There is plenty of both. It won't hurt our cause if Abreu's idea does end in failure. If it does succeed, however, America will be finished. We will give this plan a chance, as it can always be stopped if it starts to fail."

Abreu is on his third cigarette. He stomps it out on the ground when a house servant summons him to return to the meeting. As Abreu enters the room all the men are standing and talking amongst themselves. Usama Bin Ladin turns and faces Abreu,

"The council has reached a decision on your proposal. It was not a unanimous decision. I made the final determination. We believe that the potential result of your plan makes it worth the try. You will have authority over any al Qaeda cells you need and access to funds needed for this project. I don't want to be moving money back and forth, as it is too hard to keep secret. So, as we speak ten million dollars is being transferred to your account on a one time basis from many different sources. If you need more in the future it will be available to you. I trust you Abreu. I have confidence that under your guidance the plan has its best chance for success."

Mamou Satim speaks his mind to Usama, "If we are to do this, no one outside this room who knows about, or takes part in the plan, can be left alive once they are no longer needed. If they are ever captured and interrogated the effort and money for this project will have been a waste. Abreu says his plan will take years. We cannot take the chance, that anyone with knowledge of any part of the plan, will be able to keep it secret for that long of a time period."

"I agree," adds Usama, "Abreu, make it so. Protect the secrecy of your plan. Anyone who is aware of your plan and is no longer needed for its success is to be eliminated. Put nothing in writing. You will report to me personally by secret courier as the plan progresses. I will keep the council members informed as necessary."

All the cars departed the compound in different directions as the leaders of al Qaeda headed back to their domains. As he left the compound Mahed was warned to take different routes back to the city so his trip from the compound could not be tracked

Chapter 9

Abreu took a couple of days to think about the overall plan. Once he had the basic plan outlined in his mind, he made a call to Zakar at the al Qaeda camp in Libya. "I will be in your camp in three days. I want to interview the twin brothers we discussed in our last phone conversation. We will be flying in, so don't shoot us down."

Three days later Abreu observed the camp as the plane approached for landing. He saw it had grown since he had been there years before. Many large tents made up the perimeter. A rifle range was located outside the camp. People were firing rifles. Instructors were working with these people. There were camp fires with people cooking. An athletic field was located in the center of the camp. A soccer match was being played. There was a water well in a rocky area between two of the perimeter tents. Heavily armed guards patrolled the perimeter and manned the main entrance. The plane landed on the dirt airstrip adjacent to the camp. Abreu exited the plane wearing slacks and a long sleeve business shirt. He had brought his suitcase for what he planned as a three day stay.

He was greeted by the camp commander Zakar, who was wearing a grey robe and turban. The two men walked to the command tent to talk. Abreu started the conversation,

"I want to speak with the twin boys right away. With your

assistance I can complete my work here in three days. I have summoned thirty men here. As they arrive please arrange tents for them and provide each of them their choice of weapons from your arsenal. If I choose the twin boys for this project, they will remain here and insure the safety of the twins."

"I will arrange this right away" replies Zakar, as he looks outside the tent, "Both 'James' and 'John' are playing in the soccer match. We have a tent set up for you. Why don't you get settled.

I'll have the twins report to you in the large dining tent at 5 P. M."

"OK," replied Abreu, "And set up a meeting with your teaching staff for tomorrow evening in your command tent."

At five o'clock Abreu was sitting at a corner table secluded from the rest of the room. Zakar appeared at the door with two handsome and physically fit young men. He pointed to Abreu. The two came to the table and Abreu gestured for them to sit. Abreu did not waste time with small talk. He looked directly at both of them.

"I do not have the luxury of an abundance of time to speak to you. I have heard a lot of good things about you. You both fit the criteria for a long term al Qaeda operation I'm involved with. I am here to offer you an opportunity. I know who you are and that you are studying to go to America to set up cells for al Qaeda. What if I told you I want you to attend college in America in the open, then have the chance to do great harm to America and potentially kill millions of Americans, what would you say?"

'James' looked at his brother, who just shrugged his shoulders.

'James' turned to Abreu, "It sounds challenging, and exciting. But who are you anyway?

Abreu responds to 'James' question, "I am the man with the power to make happen what I just described to you. Of course it will take time and hard work on your part. Are you interested?"

"It sounds more exciting than recruiting and setting up cells.

If we do enough damage and kill a lot of Americans will we be famous in our world?" Asks 'James.'

Abreu smiles and answers, "If the plan you are to be involved in comes to fruition you will be famous beyond your dreams."

'James' speaks first, "Well, we joined al Qaeda for jihad against America. It sounds like we could do more good for our cause by being involved this plan, whatever it is, than by recruiting and setting up cells."

'John' retorts, "Kill Americans, ok, let's do it!"

Abreu acknowledges the twins acceptance, "You two are the basic part of the plan, I hope your enthusiasm is real, you'll need it."

The twins look intently at each other acknowledging silently they agree on their decision.

"Wait until we tell our parents. They will be proud," exclaims James.

Abreu admonishes both boys, "This is a secret operation you are to be involved in. It is going to take time. You will learn details of the plan as it moves along. Meanwhile, keep this arrangement to yourselves. Tell no one. And, I mean no one! Not even your parents. Study and continue to work hard in your preparation to go to America. Your hard work will be the foundation for the success of our mission. Your instructors will continue to prepare you for assimilation into American life."

Abreu told the boys he would talk to them more in the next couple of days. The twin brothers left the tent talking excitedly to each other.

The next evening in the command tent the fifteen full time instructors and the twenty part time teachers are gathered. Zakar, as their commander sits at his desk. On the wall behind him hangs a picture of Usama Bin Ladin.

Zakar addresses his teachers, "I cannot tell you the reasons behind the extra emphasis to be placed on the training of 'James' and 'John.' I don't know the reasons myself. I do know that 'James' and 'John' are brilliant young men. Our orders are to spend whatever time and training necessary to get them ready to acclimate into American society as soon as possible. These orders are authorized by Usama Bin Ladin himself. You all know Abreu. He has something to add."

Abreu stands before the group.

"From this time on the twins' names are James Henry Falcon and John William Falcon. Their real names are never to be used again. The emphasis on their studies is to be physics, space science, American history and culture, and rocket science. When they go to America to attend the universities, they are to have already achieved a strong education in these subjects, and any others necessary to back up the knowledge of these subjects. I'll let the setting up and organizing of the curriculum to you. These two young men look American, let's make them think and act American, and give them the education to back it up."

Abreu leaves the teachers meeting and walks to a dimly lighted area at the rear of the camp. He walks up to a group of armed men. They have light machine guns or AK-47's slung over their shoulders. Each one has a pistol strapped to his hip. The men are mostly clean shaven and most could pass for American. Some are American. Each has his suitcase bulging with packed belongings. In their tents they will discover new clothes for each of them. To a man they are well built, physically fit, extremely tough; and well trained.

Abreu calls the group together and begins talking, "I have hand -picked each one of you from the volunteer list. The assignment you volunteered for will be a long term assignment. It will last for two years. At that time you will be relieved and a new group of guards will replace you. This assignment is authorized by al Qaeda and Usama Bin Ladin himself. When you are relieved in two years you will either return to your cells or be re-assigned.

You have your orders. You have been briefed and introduced to the twin boys you are to protect. Starting now break into your teams and insure the safety and well being of these twin boys twenty four hours a day. As members of al Qaeda you have been paid well. I am tripling your al Qaeda pay as of right now. As an added bonus for being selected, and to give you added incentive on this job, you will be given adequate time off from the duty roster from time to time. Good luck. Now report to duty, and rest assured, your work is important to our jihad against America. In addition to serving our cause, when this assignment is over, each of you will have gained a good sum of money.

The group breaks up and Abreu walks over to a man standing by himself in the shadows. Abreu greets him, "Abib, it is good to see you again."

"Hello to you, Abreu," replies Abib, "It has been a long time. I got orders from your office to meet you here for face to face instructions. Why have you called me to ugly piece of desert?"

Abreu answers Abib, "I have a special and very important mission for you. I wanted you to know it was coming so you would keep yourself available to me and not commit to any other assignments. Consider yourself on vacation. If anyone requests your services tell them you are already committed and unavailable. I can't tell you any details now, but be ready to move when I call you. It may take a couple of months or more before I will be ready for you."

Abib acknowledged his instructions. "I'll be waiting, you know where to find me,"

Abreu met with the twin boys over the next two days. The meetings were intense as Abreu wanted to be sure the boys knew they were committing to a long term assignment. "Now that you have had the time to think about this assignment, I want your word that you understand it will take years to reach conclusion. You cannot know the details at this time, but your commitment to the time and hard work must be one hundred percent. Anything else will lead to failure."

"We don't intend to fail. All our lives we have studied and believed the Koran. There are people in the world who are our enemies. America is among them, and is the greatest threat to our world, especially because of their culture and decadence. The opportunity you have presented to us is a great honor, and we have already decided that we will do whatever it takes to be successful. The thought of someday killing Americans, and then being famous for doing it, is very exciting."

Abreu smiled inwardly. He had made a good choice. He dismissed the boys telling them, "I will be checking on your progress and preparation."

Now that the twin boys were in the plan, and their protection and training were set up, Abreu was ready move ahead.

Chapter 10

The next step of the plan called for forged birth certificates, and forged official hospital documents, to be placed in the permanent records of a small town in the United States. After several weeks of study Abreu's assistant, Kallad, recommended a town in the state of Nevada. Several other members of Abreu's staff that assisted Kallad, concurred with the recommendation. They had lived in the United States and were aware of Nevada's relatively isolated desert region. Abreu reviewed the reasons for this recommendation. The town was in a rural area of America and isolated. It was the administrative center for the surrounding county. It would be the town where the birth certificates, and other pertinent documents would be stored. Its population was large enough so that the fraudulent documents placed correctly in the permanent records would not be recognized or questioned.

Elko, Nevada was the chosen town. Abreu and his staff agreed that the small city of Elko was an easy mark in which to plant the forged documents. If anyone ever checked, the documents would prove James and John Falcon were born in Elko and therefore American citizens. This would fulfill one requirement of the plan.

Abreu insisted that the forged birth certificates and hospital documents be accurate and identical in every detail to the other official documents. He confided to his staff that every detail was critical to the current operation. His staff was not aware of the real operation. Abreu protected his staff from that knowledge so they would not have to be eliminated.

To accomplish the task of securing actual birth certificates, and official hospital documents, Abreu dispatched two members of a New York cell to Elko, Nevada. Their orders were to obtain original birth certificates and hospital documents used in the Elko Community Hospital. Then bring them to New York so an al Qaeda printer could copy the format exactly and add the names of James Henry Falcon and John William Falcon. They were to accomplish this so no one would ever know it had been done.

The two men chosen for this task were Daniel Conklin, a school teacher, and Larry Roth, a bar tender. They were members of a New York sleeper cell. These were not their real names. These were names they assumed when they came to the United States as al Qaeda operatives several years previous. They looked and behaved as ordinary citizens, so they blended in and were able to remain unnoticed when they arrived in Elko.

The school teacher was the leader of his cell. He was the only college educated member. He made sure his six cell members went about their every-day lives and jobs and did not draw any unwanted attention to themselves. The cell's operating orders were for each member to have ordinary jobs and abide by all laws. Their orders also told them to be ready to carry out assignments and attacks at any time. So far, the cell had carried out assignments from al Qaeda which included assassinations of political leaders outside the United States, and bombings of churches and government buildings in the New York area. Daniel had planned and orchestrated his cell's actions but was never directly involved in carrying out the cell's assignments. Larry Roth, the bar tender, led the other cell members in carrying out and accomplishing the missions.

To accomplish their mission in secret the two men were given enough money to buy, equip, and stock a small motor home. They stocked it with enough food and supplies so they had to do only limited shopping during their stay in Elko. They drove from New York to Elko. When the mission was completed they were to drive the return trip. They spent almost a month to accomplish the mission. The motor home was parked at differing locations so no record of their presence in Elko was ever recorded. Only cash was used for necessary purchases.

Upon their arrival they began surveillance of the Elko Community Hospital. The plan was to find a person who worked at the hospital and had access to birth certificates, and the other pertinent documents al Qaeda needed. They would offer this person $50,000 dollars for two blank birth certificates and the other State of Nevada documents required as backup to the birth certificates. They had a list of the necessary documents and the person would have to get an original of each. They had the $50,000 to show the person they chose. Anyone who refused the offer was to immediately disappear in the desert never to be found. The person who accepted the offer was also to disappear in the desert after turning over the correct documents. These were the operational orders Daniel Conklin and Larry Roth were to abide by. The school teacher was hesitant as he never killed anyone. The bar tender had killed before, so he had no qualms about carrying out these instructions.

One of the people they took an interest in was an attractive middle-aged woman. She entered the hospital at eight o'clock in the morning each work day and left at five o'clock. She wore no wedding ring. She stopped at the same restaurant and lounge each day after work. There she had a cocktail and dinner before going home to her apartment. She was a little overweight but her graying hair and her appearance were very neat. She was a quiet person and kept to herself when she visited the lounge. It took the bar tender, Larry Roth, a couple of days to strike up a conversation with her. Her name was Elizabeth Gonzales She was 42 years old and a widow.

Elizabeth was shy at first and spoke very little to Larry. As Larry spoke to her and was friendly she related to him some details about herself. Her husband had died of cancer two years ago. His illness had wiped out their bank account. She had worked in the hospital since his death. Larry learned this after cocktails each day for a week, and eventually several dinners. Larry was careful to keep a low profile and not make any acquaintances so his presence at the restaurant would not be recalled by employees and patrons. He went into the restaurant only when necessary.

Elizabeth was thrilled to have a man such as Larry take what she thought was a genuine interest in her. After a couple of weeks of seeing him almost every evening she invited him into her apartment after a dinner date. He spent the night with her. Elizabeth was thrilled, as she had not felt this good in the two years since her husband had died. She said to Larry, "I like you, you're a good friend, you've made me feel alive again." She opened up to him and talked about herself for much of the night. Larry listened attentively, so he could use the information later, when enticing Elizabeth to steal the birth certificates and accompanying documents for him.

She told Larry she was very lonely. She had a daughter and two granddaughters in San Francisco that she missed dearly. Her goal was to save enough money so she could move to San Francisco and be close them. Her son-in-law was building a small cottage on their property for her to live in. She told Larry she thought she had another year before she could move from Elko.

Larry informed Daniel of what Elizabeth had confided in him. They agreed to approach Elizabeth with the $50,000 dollar enticement to steal the documents they wanted.

Elizabeth Gonzales was stunned when Larry presented his proposal to her. He showed her the $50,000.00 in cash, it was in a briefcase. This was during a dinner date, the date was late in the evening on purpose and Daniel sat at a nearby table. Daniel was there in case Elizabeth refused the offer and had to be taken to the desert after dinner. Or, if she made a scene, she would have to be "escorted" from the restaurant.

After one or perhaps two minutes of not being able to speak, Elizabeth blurted out in a whisper, "Where did you get all that? I have never seen that much money!"

"I have developed some real feelings for you Elizabeth," Larry said softly, even though the truth was Larry had no feelings one way or the other for her. He continued, "I wanted to give you the opportunity to earn this money, before I asked anyone else. It's all yours if you do what I ask. You can use the money to move to San Francisco and be close to your daughter and granddaughters. I can come and visit you there and we can see the sights of the city together."

Hoping he had made a successful choice Larry continued his gentle urging, "Are you able to do what I ask, and are you willing to do it? No one will ever know about this, and you will have fifty-thousand dollars. You can get out of Elko and move to San Francisco to be with your daughter and granddaughters."

Larry looked around to be sure no one could hear their conversation and also to assure himself that Daniel was nearby in case he was needed.

Elizabeth had tears in her eyes, "You are asking me to steal from the hospital. I've never done anything like this before, what if I get caught?" she implored.

Larry looked at her with as comforting of an expression as he could muster, "So you're telling me, that in your job at the hospital, you have access to these documents and could obtain them?"

Larry chose his words carefully using "obtain" instead of "steal" so as to make the task seem less menacing to her.

"Yes. I would be able to get what you are asking for easily,"

Elizabeth said blandly, still stunned by the money she had been shown and the proposal Larry had made to her. She was visibly shaken and almost sobbing.

"Good," replied Larry, "Listen, if you happen to get caught and anyone accuses you of stealing certificates and state documents from the hospital we will find a way to explain it and use the money to defend you. You have never done anything wrong before and this would be your first offense, the risk is minimal and the reward is more than worth the risk."

Then Larry made a mistake but it went unnoticed by Elizabeth.

"Your American courts are stupid and allow first offenders very little punishment." He caught himself and turned the conversation back to the money. "The fifty-thousand dollars is yours as soon as you hand me the papers I have asked for. It is a simple business transaction. No one will be hurt and no one will ever be the wiser."

Larry gently urged her on, "What do you say, will you do it?"

Larry could see the wheels turning in Elizabeth's head. He decided to keep quiet and let her decide. Little did she know that no matter what her decision, she would not live to see the fifty- thousand. Larry chanced a look at Daniel and received a reassuring nod in return. Elizabeth took the last sip of wine from the bottle they had been drinking from, sighed heavily and leaned close to Larry.

"I need the money," she whispered. "It will get me out of here. I can get what you want fairly easily. If you assure me no one will be hurt, I'll do it."

On the fourth day after making the deal, Elizabeth told Larry she had all the documents he had asked for in her shoulder bag. She explained that it took her that long because she was careful and waited until her fellow workers were gone each day. She then took the keys from the supervisor's desk and opened the necessary storage cabinets. She grabbed the birth certificates and state documents and stuffed them in her bag. She then adjusted the records so no one would know anything had been taken.

They had been having a cocktail at the Elko Café and Lounge. Larry told her to come with him as he wanted to inspect the papers. He told her after making sure she had all the required documents he would hand over the money.

He said gently, "No one will ever know what has taken place."

Larry led her into the motor home and closed the door behind them. Elizabeth was startled to see a second man there. She relaxed a little as Larry introduced Daniel as his assistant. Larry and Daniel scrutinized the half dozen documents and accompanying papers.

"I trust you Elizabeth" stated Larry, "I have just two simple questions to complete our deal and transaction. Are you sure this is all the documentation needed to record a birth in your hospital?"

"Yes, there are no other forms necessary." Elizabeth responded confidently.

Larry smiled and looked at her, "Have you told or will you ever tell anyone of your actions?"

Elizabeth's last words were that she was leaving Elko and had told no one about Larry or the deal they had made.

She tried to scream as Larry plunged the butcher knife into her chest, but Daniel, from behind her, had already covered her mouth with such force that no sound escaped as she took her last breath. Daniel was shaking but he had done what Larry had ordered him to do in covering her mouth. The two men stopped the bleeding so blood would not get all over the floor of the motor home. They placed Elizabeth's body on the floor in the rear of the motor home and left Elko heading home to New York City.

Larry drove out of town while Daniel secured the documents in plastic covers and placed them in a manila folder.

Daniel looked at Larry stating, "I have pledged my life to al

Qaeda in the jihad against America. I never thought it would mean I would have to kill an individual on a face to face basis, especially a woman. I am feeling sick to my stomach. I'm not sure my faith is strong enough for this type of assignment. How can you do it and seem so uncaring?"

Larry gave Daniel a cursory glance and said, "You have been in America too long my friend. I think of our people that the Americans have slaughtered all over the world. It really pisses me off. So if I kill one American at a time, or my efforts help to kill thousands, so be it. This is jihad."

Larry had the route mapped out. He had been told by Abreu there would be no problem in disposing of a body in the Nevada desert, as there were vast areas completely void of people. About two in the morning Larry pulled off Interstate highway 80 onto a dirt road and drove several miles into the dark desert. They carried Elizabeth, along with two shovels and a pick, several hundred feet off the dirt road. It took two hours to dig her grave and bury her. It took another twenty minutes to erase the evidence as best they could of a hole having been dug.

Elizabeth's daughter and granddaughters would never know what happened to Elizabeth, or the part she played in the al Qaeda plot for the jihad against America.

Larry and Daniel completed their trip back to New York. Upon their arrival, Larry, per his previous instructions called a phone number in New York where Abreu was waiting.

"We have all the documents and the fifty-thousand dollars," reported Larry to Abreu.

Abreu replied with his instructions, "Meet me with the motor home, the papers, and the money tonight. 4:30 A.M. in the dock area under the 59th Street Bridge, East River side."

It was still completely dark at 4:30 in the morning as sunrise wasn't for another two hours. The motor home was parked next to the dock when Abreu knocked quietly on the door. Larry opened the door and stepped out right away.

"You have the documents and the money?" Abreu said without any pleasantries.

"Yes," Larry replied. "They are all here as you instructed. Here is the money." As Larry handed the papers and money to Abreu six armed men appeared. Abreu backed away from the motor home. Larry, realizing what was happening tried to run into the darkness. Two .45 caliber slugs hit him in the back. Ha had no chance of escape. Daniel was in the motor home. As he observed what had occurred with Larry he tried to close the door. His move was too late, and futile. A bullet hit him in the chest. He died wondering where his and Larry's loyalty to al Qaeda fit into this scenario.

Abreu departed the dock area in the back seat of a black sedan. The motor home, with Larry and Daniel in it, was driven onto a barge and immediately towed out to sea. Larry, Daniel and the motor home were dumped into the ocean where it was seven hundred feet deep. The six gunmen and the tug boat crew did not know the reason for this as they were just following their orders from Abreu. This was the initial stage of the plan. Abreu was protecting the secrecy of the entire plan.

Chapter 11

Abreu and an attorney, who was a member of al Qaeda, checked the documents and determined they were the correct papers needed to confirm the births had taken place in Nevada. Now Abreu had to check his resources to find a printer who could make the birth certificates and the accompanying documents authentic. The names on the documents would be James Henry Falcon and John William Falcon. The printer had to be good enough to forge the Seal of the State of Nevada onto the documents also.

The head of an al Qaeda cell in New York City gave Abreu the name of a printer who ran a small print shop in New York. Abreu preferred using resources and cells in New York City because it was far from Elko, Nevada; and New York's resources along with competent people were plentiful.

The printer was a Pakistani who had been in America for over a decade. His name was Aziz Ramji. He had brought his family to America in order to escape a severe life in Pakistan and to get away from al Qaeda. In Pakistan he had made the mistake of accepting several printing jobs for representatives of al Qaeda. He had not been aware of their connection to al Qaeda at the time. He was an expert printer and was paid well for his work. It scared him when he was given a job from these same men to print ten thousand flyers. The flyers urged "followers" to commence jihad against

Americans and kill as many as possible. The flyer was signed by Usama Bin Ladin. Aziz became frightened for himself and his family. He finished the printing job. After, he sold his printing shop, his property, and all his family's belongings. He took the money and paid the way to America for him and his family. He settled in New York and for the last ten years lived a good life. Aziz had opened his own print shop and was a hard working, honest and successful businessman.

Aziz and his family had come to love America and the life it had given them. His entire family took deep pride in becoming American citizens. He had two sons. The elder son, Amal, was twenty years old. He left working in the print shop and joined the Army. Aziz was proud of the fact his eldest son had chosen to serve in the Army of his adopted country. His wife Naisha, and the younger son Thomas, worked in the print shop with Aziz. Together they had a thriving business and a happy satisfying family life. Naisha handled the customers and her delightful personality drew more customers as the business grew over the years. Aziz's high quality workmanship became well known throughout the local area. Thomas worked in the shop after school and was learning and advancing under his father's tutoring. Aziz was generous to local charities and was well respected and well known in his community.

As Aziz built his business, he was unaware that representatives of al Qaeda had followed and tracked his move to New York. Al Qaeda had him on their list of people to approach if his services were ever needed.

Abreu was given the information and confronted Aziz in his shop.

"I have a job for you Aziz, it is the refining and completing of two birth certificates and accompanying documents. You will also have to duplicate a state seal on the papers. This job will pay you a large amount of money. It may take several days. Close your shop and tell your family to stay home. They do not need to be involved or know any details of this job."

Aziz did not need the money. He accepted the job because Abreu told him it was for the same people he had done work for in Pakistan. Aziz was afraid for his family because they were not to come to the shop during this job. Aziz confirmed the job would take several days. While Abreu was in the bathroom Aziz took the opportunity and hastily telephoned his wife.

"I have a big job and I need to close the shop until it is completed." He told her, "I'll be staying at the shop and won't be home for several days. Stay at home and do not come to the shop under any circumstances. Keep Thomas away also. I want to make sure you understand me, do not come to the shop or let Thomas come to the shop for any reason. Don't worry, I am being paid very well for doing this work. I will see you in several days."

Aziz did not give his wife a chance to talk as he hung up the phone before she could ask questions. Aziz knew his wife would abide by his wishes. He did not want his family exposed to Abreu or any of his associates. Completing the work took four days. During that time Abreu and Aziz never left the print shop. Food was delivered three times a day in a white panel truck. Abreu had ordered a local al Qaeda cell to prepare and deliver the food.

Abreu told Aziz the birth certificates and the Nevada State documents had to be exact and accurate. It took a day for the special ink to arrive. That cost them a day of work. The ink was ordered C.O.D. and paid in cash by Abreu. The invoices were destroyed. At the end of the fourth day the forged birth certificates with the names James Henry Falcon and John William Falcon were ready. By evening all the forged documents were completed. Abreu inspected each certificate and document and approved them as complete. Abreu was actually impressed with the Nevada State Seal which Aziz had duplicated and imprinted on the birth certificates and documents. He complimented and thanked Aziz and paid him fifty-thousand dollars in cash. Abreu carefully placed all the papers in a brief case. A black sedan was waiting for him at the rear entrance of the shop. Abreu shook hands and said good-by to Aziz, then departed in the sedan.

As Abreu left the print shop he contemplated the fate of Aziz. Should Aziz be spared. His work as an expert printer may be valuable to al Qaeda in the future. Should the chance be taken that the knowledge Aziz possessed would remain a secret? Abreu dismissed the thought.

Twenty minutes later Aziz finished locking his shop and exited through the rear door. As he locked the door the same white van that had delivered the food pulled up. Three men jumped out and forced Aziz into the van. The van departed from the rear of the print shop, and Aziz was never seen or heard from again.

That night the New York City Fire Department was put to work by al Qaeda as Aziz's print shop was gutted by a fire that destroyed everything in the shop. Abreu and al Qaeda were covering their tracks, no evidence of the completed print job by Aziz remained.

Chapter 12

Abreu returned to his office in Tehran with the forged documents secured in his briefcase. The birth certificates and the accompanying documents, proving that James and John Falcon were born in Nevada, were ready. Now they needed to be planted into the permanent files of the Elko County Courthouse. Abreu sent a courier to Abib with orders to report to his office on Friday. This would give Abib four days to report after being notified by the courier.

Abib was to report at three A.M. He was given specific instructions to be sure he was not followed or tracked in any way. The two on duty guards at the entrance desk of the al Qaeda building were expecting Abib. They had a picture and several questions to ask him in order to confirm his identity. Abib appeared outside the bullet proof glass doors and was buzzed in. Unknown to Abib, Abreu had stationed men in hidden locations for a three block perimeter around the building. Abreu wanted to be sure no one was following Abib. Their orders were to kill anyone following Abib, transport the body so it would never be found, and bring any identification to Abreu. Then kill, and dispose of Abib, if he had been followed.

Fortunately for Abib, none of this scenario was necessary as he arrived clean. When Abreu got the word all was clear he had Abib escorted to his office. Abreu welcomed Abib warmly and wasted no time in giving Abib his marching orders. The plan was simple according to Abreu. As he heard it, Abib wasn't so sure.

A four member cell from New York would go to Elko, Nevada and search out a person who worked in or had access to the county courthouse. This person needed to be able to file the forged papers into the permanent records of the courthouse. Abib was to go there with the birth certificates and other documents, and be sure they were filed accurately. He was to meet the cell members in thirty days at the Summerset Camp Ground just outside of Elko.

Abreu showed Abib the paperwork and made sure he knew what needed to be done. The papers were placed in a plastic protective cover and into a manila envelope. Abreu handed the manila envelope to Abib saying, "There are no copies of these papers, Abib. I did not want to take the chance of duplicates being discovered. Guard these papers with your life and be sure they are filed accurately. I am assigning two security men to be with you until you arrive in Elko. At that time they will leave you with the New York cell and return to their regular duties."

The two security men entered the office and were introduced to Abib. He knew both men from the training camps. They embraced and smiled.

"I will be happy and safe with these two guys," Said Abib.

"Go and stay at the training camp in Libya," Said Abreu. "You'll be safe and not bored there. Transportation has been arranged. Stay there until it is time to go to America and get to Elko."

"A final word to you two," Abreu said, referring to the security guards, "Protect Abib and that package as if your life depended on it, because it does."

As the three men left the office Abreu handed them passports and customs papers so they could enter the United States when the time came.

After the three men left Abreu picked up a satellite encrypted phone and dialed a New York number. The phone was answered immediately. "Are you ready to go?" Abreu asked.

The man answering was Harim.

"We're ready, and we are leaving as soon as we finish loading."

"Good, Abib will meet you in thirty days. Do your best to be ready for him." Abreu ended the call. Harim, and his cell had been assigned to New York for several years. They had participated in bombings outside the United States, but had been ordered to keep a quiet and low profile while in New York. The four men lived in a modular home located in a large mobile home park known as Riverside Estates. It got its name due to a dry river bed running along the outside of the park. The mobile home park accommodated two hundred permanent "mobile" homes. The cell lived at the end of a dead end street and worked hard to remain inconspicuous. They passed their downtime working at a restaurant owned by al Qaeda sympathizers. But their real job took place in the back rooms and basement of the establishment, where they practiced and maintained their terrorist skills. On the mission to Elko their leader figured none of these skills would be needed, as this was to be strictly a surveillance assignment.

On this night three of the cell members were sitting around the table in the kitchen. Two have beards and dark hair. Both are five foot eight inches tall. They have dark skin and look middle-eastern. The third cell member is short and stocky. He has a shaved head but has not shaved for several days. His head shows black stubble. His facial hair is ugly and straggly. They are all wearing western style clothes. The clothes are ill fitting and sloppy. They fit in with the many different kinds of people in New York and went about their daily activities without attracting any special attention.

The three men are dangerous killers, trained in al Qaeda camps as experts in disposing of individual persons, or large groups of people. They are expert in the use of every type of weapon in al Qaeda's arsenal. They know and are able to execute many various methods of killing people, from using only hand weapons to setting off explosive devices. They are learned bomb makers and experts at disguising the bombs. The cell has proven this many times by killing innocent people throughout the world. But they have never been used in the United States. These men are kept as a sleeper cell so they can be used for assignments such as the one they are embarking on to Elko, Nevada.

The fourth member steps into the kitchen. He has blond hair and a very neat haircut. It is obvious he is the leader of the cell. His clothes, shoes and general appearance are immaculate.

His name is Harim. To look at him there would be no doubt that he was an up-standing citizen, and in no way connected to an al Qaeda sleeper cell. He hadn't fired any weapon in years, and had forgotten many of the ways to make bombs. But Harim was a sophisticated al Qaeda trained leader. In guiding and directing his three cell members, they had both killed individuals and bombed buildings and gatherings of people as ordered by their al Qaeda controller. Their controller was Abreu.

Harim addressed his cell members. "We have an assignment in a place called Elko, Nevada. Our new class 'A' motor home is here. I parked it outside. It is fully stocked with food and ready to go. We cannot tell anyone about this trip or our assignment. When we get there my job is to locate a certain person. Your job will be to back me up. We will not know the reasons for our actions, but we are being well paid for this job and we get to keep the recreational vehicle. The trip to Elko is a long one so let's enjoy the ride. We leave as soon as we finish loading our equipment.

The cell members see the motor home for the first time. It is thirty-eight feet long. As they enter and look inside they are pleased to see it is well equipped and big enough to accommodate them comfortably. Harim gives final instructions.

"Make sure you have your side arms and ammo. Load four

AK- 47's and at least a thousand rounds of ammunition for each rifle. Open the locker under the kitchen and bring a couple of rocket launchers too. Make sure they are secure and hidden under the rear beds. I don't think the weapons will be needed but we'll bring them just in case."

Harim then addresses the short, stocky cell member. His name is Jasid. "Check the rear outside compartment. Make sure three picks and three shovels are there."

After the weapons are secure and Jasid confirms the picks and shovels are onboard, the men board with their suitcases. With Jasid driving, the motor home departs on the cross country trip to the Summerset Camp Ground in Elko, Nevada.

Abib and his two body guards arrived in Elko three weeks after Harim and his cell. The trip from Libya to the United States had been tiresome but uneventful. They landed in the busy San Francisco airport. Their expertly forged passports and California driver's licenses were not questioned and they passed through customs with no problems. An al Qaeda operative, who had lived in California since he was a teenager, met them. He had purchased a car, with cash, under a fictitious company name. The car was for this assignment only, after which it was to be destroyed. The operative was Abib's driver and guide. The three men had never been to San Francisco. After a driving tour of the city, and stopping to eat in San Francisco, they drove across the San Francisco-Oakland Bay Bridge to Interstate I- 80 East, and proceeded the 500 miles to the Summerset Camp Ground in Elko, Nevada. They arrived in the camp ground in the early evening. They found the motor home and greeted Harim and his cell members. Abib's body guards made sure Abib had the forged birth certificates and the other needed documents. The two body guards told Harim their responsibility was ended. With that they left the camp ground with the guide and began the journey back to Tehran.

Harim and Abib sat in the motor home. Harim reported on the assignment to Abib, and the progress he and his cell had made. "Abreu instructed me to find a person who worked in, and has access to the Elko County Courthouse Hall of Records. A person we could bribe or threaten into planting forged papers into the permanent records. I think we found the prime person to suit your needs. We have a car. We needed one so we purchased a used one here, with cash, under a fictitious name. If you want, we can drive into town now and show you the man we picked."

Abib, Harim and the three cell members drove downtown to the Elko City Casino. As they entered the casino Harim cautions his three cell members, "Stay in the background but keep alert, in case we need you or are ready to leave."

The Elko City Casino is a typical small casino. The front exterior is brightly lighted by hundreds of small pulsating lights. To the sides and rear are dimly lighted parking lots. Abib enters the front door with Harim. He sees that the casino gaming area is the size of half a soccer field. The ceiling is twenty feet high. Dozens of chandeliers hang from the ceiling providing soft light for the entire casino. The main floor is recessed down five steps from the entrance landing.

The bar is centered along one wall of the casino and is raised several feet above the gaming floor. There are booths around the perimeter of the bar area. The carpet is red with black designs running through it. There are slot machines, blackjack tables, several craps tables, and various other gaming tables scattered throughout the casino floor.

Harim and Abib are standing on the casino entrance landing. Abib observes the people throughout the casino and turns to Harim, "This is an example of American decadence and why we must continue the jihad. This is not our way of life."

Harim grunts his agreement and points out a man sitting at a blackjack table. The man is short, balding and a little overweight.

As they observe the man it is obvious that he is losing most of his bets.

Harim turns to Abib. "Our instructions from Abreu were to find someone who works at the court house and who could get you in secretly and plant the papers. My crew and I have been watching this guy for a couple of weeks. His name is Marvin. He is a clerk at the court house. As you can see he is an inept gambler, he owes the casino thousands. I think we can bribe him easily."

Abib looks at Harim.

"OK, let's not waste any time. Meet with him. Offer him enough money so he can't refuse our proposal. But, if he does refuse it, make sure he disappears without talking to anyone about us or our bribe attempt. Especially make sure he tells no one about the planting of documents."

"OK" replied Harim, "Jasid will take you back to the motor home so you can rest from your trip. I'll have him return with the fifty thousand dollars for the bribe. I'll approach Marvin tonight and show him the money."

Jasid and Abib leave the casino. Harim tells the other two cell members to stand by and observe, but do nothing. Harim looks around the casino for Marvin. He spots him sitting in a booth in the bar area with an attractive woman. She looks out of place as she is too attractive and too tall to be sitting with Marvin. Marvin has a glass of beer in front of him, the woman a cocktail. Harim walks up and sits down.

"Hi Marvin, may I buy you two a cocktail and another beer?"

Marvin looks suspiciously at Harim, "How do you know my name, do I know you?"

"You don't know me, but you're pretty well known around here," replies Harim.

Before Marvin can say anything, Harim addresses the young woman, "Would you mind? I need to talk to Marvin in private for a few minutes."

"It's OK Kathy, go freshen up, then hurry back. I'll miss you," Says Marvin awkwardly.

As Kathy leaves the booth her slender body draws attention from the male population sitting at the bar. She is oblivious to the stares and enters the ladies room. Marvin becomes defensive in her absence, "What do you want? If it's about the money I owe, I already told them I'll pay as soon as I can. They said that would be OK, as long as I paid in full in thirty days."

Harim jumps at the opportunity. "The money is exactly why I want to talk to you. I have a deal to offer you. It will allow you to pay off the money you owe and still have a lot left over for yourself and to entertain your girlfriend."

"She is not my girlfriend." Marvin replied snidely. "She's my fiancée, we have a kid together. He's two years old. We're getting married next month. You work for the casino?"

Jasid walks up and hands Harim a small satchel. Harim thanks him and Jasid walks away.

Harim continues, "No, I don't work for the casino. I do know you owe several thousand to them. What I am offering you is a private deal. It has nothing to do with the casino. My deal is this. You help my friend place two birth certificates and accompanying state papers in the permanent courthouse files and I will give you fifty thousand dollars."

Marvin is startled. "What? You'll give me that money just to plant some papers in the files?"

"Yes," replied Harim, looking straight at Marvin's face.

"It sounds too good to be true. It can't be that simple," Said Marvin, "Is this setting somebody up, or is somebody going to get hurt because of this?"

"No one is going to get hurt," Harim reassures Marvin, "You don't need to know anything more. All you need to do is plant the papers in the proper place without anyone knowing it was done.

You'll be working with my friend Abib. Look, I'm going to show you the money."

As Harim opens the satchel and shows Marvin the money, Kathy sits down in the booth and also sees the satchel full of one hundred dollar bills. "I have to have an answer now," Harim urges Marvin, "Yes or no?"

Kathy looks at Marvin with astonishment. Marvin looks at the money, then at Harim, Marvin is speechless, he takes several minutes to regain his composure. Harim closes the satchel and Marvin finally speaks.

"You will give me all that money just to plant some papers in the court house?"

"Yes," replies Harim Blandly.

"OK, I'll do it." Marvin says after a couple of seconds, giving Kathy a reassuring nod and glance.

Kathy takes a sip of her drink and says to Marvin, "Are you sure you want to get involved in this, whatever it is?"

Marvin smiles at her, "Did you see all that money? This will give us and our boy a great start. We will even be able to buy a home for ourselves. No one is to be hurt and no one will ever know the difference."

"That 's right," encourages Harim.

Harim turns to Jasid and instructs him to go and get Abib.

"Meet me in the casino parking lot in thirty minutes." Harim tells Marvin. "We will make the final arrangements with Abib."

Thirty minutes later Abib, Harim, the three cell members, and Marvin; are meeting in a dark corner of the casino parking lot. Abib confronts Marvin.

"You understand the birth certificates and documents need to be filed accurately. No one can know about this. There can be no mistakes. What is the best time to do this?"

"I understand," replied Marvin. "The best time is late at night, after midnight. I have all the keys. The rear door is the one we'll use to enter."

"Tomorrow night." Commands Abib. "We'll meet here at midnight."

Marvin departs from the group and goes back into the casino. As the group discusses the details of the next night Harim expresses a concern, "The woman, she saw the money and knows Marvin agreed to plant papers in the courthouse. She can identify me and Jasid, and place us with Marvin. Our mission here is secret. We cannot take a chance of leaving anyone who may compromise it. This woman, Kathy, must be eliminated without a trace."

"What?"Abib says to Harim, "If the woman saw the money and heard Marvin is planting documents in the court house files, she can definetly compromise the mission. Also, she can identify you and Jasid. If the authorities connect you to any pictures they may have on file that could lead to big problems in New York. It was stupid of you to allow the woman to see what you were doing!"

Harim replies sheepishly, "It was an accident, she returned to the table just as we were making the deal. We didn't intend for her to be involved."

Abib gives Harim and Jasid a hard look. "Make this woman disappear, now!"

Jasid eagerly jumps into the conversation, "I saw a steel treatment plant several miles from our campground. It is in a fairly isolated area. They must have an acid vat there. That would take care of the woman."

Abib directs Harim and the cell members, "OK, take care of the woman. Make sure she can never be connected to us."

Harim goes back into the casino to see what Marvin and Kathy are doing. Marvin is playing blackjack and Kathy is preparing to leave. Harim returns to the parking lot and tells his men that Kathy is leaving the casino, alone.

As Kathy walked through the parking lot, the three cell members grabbed her and forced her into the trunk of their car. Just as the car leaves the parking lot, Abib and Harim get in for the ride to the campground. Jasid drives cautiously so as to not attract attention. It is late and not many cars are on the road. Kathy desperately yells for help and pounds on the inner surfaces of the trunk. No one hears her except the same men who put her in the trunk. Abib and Harim are dropped off at the campground. Kathy is moved to the back seat. She is terrified. Her struggling is to no avail.

"What are you doing to me," she screams. Her strength is no match for the force of the two men pushing her against the seat. Her screams are met with silence from the men holding her down. A rag is placed over her mouth and held there with such force that she is quiet for the remainder of the ride to the steel treating plant.

At the steel treating plant Jasid drives the perimeter. It is very late and the plant seems deserted. Jasid stops the car near a large sliding door. Kathy is forced from the back seat. Jasid breaks a lock on the door and forces it open. The interior is dimly lighted by several night lights. Kathy is dragged by the two cell members as they follow Jasid. They find a steel treatment room. There are three concrete acid vats the size of large bathtubs lined up against one wall of the room.

Kathy is almost incoherent with fear. She realizes these men intend to kill her. She is thinking of her two year old son and the life she was looking forward to with Marvin. She tries to struggle with all her remaining strength. It does her no good. Next to a three foot deep concrete trough, filled with acid, she is thrown to the floor. Her head strikes the concrete floor and she blacks out.

"She's too long. We can't get her into the vat," Exclaimed one of the cell members.

"Hack her legs off and dump her in," ordered Jasid.

One cell member runs to the car to retrieve a camping hatchet from the trunk.

As Kathy regains consciousness she is crying uncontrollably. She pleads with Jasid, "Please don't hurt me, I have a young son who needs me." Her last experience in life is feeling sudden and severe pain in her legs as one of the cell members hacks them off at the knees. Her last conscious thought was that of her son's face.

The three men made sure the acid did its work. Any remnants remaining of the body could never be identified. When they were satisfied they closed up the building and departed confident of not having been detected.

The next night Marvin was in the casino parking lot at the prescribed time. Abib, Harim and the three cell members arrived at exactly midnight. Marvin ran up to their car frantic.

"I haven't seen Kathy since last night!" He yelled.

"Calm down and be quiet." Harim commanded. "We have Kathy. As soon as you and Abib file the birth certificates and the accompanying documents we will give her back to you. Now get in the car and let's get going."

Marvin gasped and stared at the men in disbelief as the color drained from his face. He felt his knees buckle as he began to collapse. The three cell members grabbed him and placed him in the car. Abib grabbed Marvin by the neck and put his face close. Abib glared at Marvin and growled,

"Gain control of yourself! File the papers and you'll have fifty thousand dollars to show her as soon as we're done."

It took Marvin several long minutes to stop whimpering and regain his composure. "You have my Kathy?" Marvin pleaded.

Harim replied sternly, "We needed insurance you would not back out of our deal."

"I won't back out!" Cried Marvin, "I've spent all day making sure we could plant the papers in the right files."

"OK" said Abib, "Let's get this done so you can get the money and your woman."

Marvin looks back at Abib. In a low, steady voice, he says, "You guys have scared the shit out of me now. I just want to get this over with and see Kathy."

The car is quiet for the remainder of the ride to the rear of the courthouse. Marvin does not take notice of the motor home parked near the court house. Earlier that night the cell had moved the motor home and parked it across the street from the back of the courthouse.

As the men get out of the car Jasid and the other two cell members spread out and check the area. Marvin is shaking as he pulls out his set of keys.

"Marvin," Abib says, "Are you sure the building is empty?"

"Yes," replies Marvin. "It's one A.M. No one is around and the security here is minimal."

Marvin is steady now and says to Abib, "I'm OK now. Let's get this over and done."

Marvin opens the rear door, he and Abib enter the courthouse. The hallway is dark. Abib's flashlight and the dim corridor night lights provide the only illumination. Abib has his flashlight in one hand with his silenced nine millimeter automatic in the other. The birth certificates and documents to be filed are inside his shirt. They pass several doors that are ten feet high and three feet wide. The doors appear to be solid steel. There are several doors marked as permanent file rooms. Marvin checks a small self drawn map he is carrying and unlocks the third door they come to. Once inside the room Marvin closes the door and turns the light on. Abib sees there are metal file cabinets from the floor to eight feet high in the center of the room, and on all the perimeter walls. Each cabinet has four drawers with labels showing the alphabetical files located within the drawer. There are two signs prohibiting smoking. Abib recognizes that the room is a vault with a fire suppression system on the ceiling.

"Let me see the birth certificates," Marvin says to Abib.

Abib hands over the two birth certificates and documents. On each one of them are the names James Henry Falcon, and John William Falcon. Marvin looks at them and is startled.

"These are real. Where did you get them?"

"You're getting paid to file them accurately. Anything else is none of your business!" Abib retorts angrily.

Marvin sheepishly finds and opens the appropriate drawer. After checking and fumbling through several folders, Marvin places all the papers into two files and closes the drawer.

"That's it, let's get the hell out of here." Reports Marvin.

As the two men exit the building Abib figures he has it made. Marvin is thinking of the fifty-thousand dollars and seeing Kathy. But both Marvin and Abib have separate surprises awaiting them.

The first surprise catches the terrorist, Abib, and Marvin off guard. The surprise is the night security guard, Jim Bentley.

Jim Bentley is thirty eight years old. He had played professional football in his younger days until a knee injury and three surgeries ended his playing days. He had been married once but it ended after three years. But that was a long time ago. Since then he had taken the easiest jobs he could find to earn a living. He was never too ambitious. He was happy to have moved to Elko and landed a job as a night security guard for the City of Elko. He spent most of his on duty nights napping, reading, and drinking coffee with brandy. Some nights he just drank the brandy and spent most of the night sleeping off the intoxication. In his five years on the job he never had to draw his weapon. In over a year now, Jim Bentley had not taken his .38 Special out of its holster for any reason. Not even to clean or check it.

On this night Jim Bentley was assigned by his supervisor to patrol the county buildings which included the County Court

House. His supervisor knew Jim was a slacker, and next to useless as a security guard. This night it was his rotation to patrol the court buildings. His supervisor did not hesitate to follow the assigned schedule, since nothing ever happened around the courthouse at night anyway. This night would change that. After finishing a thermos of half brandy and half coffee Jim Bentley decided to walk over to the court house and use the bathroom to relieve himself. As he approached the corner of the adjacent building he found he could not wait any longer. Getting close to the building he unzipped his uniform pants and began urinating.

As Abib and Marvin exited the rear doorway Jim Bentley was ten feet away. It was now after two A.M. The exterior walkways were not well lighted. Jim Bentley hesitated as he saw the two figures coming out of the door. Without zipping his pants, or finishing his relief, he yelled at the two men.

"Hey, what are you doing here!?" He drew his weapon and pointed it at the two men.

Abib had been in this type of situation before, when a plan had been interrupted by the unexpected. The execution of this plan had gone well up to this point. Now, the security guard, Jim Bentley, who had been asleep fifteen minutes earlier, was complicating the plan by having finished his thermos of brandy, and walking to the court house to use the bathroom. Marvin started to reply. Before he could say a word Jim Bentley died immediately when two nine millimeter bullets from Abib's gun entered his chest.

Marvin's eyes were wide with fear as his bladder lost control and he urinated in his pants. Harim and his cell appeared from around the corner. One of the cell members went directly to the downed security guard.

"He's dead." The cell member said as he stood up.

Harim ran up the Abib. "Are you alright?"

Abib nodded in the affirmative.

Harim continued, "Are the birth certificates and documents filed?"

"Yes," said Abib.

Harim shoots Marvin with a silenced .357 Magnum. As Marvin falls to the sidewalk he has two dying thoughts. The first is Kathy saying, "Are you sure you want to get involved with these people?" His second and last thought was of Harim saying, "No one is going to get hurt."

Abib addresses Harim and the cell members, "Alright, we have an extra body to bury in the desert, but the secrecy of the operation is still intact. Load them into the motor home while I report to Abreu."

Harim and the three cell members clean up the area so no blood or evidence of what had occurred remained on the scene. Two bottles of Hydrogen Peroxide did the trick. The bodies of Marvin and Jim Bentley are then loaded into the motor home.

Abib dials a secure satellite phone, it is answered immediately. "Abreu, the birth certificates and other documents are filed. No one will ever know the building has been violated or what took place here tonight. The only difference in the plan is we have one extra body to bury in the desert." After he hears acknowledgement he disconnects the call. As Abib turns around he faces Harim and Jasid. Without warning Harim violently thrusts a six inch serrated knife into Abib's abdomen and forcefully jerks up on it.

As Abib's world goes black he directs his last gasp at Harim, "What the hell!"

"Get him into the motor home and get the others to clean up the blood." Harim orders Jasid.

Harim picks up the same satellite phone and dials the same number Abib did several minutes previous.

"Hello Abreu, this is Harim, The mission is accomplished. I

have made sure no one will ever know what happened here. Abib is dead as you ordered. We have one extra body to bury, a security guard we had to kill. There are miles of isolated desert just as you told me. The bodies will never be found."

The phone clicked dead and Harim turned it off.

Chapter 13

With the three bodies covered in the rear of the motor home the cell left Elko, Nevada and began the journey to New York. They planned to make a stop in the desert to bury the three bodies.

Jasid drives the motor home out of Elko as Harim studies a map. "There is an isolated spot about fifty miles out. We'll stop there and bury these guys before dawn."

A little less than an hour later Jasid says, "I haven't seen another car for over a half an hour."

"Good," replies Harim, "Stop at those bushes ahead."

The motor home pulls off the road and parks in an area of large bushes. It is pitch black as no moon has shown. The only illumination is the interior lights of the motor home.

Suddenly Jasid jumps from the driver's seat. In a panicky voice he reports, "A police car just went by in the opposite direction. I'll get the guns ready!"

"Get the AK 47's out and loaded. Keep the weapons in the back. That police car probably won't even come back." Harim orders his men.

The four men waited tensely for several minutes. Their fears were answered in about five minutes. A Nevada Highway Patrol cruiser pulled up fifty feet behind the motor home. A spotlight is shined on the motor home. Two Highway Patrolmen stood on either side of their patrol car. They did not move and nothing was happening.

Highway Patrol Sergeant Tim Ruthers stands beside the driver's door of his patrol car and orders his partner, "Eric, hold your position by the car. All the lights are on so they are not trying to hide or anything. I'll talk to the driver."

Seven hours earlier at the Highway Patrol Station in Elko, Sergeant Ruthers had greeted his young partner, Eric Richardson, as they reported for duty. The sergeant's wife had just dropped him off and he was waving good bye to her as Eric drove up with Judy, his fiancée. He waved at her also as she drove off. He and Eric entered the station together. In the briefing room the shift commander addressed the twelve officers coming onto the night shift. After reading the daily announcements and reports from the previous shift commander, he dismissed the twelve patrolmen with this word of caution, "Be careful out there tonight, especially along highway 80. There have been several drug smuggling arrests on the day shift recently, be aware of suspicious vehicles and watch your butts out there."

They entered their patrol car, but before Tim could start it Eric blurted out, "I want to ask you something. Will you be best man at my wedding next month? I've been afraid to ask you but time is getting short so I'm asking now. Judy wants you in the wedding also and has been bugging me to ask you. You don't know it yet, but your wife is in the wedding party also."

Tim looked at his young partner. They had become friends since being partners over the last six months. Tim's wife and Judy had also become rather close and she had spent a lot of time helping Judy with preparations for the wedding.

Tim laughed and said, "No wonder she has been so smug lately. She never gave me a clue Judy had included her in the wedding." Then Tim got serious. "I'm a lot older than you. I figured you would have a younger guy as your best man." He paused, and then smiling he simply said, "Hell yes, I'm your man!"

They smiled at each other, Tim started the patrol car and they began their shift. The shift turned out to be completely routine. They had issued one citation to a trucker who was speeding and pulled over several drivers for minor violations but did not ticket them. Now, it was the end of their shift and they were heading back to the station. They passed the stopped motor home facing the opposite direction.

"Well," said Tim, "Shall we turn around and check that RV or leave it for the on-coming shift? Our relief is on the road already and we're over due at the station."

Before Eric can reply Tim continues, "Shit, call for backup, let's turn around and check them out. That's what we're getting paid for, and besides, I can't help but to do this job all out."

"I'm with you, sarge," Eric replies.

Several minutes later the two patrolmen pull up behind the motor home. Eric picks up the radio mike, gives their location and calls for backup. He writes down the description of the motor home and the license number but does not call that information in because his partner has opened the door and is standing outside the patrol car. Eric throws his clipboard onto the seat and exits the patrol car also.

In the motor home Jasid began to panic.

"Let's kill them while they are standing there!" Jasid said as he began to shake uncontrollably.

Harim grabbed Jasid's neck with both hands and squeezed. "I need you to gain control of yourself, be the soldier I know you are," Harim commands.

As Jasid calms himself Harim issues orders, "American Policemen can only enter and search us if they have what they call reasonable cause. So, don't do anything unless I say. If we kill these policemen, U.S. law enforcement will be relentless in their search for us. We might never make it back to New York, and the secrecy of our mission would be compromised. The best option is to talk our way through this."

From the opposite direction a second patrol car parks thirty feet from the front corner of the motor home. The two patrolmen stay inside their car.

Harim silently talks to himself as continues to consider his options, "These Highway Patrolmen look menacing, if we can't talk our way out of this and a fight breaks out, they might kill us. In which case the bodies would be discovered and an intense investigation would follow. Maybe they will just talk or maybe we should gun them down before they can react?"

Harim runs out of time to continue his thinking, and his options are decided for him.

One of the patrolmen from the first car walks cautiously up the side of the motor home to the driver's window. Harim is sitting in the driver's seat and opens the window.

"Hello," the officer says to Harim, "Any problem?"

"No sir," Harim replies. "We just stopped to change drivers. We'll be on our way in couple of minutes."

Tim Ruthers replies, saying the last words he is ever to speak, "It's pretty late. We don't usually see motor homes stopped in the middle of nowhere at this time of night. We're just checking to make sure everything is ok. If you don't mind we'll come in and just take a fast look around?"

As usual in America, the law enforcement officer has given an unknown enemy the first shot.

Before Harim can answer Jasid starts shooting at the patrolman. The first shot destroys the patrolman's face and head. The other cell members immediately open the back window and fire at the patrolmen to the rear of the motor home. The sound of the AK 47's is deafening and reverberates throughout the surrounding desert. The second patrolman tries to use the radio, but is hit multiple times, and goes down pulling his revolver from its holster. He dies before returning fire. The two patrolmen in the front vehicle are unaware that the second patrolman to the rear has been killed. They exit their vehicle and take cover behind their open doors. They begin firing at the motor home with their .357 Magnum revolvers. Harim and Jasid exit the motor home and open fire on them with the AK-47's. The two patrolmen see the two leave the motor home. They concentrate their fire on them. Their aim is accurate and force Harim and Jasid to retreat and take cover. But the patrolmen's .357 revolvers are no match for the terrorist's AK-47's. The patrolmen are out gunned, and are killed as the rounds from the terrorists' weapons tear through the car doors. The gun fight has lasted less than a couple of minutes.

Al Qaeda has forced a funeral to be scheduled instead of a wedding.

"Quick!" Harim commands, "Load the bodies into their cars. Drive the cars behind the bushes so they can't be seen from the road. We have to put a lot of distance between us and this place before they are found. We'll keep the three bodies we were supposed to bury on board and let Abreu figure out what to do with them when we get home."

After the patrol cars are driven behind the bushes and hidden. Jasid runs up to Harim, "I found this on the front seat of the first car. It was upside down. It has our license number on it!"

"I don't think he had time to use his radio to report this information," Harim states. "In either case we need to get the hell out of here now!" The motor home speeds off continuing its journey towards New York. The bodies of Abib, Marvin, and the security guard, Jim Bentley remain in the rear floor area, wrapped completely and tightly in plastic.

The dead patrol officers were found at dawn. There was nothing at the scene to help determine what had happened except tire tracks. But, there were so many different ones they proved to be of no consequence. Al Qaeda had dodged a bullet.

Three days later the cell pulled into the Riverside mobile home park. Several police and highway patrol cars had passed them, but none had paid the motor home any attention. They parked on the street in front of their permanent modular home. The three bodies were still in the rear of the motor home. The plastic wrapping remained intact so no smell of the dead bodies escaped.

"I'll call Abreu and see what he wants to do about the three bodies. He is in town to pay us. You three stay close and don't let anyone in the motor home," Harim orders

Harim steps outside and makes the call to Abreu.

"Abreu, we are parked at home. We had a problem in Nevada. We had a shoot out and killed four police officers. It could not have been avoided. I made an on the spot decision. We still have the three bodies in the motor home. We didn't take the time to bury them in the desert like you ordered. We needed to get away from there. I figured you would know what to do with them when we got here."

On the other end of the call Abreu's face grimaces in anger. He says as calmly as he can, "You and your men stay in the motor home while I figure this out. Don't let anyone inside. I'll decide on how to get rid of the bodies. I'll call you back."

After the call Abreu's face still showed his anger at the cell. Not only did they know too much, but what they knew could compromise the entire mission, especially if the three bodies in the motor home were discovered and identified. Abreu placed a call to one of his al Qaeda assets, "This is Abreu, I need one of your bombs from the storage bunker. It must be powerful enough to vaporize human bodies and completely destroy everything in a one-hundred foot radius. Do you have one?"

The voice on the phone replies, "Yes, we have several ready to go."

Abreu asks, "Will it fit in a small suitcase?"

The voice replies, "Yes, it is made to fit in a back pack."

"I need it today, is that a problem?"

"No problem, Abreu."

Abreu gives his instructions, "Put it in a back pack and rig it to detonate when the pack is opened. Have a driver deliver it to me by noon. I am at the Continental Hotel, he can pick me up in front. Tell him he'll be working with me for a couple of hours."

At noon a sedan stopped in front of the hotel where Abreu was staying. He had registered under one of his many fictitious names. Now he had checked out, paying with cash, and was waiting on the sidewalk. He got in the back seat and seeing the back pack said to the driver, "Drive careful, we don't want to have an accident. Take us to the Riverside Mobile Home Park."

The sedan pulled from the curb as Abreu made a phone call. "Are the bodies secure?" He inquired when Harim answered the phone.

"Yes," Harim answered. "My men are having lunch in the motor home right now."

"Good," said Abreu. I am sending a driver to you with your money for the mission. Watch for him and come outside and get it. I will call you later and tell you what to do with the bodies."

Abreu tells the driver, "Let me out at the entrance to the park. I don't want to be seen. Take this back pack and give it to Harim, he is in the motor home parked in front of this address. Then come back and pick me up. Don't delay, leave immediately after giving it to Harim."

Abreu hands the driver a paper with the address, and a map of the park and gets out of the car.

Harim met the sedan when it parked next to the motor home. He took the back pack from the driver and they exchanged nods. The sedan drove away and stopped at the entrance to pick up Abreu.

Harim eagerly charged into the motor home and set the back pack excitedly on the table.

"This is our big pay day men. After the bodies are gone we'll divide it up and have a party!"

Harim eagerly unfastened the clips and opened the back pack. A tremendous detonation immediately occurs. The interior of the motor home is instantly engulfed in white hot fire. Extreme, terrified screaming is heard from the four men for only a split second. The explosion and resulting fire completely disintegrates the motor home and damages a dozen surrounding modular homes.

Abreu witnesses the detonation and fire from the sedan at the park entrance. He and the driver can feel the heat from the fire. Abreu sadly smiles and says to himself, "That takes care of anyone who could tell of the Elko operation. The papers are filed and if anyone ever checks, both James and John Falcon are American citizens. The secrecy of my plan is intact."

The sedan drives away from the mobile home park. They pass the FDNY fire engines and trucks responding to the tremendous hot fire now burning.

Immediately after the explosion the first of the many 911 calls came into the New York City Police Department switchboard at one ten in the afternoon. As per the New York City Emergency Operations Plan, the call was transmitted less than one minute later to the FDNY dispatch center. The initial response consisted of Engines 233, 217, and 222 along with Ladder Truck 176 and Battalion 37. Upon their arrival Battalion 37 called for a second alarm assignment. This dispatched Engines 214, 230, 238 and Ladder Trucks 111 and 102 along with Battalion 57. In all, six Engine Companies, three Truck Companies and two Battalion Chiefs responded to the al Qaeda caused conflagration.

Four hours after the first alarm the fire is completely out. The Battalion Chiefs are at the command post viewing the fire scene before them. The "first-in" fire captain and the a FDNY Fire Investigator approach. The captain reports to his Chief.

"That was the hottest fire I have ever seen in my twenty two years on the line, Chief."

The Fire investigator added his preliminary findings, "We can't tell how many people were in the motor home Chief. The fire was so hot the bodies were almost vaporized. Identification will be impossible. The motor home itself got so hot there is not enough left of it to find the VIN number or any identifying markers.

The fire was investigated extensively. It was never remotely connected to the terror cell. The names of the four men who lived in the mobile home proved to be untraceable. The motor home was not able to be identified. The cause of the fire was determined to be an explosive device, but the destruction was so complete there wasn't enough evidence left to trace the explosive. Al Qaeda had covered its tracks.

Chapter 14

While the placing of the forged birth certificates into the Elko files was being carried out and completed, another aspect of the overall plot was being put in place in California.

It was a beautiful spring morning in Sunnyvale, California. Airman Steven Housten approached the main entrance guard station and presented his identification packet to the U.S. Air Force security guard. Even though the guard knew him well due to many nights drinking at 'Rocky's, a local bar and restaurant, the ID was scrutinized as though Steve Housten was a complete stranger. Above the guard station and entrance to the Air Base was a large lettered sign which read:

AUTHORIZED PERSONNEL ONLY-
-DO NOT ATTEMPT ENTRY
DEADLY FORCE AUTHORIZED

It was a Saturday. Steve Housten had been stationed at the Sunnyvale Air Force Base for almost two years. The base was located adjacent to the former Moffett Field Naval Air Station, now a NASA facility. This morning Airman Houston tried to hustle through the security check point to his duty station. This was the third time he was late for duty in a month's time. He knew his supervisor, Sgt. Chet Daily, would be pissed at having to cover for his lateness again. Steve's tardiness was amusing the first time, and even tolerable the second time. In his previous eighteen months at this duty station he had never once been late in reporting for duty.

But now he had met a woman. Steve was well liked by his comrades, and some of them knew he had just become friends with pretty girl. They also knew he was a novice with women. Because he had covered their shifts on numerous occasions, and because he was extremely competent at all the computer stations in his section, his first two instances of tardiness were overlooked. But this time Steve knew his sergeant was going to chew him into the next century. Sgt. Daily was also going to warn him, as a superior and a friend, that no woman was worth the risk of being placed on report. Being placed on report would mean possibly losing his security clearance, and his position at one of the most secure U. S. Air Force installations in the continental United States.

Steve Housten worked in the Satellite Tracking Station. When on duty his job, along with rest of his section, was to monitor the orbits of the satellites circling the Earth. This included monitoring the movement of the manned space station.

The Sunnyvale Air Force Base was small in comparison to most other bases. It consisted of only eight concrete block buildings. Regardless of size, its importance was paramount to the manned space station, the satellites, the space junk, and other debris which orbited the Earth.

Airman Steve Houston was twenty-one years old when he was assigned and stationed at Sunnyvale. In junior high and throughout his high school years Steven was a straight "A" student. Although he was sociable and had many friends he spent most of his spare time in his room and garage, which were full of computers and technical gadgets. He was recognized by his teachers and fellow students as the computer wiz kid. He did play on the basketball team. This was only due to the coach's insistence, peer pressure, and his parents forcing him to 'leave the computers alone' and get some exercise. His friends urged him to go after the girls that liked him, but he remained shy and mostly avoided interaction with girls. Several of Steven's teachers informed an Air Force recruiter of his ability and potential as a computer expert.

During Steven's junior and senior years the recruiter worked hard to entice him to join the Air Force. He took Steven on trips to Air Force bases and showed him the computers and advanced technology used by the Air Force. The result was that Steven joined the Air Force right out of high school, without ever having a girl friend. He never had time for one. His whole life had been his computers and the technology surrounding them. Once through basic training, he qualified for, attended, and graduated from the Air Force computer technology schools. He became an expert at U.S. Air Force computer systems. This expertise earned Steven his current premiere assignment at Sunnyvale.

The duty and responsibility of Steve Houston's section of the base was to track all satellites orbiting the Earth. This included the manned space station. Any unauthorized change in any satellite orbit would be transmitted via secure channels to NORAD, the North American Aerospace Defense Command.

NASA also tracked the satellites and monitored the manned space station. The difference being NASA was civilian. Its concern was the safety of the manned space station and the orbiting satellites. NASA controlled and could adjust the orbits of U.S. satellites to avoid collisions between them, space debris, and the manned space station. NASA also reported to NORAD if any problems were detected. NASA, however, was not responsible for the defense and protection of the North American continent.

NORAD, The North American Aerospace Defense Command, was responsible. This was the reason for the existence of the Sunnyvale Air Force Base and the section in which Steve Housten worked.

By order of the Chiefs of staff of the United States Air Force, Navy, and Army, in concurrence with the Secretary of Defense and the National Security Advisor, any deviation in the established and authorized orbits of any satellite, or the manned space station, was to be considered by NORAD as a threat to the United States. An orbit change could be by natural causes or by an enemy's action. Any unauthorized orbit deviation would bring the defensive and offensive military capability of NORAD to full alert until the situation was deemed peaceful, and not a threat in any way to the United States or the North American Continent. Command officers at NORAD knew they would become heavily involved with any problem in space, whether military or civilian.

After chewing out Airman Housten for being late, and giving him a lecture about letting love or lust for any woman interfere with Air Force duty, Sgt. Daily calmed down. There was several tense minutes of silence between the veteran sergeant and the young airmen. Then Sgt. Daily called the men and women of his section together. A stern discussion outlining the importance of their duty station ensued. The sergeant touched on the importance of each man and woman doing their job one hundred percent. Unknown to the veteran sergeant, the young airman under his command, Steven Housten, never had a girlfriend, nor had he ever spent the night with a woman before now. Had he known this, an additional lecture, and warning about women interfering with duty would have taken place. It would have been much more severe, intense, and detailed. It would have been in private.

The officer in command of the section, Captain Hal Roberts, listened intently from a corner of the room. He had observed the chewing out of Airman Steven Housten. He heard Sgt. Daily emphasize to his subordinates the importance of their mission in monitoring the orbits and reporting any deviation to NORAD.

The Captain was satisfied that the sergeant understood the importance of the section's work and had motivated his people in carrying out their mission. He walked away knowing his input was not needed. Captain Roberts had never taken a personal interest in the young airmen with reputation of computer brilliance. Later, he would wish he had.

Olivia Marchan had spent the afternoon shopping for a new dress at the downtown Sunnyvale Macy's. She was getting to know what he liked. The dress she picked was short and sexy. Olivia thought this would bring her and Steven one step closer to being a couple. That was her goal. As she entered her apartment the secure satellite phone buzzed from its hiding place. Olivia picked it up and spoke her identification code into it.

A voice asked, "Have you made contact yet?"

"I have," Olivia reported. "We are having dinner again tonight. I think he is the right one for us." The phone clicked dead. Olivia returned it to its hiding place. She then continued putting on her make up in preparation for her dinner date with airman Steven Housten.

Olivia Marchan was twenty five years old. She looked like she could be a movie star. She had immigrated to the United States from France as part of an al Qaeda sleeper cell made up of four people. She entered on a student visa and was set up to attend the University of Southern California full time.

The cell paid her tuition, rent and living expenses. Olivia also received five thousand dollars a month as a salary from al Qaeda. The money was paid to her by the cell leader on the first day of each month. It was paid in cash. Olivia placed the money in a long term savings account. She considered it her nest egg and retirement money when her life in al Qaeda was over. As part of her instructions to maintain a low profile she made sure her ravishing good looks were disguised. She took a part time job at the library to enhance her in keeping a low profile. She was told to be ready at any time for an assignment from her controllers in the higher levels of al Qaeda.

Olivia lived with her other cell members in a small apartment complex. She had her own apartment and spoke only occasionally with her cell leader. She had blazing red hair and a body and personality to match. It took a real effort for her to maintain a low profile. She enjoyed an easy life style. Going to school allowed her to participate and enjoy the many activities such as tennis, swimming and an active social calendar. She had orders not to have sex. She was told her pending assignment was too important to risk any sexual problems. Since attending college had no real purpose she was quite carefree and enjoyed her daily activities. She was tempted more than once to have sex but refrained knowing that if caught she would be in dangerous trouble. Without warning one afternoon the head of her cell called her into his apartment.

"Pack your belongings and be ready to move within the next couple of days," he told her.

Three days later Olivia was once again summoned to her cell leader's apartment. She was introduced to a man named Abreu. He gave her three separate checks. Each was for twenty thousand dollars drawn on three Los Angeles banks. Abreu identified himself as their superior in al Qaeda and proceeded to give Olivia her orders and instructions verbally.

"Move to Sunnyvale, California and open three checking accounts, each at a different bank. Find the entrance to the Sunnyvale Air Force base and rent a nice apartment within a one mile radius of the base. The apartment is to be at least on the second floor level. Furnish the apartment and wait for further instructions. Make sure it is a nice apartment and furnish it with expensive, classy furniture. Make the bed and bedroom very plush. Report in to your cell leader every day at noon. Send him the address to your apartment."

Olivia followed her orders. After living in the apartment for a month she received a visit from her cell leader and the man named Abreu. She was given a photograph of a young United States Air Force technician. His name was Steven Housten. She was told she could meet him at 'Rocky's' Bar and Restaurant. She was also given a fire proof lock box with two keys.

Abreu instructed her, "Begin a relationship with him. This is the first part of your mission. It will be your responsibility to get as close to Steve Housten as possible and gain his absolute trust. You will be given further instructions after you accomplish this. I caution you to go slow in seducing him as this needs to seem like a normal and sincere love affair. No one is to suspect you are playing him. Keep the contents of the box safe and locked. They are gifts to be given to Housten as your relationship matures. There are radio transmitters built into these gifts. They are tuned to the receiver in your apartment. You will be able to hear whatever is going on around Housten when he is on duty. Make sure your affair with him is strong before you start giving him the gifts."

After Abreu and her cell leader left Olivia looked in the box before locking and hiding it. In it were three watches, a dozen pens and three pair of glasses. She noted the plastic box which held the glasses was labeled: "Glasses / prescription: Steven Housten."

As she locked and hid the box she wondered what all these transmitters were for. Unknown to her, al Qaeda wanted to be sure that when the time came, Olivia would receive certain information. This information would concern the movements of the International Space Station. The information would come to Olivia from the Satellite Control Center via transmitters worn or carried by Airman Steven Houston. When Olivia received the report that the space station was changing its orbit, she was to notify Abreu right away. This was the trigger to initiate the start of another al Qaeda plot.

Chapter 15

Abreu now had the plan in motion. He now wanted to assure that James and John were really committed, both to the long term plan, and to the mass killing of Americans. He placed a secure call via the satellite phone to Paul Macal and Michael Heilman in Washington, DC.

Abreu directed the two spies, "I want you to inform your superiors in the National Security Council, that one of your reliable sources is going to give you the location of a large al Qaeda training camp in Libya. Tell them hundreds of terrorists are being trained there. In this camp terrorist training of every kind is taking place. They are being taught to use weapons and make bombs. Bombs are actually being built there and hundreds of people are learning how to use them. These bombers are being dispatched to secret cells throughout the world including the jihad against the United States. Unassembled bomb parts are smuggled to existing cells. I will send you the camp location and coordinates. Recommend that the camp be bombed and destroyed. It will then be imperative for you to tell me the time and date of the bombing attack.

Three days after the phone call an al Qaeda courier placed an envelope in a post office mailbox. It was not delivered to the apartment because in al Qaeda, only Abreu and his assistant knew of the apartment. Paul and Michael opened the envelope. Inside was

a map and coordinates showing the location of the training camp
to be bombed. The same camp where James and John Falcon were
now finishing their schooling.

"I wonder why al Qaeda wants their training camp bombed,"
Michael queried.

"I don't know," replied Paul, "Maybe because too many people
know its location. At any rate we apparently don't need to know
why or they would have told us. Our problem now is how to give
the information to our bosses, explain how we got it, and convince
them it needs to be bombed and destroyed."

It took a couple of days to formulate a plan so no suspicion or
doubt would fall on Paul or Michael. They had to protect the fact
that both of them were pseudo members of the National Security
Council, but real spies for al Qaeda.

The two spies went to Virginia and purchased a computer and
printer. They printed out a message and mailed to themselves. It
read:

> "Paul,"
>
> "I am sending you this information because
> you have paid me much money in the past. I expect
> to be paid for this information also. The usual fee
> is twenty-five thousand, I want fifty-thousand for
> this as I am risking a great deal, including my life.
> I can't tell you how I came by this information.
> Wire the money to the usual place. Tell no one
> where you got this. It is a highly protected secret.
> Enclosed is the location of an al Qaeda training
> camp. This camp trains terrorists who are sent all
> over the world. There are at least several hundred
> in training at this time. The camp includes ex-
> tensive facilities for teaching bomb making and

bombs are actually built there and the parts are shipped all over the world."

The note was not signed.

They addressed the note and maps to themselves and mailed the package from Virginia. They made extra copies of the maps in case the package was lost in the mail. The two spies then beat the computer and printer with a hammer and destroyed them. Then, they threw them into separate dumpsters and set them on fire.

Paul and Michael requested an urgent meeting with Deputy National Security Advisor Geraldine Francis. They told her secretary it concerned al Qaeda. The meeting was scheduled and held the same day.

Geraldine Francis, Assistant National Security Advisor, frowned deeply as she read the message and looked at the map of Libya. She immediately called her boss and told him what she had been given by two staff members. She was instructed to set up a meeting for the next morning.

Paul and Michael were told to wait in the outer office as the meeting commenced in the National Security Advisor's secure meeting room. Everyone Geraldine had advised of the meeting was in attendance. This included representatives from the CIA, FBI, State Department and several of the President's personal staff. The military was also present including General Snyder, recently appointed Chairman of the Joint Chiefs.

Geraldine had an enlarged copy of the note and map displayed on a screen so everyone in the room could see it. The CIA people questioned the validity of the information as they had no information about this "camp."

"If such a training camp existed, we would be aware of it." The CIA Director insisted.

The FBI stated they had no known spies in the United States that would have such high value information. They wanted the identity of the person who sent this note. Paul and Michael were summoned into the meeting. The CIA re-stated their position that the information probably was not authentic or real. The FBI insisted on knowing the identity of the person supplying the information.

Paul started to speak, "Our source has presented information to us in the past and it has always been true and accurate."

He was about to say he would not reveal his source, but was rudely interrupted by Robert Duncan, the current National Security Advisor.

"We're missing the point here people. It is irrelevant at this point if the CIA has information on a secret camp or not. And, it does not matter who the source is. What matters is that if this camp does exist we need to know it and its location. Paul and Michael have fulfilled their job and brought that information to us. Now it's up to us to act on it. Paul, Michael, do you have anything else to add?"

Paul took this opening to express what Abreu had instructed him. As professionally and evenly as he could muster, he managed to say, "Well, it seems to me that if an al Qaeda training camp exists, and is making bombs to be sent throughout the world, that camp should be destroyed."

Paul and Michael were dismissed from the meeting.

Air Force General Snyder stood and studied the map of Libya for several minutes, then addressed the room, "This camp, if it does exist. Is in the middle of a desert at a location that none of our satellites cover. Rather than change any satellite orbits I say we send a high altitude Air Force reconnaissance plane over this location. This mission can be commenced within hours and have the information to us within two days. It can determine if a camp does exist, take pictures of what is going on and pinpoint the co-ordinates of the camp. If it is determined to be a terrorist camp, we present the info to the President and he decides what to do about it."

It was decided that a high altitude Air Force reconnaissance aircraft would be dispatched to confirm the existence of the training camp, and take pictures of the activity happening in the camp. If the information from Paul and Michael proved to be accurate then it would be presented to the President along with the recommendation that the camp be destroyed.

Chapter 16

It was four o'clock in the morning at Spangdahlem Air Force Base, Germany. The base is home to the 122nd Reconnaissance wing and two fighter aircraft wings. The commanding general's aide knocked on the bedroom door and waited for the General to give him permission to enter. Once inside he addressed the General's wife, who was lying in bed, "Please excuse the intrusion ma'am." He then saluted the General and reported, "Sir, the communications center just received a secure 'execute immediate' order from the National Command Authority. They have confirmed the order as authentic."

The General read the order which was addressed to him. It read:

TO: COMMANDING GENERAL, SPANGDAHLEM
AIR FORCE BASE
    FROM: NATIONAL COMMAND AUTHORITY
    EXECUTE: IMMEDIATE:
    DISPATCH HIGH ALTITUDE RECONNAISSANCE
AIRCRAFT OVER LIBYAN AIRSPACE: STOP
    TAKE HIGH RESOLUTION PICTURES OF AREA IN
COORDINATES LISTED: STOP
    PROTECT AIRCRAFT WITH FIGHTER ESCORT:
STOP

MAINTAIN MISSION STEALTH: STOP
RETURN FILM IMMEDIATE TO ANDREWS AIR
FORCE BASE. STOP
ADDRESS FILM CONTAINER TO: JOINT CHIEFS OF
STAFF: STOP
REPEAT: IMPERATIVE - MAINTAIN SECRECY OF
MISSION: STOP
INFORM PERSONNEL INVOLVED: MISSION NOT
TO BE DISCUSSED OFF BASE:
END

The General looked at his aide and issued preliminary orders, "Wake the executive officer and have him read this message. Then you keep the actual message for our mission briefing. As of now you are to take charge of this message. No copies are to be made and any that exist are to be destroyed. Notify security to quietly lock down the base, no one in or out. Ask the exec to wake the duty flight crews. We'll send one picture plane with six fighter escorts and three refueling tankers. Tell the exec I want a fighter squadron orbiting fifty miles out over the Mediterranean in case they are needed. Have all the crews report to the briefing room. We'll solidify all this at the mission briefing."

"Yes Sir, and good night ma'am," The aide saluted and left to carry out his orders.

The lights went on in the crew barracks as airmen were roused from their bunks. Pilots were summoned from throughout the base. Colonel Roger Dillon had spent a late night at the officer's club trying to land a woman. He failed to seduce any and went to bed alone and intoxicated.

Being drunk was ok, because he was not on the duty roster for that night. He could not believe it when the lights went on in his room and a sergeant shook him awake.

"What the hell do you want," Colonel Dillon growled at the sergeant.

The sergeant stood back and said, "Sir, the executive officer sent me to get you. He said to tell you that you're going to command a mission."

"What!" Responded Dillon. "Hell, I'm still half drunk."

"I know," Said the sergeant, "The exec said to tell you to take a cold shower, brush your teeth, gargle with mouth-wash, drink some strong hot coffee, and in his words, not mine, get your ass to the briefing room."

"Shit," exclaimed Dillon as he headed for a cold shower. "Tell the exec I'll be there in twenty minutes."

A half an hour later Colonel Dillon still had a headache when the executive officer grabbed his arm and pulled him aside for a private conversation.

"Roger," the exec began, "You're up because your counter part is sick and can't get out of bed. I saw you at the officer's club last night. I know we're going against all regulations, but we have a serious mission and you are the best man available at the moment to command it. I want you on this mission. Tell me now if you can't do it."

"I can do it, if it's a serious mission I don't want to miss it."

"I figured you would say that. Let's get to the briefing."

The actual briefing lasted an hour. All the details of the mission were addressed. Colonel Dillon would fly the reconnaissance plane. Six fighter aircraft would fly protective escort. A squadron of fighters would orbit and would only fly into Libyan airspace if needed. Refueling would take place over the ocean. All personnel were sworn to secrecy and ordered to not discuss this mission.

Ninety minutes later the mission launched. As the planes approached Libyan airspace Dillon's co-pilot turned and said, "Why are we taking pictures of the desert from such a high altitude?"

"I don't know the reason for the pictures or the urgency,"

Dillon replied. "But we're over a desolate area of the Earth and high enough that no one will know we've been here."

It would be several weeks later that Dillon and several other pilots would find out the purpose of what was referred to as "The picture mission."

Three days after the meeting the report and pictures from the Air Force came back and convinced everyone involved that the camp was an al Qaeda training center for terrorists. The high resolution film showed details of the camp with tents and large numbers of people. Several of the pictures showed armored vehicles, people shooting at a gun range, and a commando type training area. Outside of three large tents were stacks of small and large boxes. The smaller boxes were labeled: EXPLOSIVES and DYNAMITE. The report was presented to the President. He determined the camp was a clear and present danger to the United States. He ordered the military to destroy it.

Paul and Michael were informed their source had given them accurate information. The NSA and the CIA coughed up the fifty grand and gave it to Paul to pay their source.

Paul and Michael had no choice but to split the money, and keep it.

Several days passed. Paul and Michael became concerned they would not be privileged to know the time and date of the attack. On the following Saturday each man got a phone call ordering them to a special meeting at five A.M. Sunday morning. At the meeting, the Chairman of the Joint Chiefs questioned several people in the room. He wanted to be sure this was not some kind of trap for the United States. Paul and Michael were both asked questions about their source. They told the Chairman their source was reliable and had given accurate information on previous al Qaeda situations. Satisfied, he announced the attack would be executed. It would take place ten days later, September 30th at the Libyan time of 2 P.M. The two spies looked at each other across the room and their hidden smiles showed the relief of knowing the attack date and time. They passed the details to Abreu Sunday afternoon. He praised both the spies for successfully completing their assignment. This time the mission assignment to the U.S. Base in Germany was not a last minute order. The base was ordered to bomb and obliterate the camp at the co-ordinates where they had taken the reconnaissance photos. The date and time were specified so the U.S. government would be ready to respond politically, or militarily, if necessary.

Abreu had to work fast in order to have everything in place for the attack. Al Qaeda announced that a celebration was to take place at the camp schools on September 30th to celebrate the graduation of several classes. A special invitation was given to James and John Falcon's family. The RSVP from James and John's father said he would bring his entire family, his wife, his two daughters and his mother. His mother was exceptionally close to James and John, and the two boys had strong emotional ties to her.

On the morning of the attack Abreu assigned extra guards to James and John and gave confidential orders to them and the body guards on duty, "Just Before two o'clock this afternoon James and John are to be summoned and taken out of the camp for a private meeting and celebration of their academic success. Be absolutely sure they are out of the camp and in the hill area surrounding the camp for their two o'clock private meeting. Leave their family in the camp."

At noon on September 30th James and John greeted their mother, father, grandmother and sisters at the main entrance to the training camp. The celebration was well underway with many families and visitors roaming the camp, enjoying the food and activities. Abreu stood at the edge of the camp. He actually felt a twinge of guilt saying to himself, "It's too bad all these people have to die today, including James and John's family. But this will assure the boys will want to commit to the plan and be intensely motivated to see it through to its conclusion." His contemplation made him feel better. He muttered out loud but only he could hear, "To sacrifice a thousand or more lives to insure the potential killing of millions of Americans and the destruction of American cities is definitely worth the trade." He then walked to a location where he could watch and be sure his future terrorist astronauts were being well guarded.

James was showing his family around the camp. In addition to the food and drink there were demonstrations of martial arts, knife fighting, shooting, and hand-to- hand combat. Most of the classrooms were open. The bomb making classrooms were closed up tight and sealed shut. John was walking behind the family speaking with his grandmother. Then the pleasant afternoon turned to sheer terror.

Suddenly there was the distant roar of jet engines. People looked up to see where the sound was coming from. Abreu looked at his watch. Like many well laid plans this one was askew. The attack was happening earlier than scheduled. Abreu charged forward and quietly told the guards to get the brothers behind the large boulders at the edge of the camp. James' body guards grabbed him and started running towards the edge of the camp. The roar of the jet aircraft was now deafening as the planes neared the camp. John's guards were farther away and it took several seconds longer for them to reach John. As they grabbed John and started running they tripped and fell to the ground. The brothers' family stood near where John fell. They were frozen in place as they did not know what to do.

Now there was a sudden thunderous roar in the sky. Explosions and tremendous fireballs engulfed tents and people all around them. Abreu had reached the large boulders at the edge of the camp. He helped James and his guards to take cover behind the boulders. James looked over the shoulder of the guard carrying him. He saw his brother John burning up and engulfed in flames. His face and head were on fire as he screamed in agony. James' sisters and grandmother were near his brother. They were panic stricken; crying and screaming uncontrollably at the horror that surrounded them. His father and mother were both trying to cover John with a blanket to put out the flames. In the next moment they were all engulfed in a sheet of white hot flame and disintegrated before James' eyes. James was in sudden shock. Abreu ordered James's guards to take him from the camp to an al Qaeda compound where he would be safe.

"Guard him with your lives!" Abreu commanded. Abreu looked back over the death and destruction he had ordered. For whatever reason, the bombing attack had come earlier than anticipated. The Americans, as usual, had used their power to its fullest extent. They had not known that a festival was planned and many innocent people would be there. There were dead lying everywhere and the camp was in ruins. Abreu said to himself, out loud but under his breath, "This is the price for jihad against America."

The middle eastern news papers had a field day accusing the United States for the destruction of what was termed a Libyan refugee camp. Abreu's only thought was that with John dead it only left James to carry on with the plan. The quick action by James guards had saved his life. The surviving guards who failed to save John were later executed for that failure. Back at the safety of the compound James wept for hours at the memory of his family's horrid death. He stopped weeping whenever Abreu comforted him. For many months Abreu was with James every day. He was his constant companion. James felt Abreu's love for him and was comforted. Abreu worked hard to get James back on track for the plan. Abreu did have genuine feelings for James, so it was easy to spawn a loving relationship. James never knew the reason all his guards disappeared and were replaced by new ones. Abreu could not take the chance of any guard questioning why James was to leave the camp before two o'clock. He certainly could not allow any chance of James finding out it was he who planned the attack that intended to kill James' family. So anyone who might ask a question about the timing of the attack was sent back to the cells from which they had come.

During the period of healing the explanation of what happened and why it happened was presented to James many times over. Abreu and others told James the evil people of America had done this with their jet airplanes and bombs. Abreu had many sessions with James explaining that the Americans killed many of his people, and did this kind of evil all over his part of the world. He was told that someday, he would have the opportunity to do great harm to America as punishment for what America had done to his family, and his world. He was to show the world that America could be harmed greatly and ultimately be brought down. James pondered the many things he was told. He knew his training was coming to a conclusion and he would be going to America. He concluded he hated America and vowed to himself to do whatever Abreu had planned in order to attack America.

Chapter 17

I t was at this point in time that Paul Macal and Michael Heilman, the al Qaeda spies in the Security Council, were ordered by Abreu to use their congressional connections to get James Henry Falcon an appointment to the Air Force Academy. They were also ordered to use the same group of people to instruct NASA that James Henry Falcon was to be inducted into the Astronaut Training Program upon his graduation from the Air Force Academy.

The first part of the assignment proved to be rather easy. Paul went back to the office of former congressman Pete Homier. This was the congressman who first hired Paul into a government job. Paul had kept in touch with the people who worked in the office and was close friends with two of the aides to the present congressman. He recommended to them that a student at the University of California be given an appointment to The Air Force Academy. Paul's friends manipulated the paperwork for the congressman they worked for, and James Falcon was given an appointment to the Academy.

The second part of the assignment, to get James into the NASA Astronaut Training Program, proved to be more difficult. Michael Heilman, with Paul backing him up and helping him, took on this part of the assignment. As a senior aide to members of the National Security Council, Michael maneuvered himself into a position of representing the council at the Senate appropriations committee meetings. This allowed him to meet and establish a business relationship with Senator Cheryl Konlin, the chairman of the appropriations committee. In her position she had extensive political power, as she influenced the determination of where monies would be allocated. Michael and Paul quietly gathered all the information they could about Senator Konlin. They discovered she was a solid citizen, a good wife, a respected senator, and a shrewd politician. Because she was a powerful senator, as well as an ambitious politician, they decided that Michael needed to get close to her, do her some favors and become a political ally.

After several months of attending appropriation meetings, Michael made sure he became well known to the senator. Once he established a relationship with her, and gained her trust, he was comfortable in giving her certain Security Council information. She used this information to enhance her power as a senator. He started slow at first, dropping hints to her about information from the Security Council that she might be interested in knowing. Once Michael found that she was open to him informing her of Security Council information, he made it a point to speak to her whenever an opportunity presented itself. Eventually, as the two came to know each other, he would discretely stop by her office to entice her with happenings in the Security Council. At one of these meetings she asked him if he would be willing to do her a favor occasionally. He said he would be happy to. She would supply him with questions to ask her at the appropriations meetings and press conferences. This allowed her to answer these pre-arranged questions making her look good in the meetings.

Michael now had her in a position where he felt comfortable in asking her a favor. He did so by telling her he was aware of a brilliant young man about to be appointed to the Air Force Academy. He would be a solid astronaut candidate at NASA. He asked her if she would use her influence to get this young man

into the NASA Astronaut Training Program upon his graduation
from the Academy. She replied that she would be happy to do this
favor in return for what he had done for her. Several weeks later,
at one of his visits to her office, she told him it had been arranged
and that upon his graduation, James Falcon would be assigned to
the NASA program.

The two spies reported to Abreu that his instructions had
been accomplished. James had his appointment to the Academy.
After graduation NASA would recruit James and assign him to
the NASA Astronaut Training Program.

The two spies now felt secure both in their standing with al
Qaeda and with their positions in the National Security Council.
They had informed Abreu and al Qaeda of the Laser weapon,
were successful in getting the Libyan camp bombed and now had
fulfilled Abreu's instructions concerning James Falcon.

Chapter 18

James Henry Falcon was seated with on stage with fifty other graduates. He had just completed and was graduating from flight school. There were over three hundred people in the audience, made up of families, friends and well wishers of the flight school graduates. James had no one in the audience. He had no family, except his pseudo American parents who had helped him when he came to America. It had been several years since his real family had been killed in the bombing raid by the American planes. James had a vivid memory of the day. He could not help himself as he often thought of his brother on fire from the bombs. He remembered his sisters screaming in sheer panic, and his parents helpless in trying to save his brother. He hated the memory of seeing his brother's face and head engulfed in flames. Then from the safety of large boulders, where his guards had taken him, he witnessed his entire family disintegrate in a sheet of white hot flame from an American bomb. This fact caused him uncontrollable bitterness and hatred towards America. The only reason for James' self control was Abreu's promise. The promise that one day, James would be able to do great harm to America.

The dean of the flight school stood at the podium and addressed the audience. "Ladies and gentlemen, on behalf of the Northern California Aeronautics Academy I present to you our tenth graduating class." The audience applauded loudly. When the applause ended the dean continued.

"It is now my privilege to present the award for the most outstanding student. This student finished our course with the highest score in the history of our Academy. I present this award to James H. Falcon along with my sincere congratulations."

That evening following the graduation ceremony James Henry Falcon was in his dorm room contemplating his time at the University of California at Berkeley. James sat on the edge of his bed reminiscing of his boyhood and his beloved brother and family. In his mind he visualized their horrible deaths. He became angry all over again as he did every time he thought of his family. He had been promised by Abreu that he would have the opportunity to potentially kill millions of Americans as retaliation. James was tired of waiting. He had accomplished all the goals Abreu had asked of him. He had a commercial pilot's license and had logged many hours of flight. He had excelled in school both scholastically and athletically. He was tired and bored, and ready to kill Americans. This night he would find out the plan.

Abreu was coming to his college dorm room for a meeting.

As Abreu approached the door to James' room he could not stop his mind from reviewing his history with James. He had recruited James and his brother John in an al Qaeda training camp. He had made sure the staff at the camp had given the necessary effort to prepare them for American society. James and John were never to know their parents and sisters were to be killed in the bombing attack by the American aircraft. The attack he had planned. If the bombs did not kill them, Abreu had men in the camp that would complete the killing and make it look as if they died as a result of the bombs. The men had explosives, grenades, and flame throwers to complete the killing, if necessary.

It was bad luck for the overall plan that John was killed with his family during the attack.

What Abreu, and other leaders of al Qaeda involved in the plan considered fortunate, was that James had witnessed the horrible deaths of his family. They considered, and rightly so, this would add to James' hatred of America. Americans had killed James's family, and James repeatedly proclaimed to his al Qaeda colleagues, that he would do whatever necessary, to kill as many Americans as he could in his lifetime because of what they did to his family.

As the result of the death of James' twin brother John, it meant only one brother was left to carry out Abreu's plan to completion. Abreu remembered how he comforted James and was his mentor for many months following the death of his family. During that time he and James had become very close. Abreu had become very fond of James even though he had to bury deeply within himself the fact that he had ordered the deaths of James' family. John's death also meant that James needed to be protected from any harm at all times in order for the plan to move forward.

Abreu knocked lightly on the door. Both his thoughts and James' contemplating ended. James opened the door. Abreu walked in. Mentor and student hugged tightly for a full minute. Their deep feelings for each other were evident and sincere. After their greeting Abreu stated he should not stay long and he would get right to the point of the meeting.

At that moment the door crashed open and James' two body guards charged into the room with their silenced guns in hand. They immediately relaxed when the saw Abreu.

"It's good to see your guards are still being diligent." Abreu said.

"They respect my privacy mostly, but they are always around," replied James.

"You may go," Abreu ordered the body guards. "James is safe with me. Abreu and James sat down. Abreu looked intently across the table at James. Before Abreu could speak James' anger from his previous thoughts flared, James seethed loudly at Abreu, "When will I start killing Americans like you said I would? I have done everything you asked me to do, I'm tired of waiting!"

Abreu retorted, "Quiet down, and calm yourself my young friend. You will like what I am about to tell you. First let me tell you that your leaders, including Usama Bin Laden, and myself, are highly pleased with your hard work and success so far. It is everything we expected and hoped for."

James interrupted, he was calmer now.

"I want to start killing Americans right now. I'm tired of all this bullshit of school and flying."

Abreu continued gently, "Listen to what I have to say to you. I appreciate your patience and now you will know what part you are to play in the killing of millions of Americans. You have been accepted and will enter the United States Air Force Academy next semester. Our people in Washington arranged a congressional appointment."

James sat up in his chair. Abreu had his full attention now.

"We have prepared you, and you have prepared yourself, to be successful at the Academy. And, you are going to be an astronaut!" Abreu continued excitedly. "It is already arranged, by the same people in Washington. You are to be selected for astronaut training after graduation from the Air Force Academy. This information is only for you to know. It must be kept secret. Tell no one of this."

James was astounded. All he could mutter was, "You have got to be shitting me!"

Abreu Continued, "You must continue to work hard and excel. Become a trusted astronaut. You will receive further instructions when you reach that level. Until then you may not hear from me. I assure you, that as an American astronaut you will deliver a deadly blow to the country that killed your family, and has done so much evil to the people in our world. If our final plan

works, you will kill millions of Americans. Our leader, Usama
Bin Laden, and I agreed, and he gave permission to tell you this
information. I'm telling you this so you know where all your hard
work is leading. It is imperative that what I have told you is kept
secret. Tell no one!"

Abreu continued, "You will be on your own at the Academy.
I have no doubt you will be successful in graduating."

All James could do was nod his approval. He was speechless.
The meeting was short. It lasted only fifteen minutes. James had
many questions that were unanswered.

As he left, Abreu said, "All your questions will be answered
at the proper time. Good luck at the Academy, I know you are
prepared and will do well."

Then, even though Abreu was concerned about the length of
time and the security of this meeting, he hugged James again for
several long minutes before leaving.

The decision to tell James that he was going to attend the Air
Force Academy and become a NASA astronaut was a hotly debated one. The several men controlling the over-all plan, including
Abreu, requested and were granted a top secret meeting with the
al Qaeda top echelon council, and Usama Bin Ladin himself,
to discuss the issue. The meeting took place deep in the isolated
mountains of Afghanistan.

"That is too much information to give Falcon at this time,"
argued the head of the inner council of al Qaeda, "We are still
seeing if a second operative can be placed in NASA as a back-up
to Falcon."

Abreu argued, "First, trying to slip a second person into
NASA is dangerous to the plan and not needed. NASA security
screenings are very intense and thorough. Any operative who has
not been prepared for years, as we have prepared James, will not
make it through the vetting process. Anyone who tries and is

discovered will make it more dangerous and difficult for James to succeed."

Abreu had Usama Bin Ladin and the Council's attention now. He pounded home his point.

"Secondly, James is dedicated to doing great damage to America. He has worked long and hard to get to where he is now. He is very intelligent and for him to know the result of his on-going efforts would be beneficial to him. I can think of nothing more motivating to James than to know he is to be an American astronaut with the potential to bring down America."

Bin Ladin made the final decision.

"Abreu is closest to our man Falcon and is responsible for the plan to come to fruition. Therefore, we will go with Abreu's wishes. Also, cease any plans to place a second operative in NASA. I agree with Abreu that Falcon operating alone is the best plan."

The decision was made. James Henry Falcon was informed that he was to be an astronaut.

James sat silently in his room for many minutes thinking of his meeting with Abreu. He was satisfied with his life so far. He actually enjoyed coming to America. He remembered the ship and the fun he had aboard with his body guards during the ocean crossing. James recalled that he was a little scared when he and his body guards left the big ship and boarded the small rubber boats while still miles out to sea. The little boats were fast and it took only twenty minutes of a rough ride to reach land. He was relieved when the small boats ran up onto the beach. It was very late at night. Several men were waiting. They took him and his body guards to meet the couple who were to be his parents in America.

The couple had been in America several generations. Their name was Falcon. The woman was a school administrator. She had set up James' school records in California including a copy of his forged birth certificate from Elko, Nevada. The husband was a professor at the University of California at Berkeley. Although

James' grades were legitimate for the year he attended, the professor used his position to enhance James' college records and make his identity foolproof as far as college transcripts and records were concerned.

James decided that he was excited to be going to the United States Air Force Academy. He wondered for several minutes how it had been arranged for him to be accepted to the Academy. Then he dismissed the thought. Regardless of how he got in, he would give it his best effort. But, the idea he was to be an astronaut caused his entire body to tremble uncontrollably for several minutes. He did not know, and decided not to ponder how that was to come about. Then he stopped trembling and smiled at the prospect of being an astronaut. James Henry Falcon was happy with his accomplishments and slept well that night.

Chapter 19

UNITED STATES AIR FORCE ACADEMY
COLORADO SPRINGS, COLORADO, UNITED
STATES OF AMERICA

James was six months into his first- year orientation. On a Sunday afternoon he received a phone call in the common study area of his dormitory.

A familiar voice on the phone asked, "I hope you are well, how's it going?"

James recognized Abreu's voice and replied, "It's much more difficult than I had anticipated. This is serious business. I want you to know that it will require my best and continuous effort to get through this."

"You and I both know you have the guts and ability to make it on your own," replied Abreu.

"I know that," said James. "No outside help would be able to penetrate this academy. The manipulations you made happen, and that I was not privileged to know about, may have got me into this Academy, but the honor here is real and no manipulations would help me to succeed."

"My dear young friend," implored Abreu, "I hope that is not despair I hear in your voice. Be assured our plan is moving forward."

James took a cursory look around the study area to make

sure no one was paying attention to his conversation. Satisfied his conversation was private, he ended by telling Abreu, "Don't even worry about me, I feel good and will be able to see this mission through successfully. You can count on it."

"It is good to hear your voice and what you just said, I will report that you are doing well, good bye."

The phone clicked dead and James felt sad he did not have the chance to say more to Abreu. As he hung up the phone he was amused for a moment. These Americans have no clue as to what is coming at them.

James Henry Falcon stood many morning formations during his four years at the Air Force Academy. He spent his time study-ing intensely and playing hard at intramural swimming, self-de-fense classes, and gymnastics. He kept a low profile during school and kept to himself during spring and summer breaks. He used the time to log more flying hours.

He kept his determination and dedication to the fulfillment of the plan. It did not matter to him that he was not aware of the whole and complete plan. Always in the back of his mind was the idea that all this education and preparation was leading to some kind of culmination, and an attack on America.

James' intelligence, his early educational background and learning, and his athleticism; were large factors in his success at the Academy. What carried him through any tough times, though, was his motivating factor, that being successful at the Academy was another step to doing some kind of great harm to the United States of America.

In the last weeks of his senior year he was called to the com-mandant's office, along with two other cadets. As they sat in the outer office the two cadets talked about what their assignment might be. James Henry Falcon had a good idea why he had been summoned and he kept it to himself. When his turn came he was led into the office. He met the Commandant of the Air Force

Academy, several staff officers, and three representatives from
NASA.

James knew what they were going to offer him. It took su-
preme effort to act surprised as he humbly accepted their offer to
try out and train for the NASA Astronaut Corps. His four years
in the Air Force Academy had gone by smoothly and easier than
anticipated. When it was over James looked back and realized
he had actually enjoyed the intensity of the all out effort it took
for him to succeed. He also relished the irony of the fact that the
United States Air Force Academy was giving him the means to
destroy what it was sworn to protect.

Normally, a graduate from the Academy would spend time
fulfilling an Air Force assignment. But the two spies, Michael
Heilman and Paul Macal had done their job well. Unsuspecting
members of Congress, including Senator Cheryl Konlin, along
with several officials in the National Security Council, had ordered NASA to request James Falcon be assigned to the Astronaut
Training program. These elected and appointed officials had un-
knowingly advanced the al Qaeda plan to attack the people and
nation they represented.

The order to admit James Henry Falcon into the astronaut
training program, direct from the Air Force Academy, did not go
unquestioned. NASA Deputy Director Jay Hart received the di-
rective and immediately confronted NASA Director Terry Walsh,
"Are you aware of this?"

Terry Walsh took the written order from his Deputy and
read it. "Yes," he replied, handing the paper back. I received a
phone call from Senator Konlin. She said she had received several
recommendations that this young man was highly qualified and
would be an excellent candidate for our Astronaut Program. She
'requested' that I recruit him upon his graduation. Since she has
a lot of authority and influence over our budget and the money
we receive, I honored her request."

"Well, I can see we don't have any choice," Said Jay, "This is highly irregular though, I hope this guy is for real. If he washes out of the training program it would be embarrassing to the senator and bad for us."

The Director ended the conversation, "If he is as good as she described, he will be an asset to the Astronaut program. But I don't want any special treatment. He makes it or doesn't make it just like any other candidate."

After his graduation James was assigned to NASA's Astronaut Training Program. The years of education and training from al Qaeda, along with his dedication and effort in college, and the Academy, served him well at NASA. After two years in the training program he was assigned permanently to NASA as an astronaut. The al Qaeda plan was moving forward.

During these two years the whole al Qaeda plot almost became unraveled because of a woman. On his first day at NASA James noticed a young receptionist working at the main entrance desk. She smiled at him. James was immediately infatuated by her. As the first weeks went by he occasionally spoke to her. One afternoon he got his nerve up and when no one else was in earshot he asked her out to dinner.

She smiled and replied, "I'm flattered. Let me think about it, sir."

He immediately told her, "Don't call me sir, it makes me feel old."

She smiled again and insisted, "I'll let you know. I think it would be fun."

James had never been a "ladies man," as he had spent his time studying, working out in the gym, swimming, and reading the Koran. He read the Koran only when he was alone. He had not thought about women except to satisfy his sex drive when it surfaced. But this young woman was different and James was drawn to her. When she finally accepted his invitation to dinner it gave him a warm feeling he had never experienced. After several weeks of dinner dates, and weekend afternoons together, she let James make love to her. It happened in James' apartment and it gave James a feeling he had never felt in his entire life. Her name was Sonya. James was developing deep feelings for her. Even though he knew his parents would not have approved of his behavior with Sonya, he wished his brother and family were there so he could introduce her to them. As the months passed James' feelings for Sonya became more intense as he spent more time with her. He thought and assumed she was his girl exclusively.

It was a tremendous and satisfying feeling. It even made James almost start to re-consider his ultimate goal of doing great harm to America. One evening after a long day at work he decided to surprise her. He picked up a bottle of red wine and flowers from a local flower shop. He arrived at her apartment around eight o'clock. The windows in her apartment were dark as James knocked on her door. After waiting a few minutes he knocked again. It took several minutes for the porch light to go on. The door opened only a couple of inches. James could see Sonya's face through the slightly opened door.

"James," Sonya exclaimed, "What are you doing here, I didn't expect you to come over today."

"I thought I would surprise you," James started to say.

He was interrupted by a male voice inside Sonya's apartment. "Who's at the door, Sonya?"

Through the now partially opened door James saw a male figure in a robe come out of the bedroom. James pushed the door open a little more and saw that Sonya was also in a robe. James was dumfounded. Not only was Sonya with another man, but they were both wearing the matching robes James had given to her as gifts. James stared at the man. Sonya did not say a word. James did not know what to do. He gave Sonya the flowers, turned and walked away without saying a word. Sonya took the flowers, remained silent, and closed the door.

He drove away with tears in his eyes. He tried to organize his thoughts and reaction to what had just happened. By the time he arrived at his apartment he had reached a conclusion and made a couple of decisions. His conclusion and decision was that he would not ever allow himself to feel close to a woman again. He told himself that he had just discovered another evil of America. The freedom American women have to act and treat men the way Sonya had just treated him. Sonya added yet another reason for which America needed to be punished. James decided he would rededicate himself in preparing to do whatever Abreu and al Qaeda had in mind for him. He never looked at or spoke to Sonya again. Sonya did not seem to mind as she never approached James again either.

For the next year James excelled in his training as an astronaut. He wanted to be sure he was ready when Abreu and al Qaeda unleashed him and told him what to do in order to kill Americans and bring down America.

Chapter 20

NASA Headquarters
Office of the Director

Jay Hart, Deputy Director of NASA knocked on his boss's door and stepped into his office.

"Here is the file you wanted on astronaut James Falcon." Jay Hart said to his boss.

NASA Director Terry Walsh took the folder from his Deputy and motioned for him to sit down. Jay Hart felt a knot in his stomach. The Director never asked him to sit unless a serious discussion was about to take place.

"What do think of Astronaut Falcon?" The Director asked without hesitation.

Jay Hart, as was his style, answered immediately. "I don't like him, but he consistently performs above an acceptable level."

"Yes," the Director replied, "and we are going to send him to the Space Station as the pilot of the shuttle. He is the back up to Henry Irving. Irving has developed high blood pressure. He's been grounded, so Falcon goes in his place."

Jay Hart spoke up and stated he did not like it, but it followed standard NASA protocol, so that was it.

While the meeting in the NASA Director's office was taking place Astronaut James Falcon was in the astronaut locker room. He looked around to be sure he was alone among the lockers.

He then spun the dial on astronaut Henry Irving's locker and opened it. It had taken months to get the combination to Irving's locker. James had accomplished this task painstakingly, one number at a time. Since none of the other astronauts suspected what he was doing, James had watched Irving open his locker many times until he had the complete combination.

He opened Irving's locker and removed the bottle of replacement pills he had planted there. He replaced it with Irving's original bottle of vitamin pills. Starting a month previous Falcon had replaced the real vitamin supplement bottle in Irving's locker with an identical bottle, containing identical looking pills. These replacement pills were designed to raise blood pressure slowly, over a period of time. Irving never suspected he was taking replacement pills. Each time Irving had brought in a new bottle Falcon replaced it with an identical bottle containing the replacement pills, which caused Henry Irving to develop high blood pressure.

The ploy had worked. Irving was grounded due to developing high blood pressure and Falcon was headed to the Manned Space Station. Falcon gathered up the remaining replacement pills and flushed them down the toilet. He placed the replacement bottles in his brief case to be destroyed when he arrived at his apartment. Falcon finished putting the real bottle in Irving's locker, closed it and left the locker room.

The phone was ringing as James entered his apartment. He answered it, listened and responded, "Yes, our ploy with the pills worked. Irving is grounded and I'm scheduled to pilot the shuttle to the space station on the next mission."

The phone clicked off.

Astronaut Henry Irving was angry. He could not figure out why his blood pressure had increased inexplicably over the last month. He had never experienced any blood pressure problems his entire life. Now he had been grounded and relieved from the crew going to the manned space station. He had been very excited about his first flight into space. He was looking forward to living aboard the space station and to the science experiments he and his assistant, Lisa Conrad, were to perform. The other part of the situation which was really pissing him off was his chosen replacement. He did not like James Falcon. The two had never become friends. Now Lisa Conrad would become the science officer and Falcon would be her assistant. Henry Irving was a shuttle pilot with plans to fly future missions in space. This blood pressure situation was throwing a glitch in his career plans.

Irving was given a six month sabbatical. His orders required him to rest and relax during his stay at home. He was to take periodic medical exams to determine his fitness for duty. Henry had a good home life. He had a beautiful and intelligent wife, who understood the commitment to his career, and backed him one hundred percent in their marriage. He and his wife had three young sons. Ronald was seven years old, David ten years, and Gavin twelve. The Irving's had a large two story home in Florida. They had lived there for fourteen years. Henry was an active member of the Shepherd Lutheran Church. His faith was deep and sincere. Henry believed, without understanding it, that God created the universe, and Henry Irving was exploring it in his lifetime.

Henry Irving had been a young pilot in the Viet Nam War. It had repulsed him to drop bombs and napalm on the enemy. One aspect that helped him feel better about the bombing was that he was protecting American troops on the ground. Through many hours of prayer and meditation he had come to grips with his actions as a human being. Although he did not understand why God allowed such things to happen, he was confident that God did understand. However, it did bother him that because he was a damn good pilot and rarely missed his target many people had died. All in all Henry Irving was an asset to NASA. Both he and NASA were anxious to determine why his blood pressure had increased causing him to be grounded just before a scheduled mission. His superiors wanted him back to full duty.

There were three other astronauts on the team headed for the space station along with Lisa Conrad and James Falcon. The additional crew members were Cecil Roberts, Roger Lawrence and Dave Ash. Two of the six astronauts now on board the space station would remain. Four of the astronaut crew would end their tour on the station and return to Earth as part of the personnel rotation. Usually, there were only six American astronauts on the station at one time. Due to the work load and experiments to be conducted on this rotation an extra astronaut was to be sent. James Henry Falcon was the added 7TH Astronaut.

Cecil Roberts and Dave Ash had been on previous deployments to the space station. They led the team in the group training sessions in preparation for their time on the station. Most of the team training time included life support systems and emergency procedures. It was imperative that each person on board the space station be an expert in the life support systems. Each team member had to be able to conduct emergency procedures without the help of other astronauts. In addition to the group training, each astronaut would have their own experiments and individual work to prepare for, and then perform them on the station.

There were also reviews of work schedule routines, sleep and eating cycles, and hygiene routines. Practice included hours of manipulating the articulating boom, simulated space walking and reviewing all the working parts of the space station. The training was intense and time was running short. The training was set up so the sessions were at different hours throughout the twenty-four hour day. This schedule would help to acclimate the crew to the life schedule once onboard the space station. Four afternoons per week were allotted for outdoor physical fitness. The crew worked out on the football field. As Cecil, Dave and Roger did stretching exercises Lisa and James ran together around the track.

"Those two are getting awful chummy," remarked Dave, "I hope that does not lead to problems on the station."

"Don't worry," Cecil chimed in. "I've known her a long time. Lisa is a pretty level headed girl. She is a hell of a competitive bitch too, as well as a good astronaut. Falcon doesn't have a chance with her. She's strictly professional."

"I don't particularly care for Falcon, but he is a great pilot," added Roger. "I don't think he has anything on his mind except the mission. They are just crew mates."

As Lisa and James jogged around the football field Lisa said to James, "So, how does it feel to be the seventh astronaut assigned to this mission?"

"Feels great," replied James. "How about dinner again tonight and I'll show you just how great."

"Well," said Lisa, "if you're going to pilot me to the space station, I need to have confidence that you can fly. Let's skip dinner. I'll be at your apartment at seven. Have the wine open."

Lisa arrived just after seven. After a bottle of cabernet and half hour of dancing to slow romantic music Lisa found herself in Falcon's bed. After she was able to catch her breath she looked at James.

"Oh God, two glasses of wine and you can do whatever want to me? I like you James Falcon. I hope I'm not falling for you."

Falcon returned her look. As Lisa rolls over and falls asleep, James Falcon's mind is racing. The memory of Sonya jumps into his head. He can't shut his thoughts off so he vents silently to himself as he stares at Lisa's back,

"Just wait you bitch. You are just like the rest of American women. Your freedom allows you to do whatever you choose. I'll play along with you and your weak morals, even though my mother would be sickened by them and your western ways. Ha! She would punish me for these moments of pleasure with you. It's fun playing and taking advantage of you. But you're going down with the rest of them."

Chapter 21

The next morning a special training session was scheduled in building 39. Lisa and Falcon were late. They did not know where building 39 was located. No training had ever taken place there before today. The pair had gone for a run early and had their sweats on. When they spotted the building they jogged to it. The building was made of grey cement blocks. It was at least fifteen feet high with a flat roof. Two ten foot high steel doors were apparently the only access. A large bold black lettered sign above the doors read:

NO ADMITTANCE-AUTHORIZED PERSONNEL ONLY
IDENTIFICATION REQUIRED
DEADLY FORCE AUTHORIZED
DO NOT APPROACH

As they approached the building they were suddenly confronted by two armed Air Force Policemen. With their wicked looking weapons pointing at the two NASA Astronauts, one policeman growled at them.

"Halt, continue your approach and we will open fire on you!"

Lisa and Falcon stopped their movement.

"What is this?" Falcon said. "We're astronauts, everybody knows us, both of us are supposed to report to building 39."

"I don't give a shit if you're the man in the moon! One more step toward this building and NASA will be hunting for your replacements!" The policeman loudly retorted.

At that moment the doors opened and four more armed Air Force Police came out. The officer in charge had a large gold badge pinned on his shirt. He approached the two astronauts.

"Don't move." He ordered. "I know who you are. You're late. The group you were scheduled with arrived a half hour ago. Wait here while I get permission to let you into the building. These guards have strict orders to shoot anyone trying to approach this building, no matter who they are, so please don't move until I get back."

Lisa and Falcon were not aware of it, but these guards were part of an Air Force Police detachment numbering one hundred men. The men were housed in a barracks building behind the grey block building. These Air Police did not know what they were guarding in building 39.

Their orders were never to discuss with anyone where they were stationed or what they did. There were always eight men on duty. Twenty four hours a day, every day. They were backed up by a standby force of twenty men in the barracks. They had anti-tank weapons and heavy machine guns. Since this was a secure NASA facility, it allowed for the building to be located in an isolated corner of the complex, out of sight of NASA workers and the public. Two fighter jets and an Apache helicopter squadron were stationed at a nearby Air Force Base as additional back up to defend the building. When the men went off duty they left in civilian clothes and blended in with the other thousand or so workers.

The Air Police commander and Cecil Roberts appeared at the door. Cecil confirmed the pair's identity. The armed guards were ordered to stand down and the astronauts were allowed into the building.

"What the hell was that all about?" Lisa seethed at Cecil.

"You will find out in about two minutes." Cecil answered.

The three astronauts entered through the large doors. Inside they encountered a block wall four feet high and twelve feet long. Behind the wall were the four guards who had come outside. Lisa and James followed Cecil around the interior block wall to another wall which ran the full width of the building. There, they went through a second set of steel doors and entered a large room. Their fellow crew members were in the room. There were three uniformed Air Force officers also in the room, a colonel and two sergeants. Lisa and James barely noticed the men in the room. What grabbed their full attention and caused them to disregard everything else was a large control console with many dials, knobs, and a trigger type mechanism. On the wall behind the console was a full scale map of the world. The map ran the full length of the wall and from floor to ceiling. Large letters running across the console identified what it was. The large bold letters read:

LASER FIRING CONTROL CONSOLE SIMULATOR

"You're late," said the colonel. "Be seated and we will begin."

The five astronauts took seats at individual desks. On each desk was a binder, on the cover of which stated:

LASER WEAPON OPERATION MANUAL
DO NOT REMOVE FROM BUILDING 39

The Air Force Colonel introduced himself and began the training session. "I am Colonel Frazer. You do not need to know the names of the two sergeants who will actually be in charge of the training. If you come across these men outside this building you are not to acknowledge them. Another thing, don't ever try to approach this building without an authorized appointment.

This phase of your training and operation is top secret. You gave your sworn oath when you became an astronaut. This is one of the secrets of that oath. This is a secret you are sworn to keep the rest of your life. Sergeant, take over."

The Colonel sat at the rear of the group. One of the sergeants stood between the seated astronauts and the laser weapon control console and began.

"This is the simulator for the laser weapon that is built into the American module of the Manned Space Station. It was secretly built into the space station. As you can see by the security around this building, the existence of this weapon is a highly protected secret. Cecil and Dave are already qualified on the use of the weapon. Our job now is to qualify the rest of the crew."

The astronauts look at each other questioning what they just heard.

Cecil Roberts, the crew commander, addresses the other astronauts, "As part of our duty as military officers and NASA astronauts, the potential use of this weapon is part of our mission whenever we're onboard the space station. So let's be sure we are capable of using it."

The sergeant waited until Cecil finished. He then continued with his introduction of the laser weapon, "This weapon will burn and disintegrate anything it is aimed at. Its main use is to defend the station against sizable space junk that is on a collision course and would strike the station. It can be used to defend the station against possible future missile attacks from an enemy. The laser can be set as a single narrow beam to strike individual targets or as wide as a ten mile spread. It will only be aimed at the Earth by order of the President to defend the United States and the North American Continent from an enemy attack. If aimed at the Earth it has the potential to devastate entire cities and kill millions of people. That is why only the President can authorize its use towards the Earth and only to defend America. One point

I will emphasize is there is no defense against this weapon, and once fired it cannot be deactivated. Each of you will become an expert at using this weapon."

The Colonel interjected. "We must maintain the secrecy of this weapon. If our enemies, and for that matter, even our allies knew this weapon was overhead there would be hell to pay."

James Henry Falcon sat frozen in his seat and became very pale. He hoped no one noticed. He realized in a split second this was what all the years of hard work and preparation were for. Abreu had led him to this weapon and it was the means to bring America to its knees. It took several minutes for him to regain his composure.

"Starting today," the sergeant continued, "We will have a two hour training session every day until each of you is proficient at manipulating the weapon. The laser is computer controlled. The console is for the operator to feed the aiming and power settings into the computer. The trigger mechanism in the middle of the console is for firing the laser. The weapon can only be fired by a human operator."

Two hours later a shaken crew of astronauts left building 39. Each one left to ponder the new potential responsibility they had just inherited. James Henry Falcon had a whole new outlook on why he was at NASA.

Chapter 22

Abreu had been summoned to a secret meeting in Pakistan. He was ordered to wait in the city of Sahidan, Iran. He would be called to the meeting from there. Abreu checked into a hotel as instructed and was happy to enjoy several days of relaxation. He had several al Qaeda friends from the training camps living there. He went with them to a soccer match and some late dinners.

He actually relaxed, the final meeting was scheduled to bring the overall plan to fruition. On the fourth day the phone rang and Abreu's little vacation was over. He answered the phone.

The voice on the phone simply said, "We will pick you up in three hours in the parking garage. Settle your affairs. You will not be returning here."

Abreu packed his one suitcase, settled his account in cash with the hotel manager, and went to the parking garage to await pickup. His friends had given him a nine millimeter automatic and two clips of bullets. He took the weapon, even though he did not feel the need for it, as he felt safe and was comfortable waiting in the garage. There were not many parked cars and very little traffic. His friends knew he was there on holiday. No one else knew of him. There was a cool breeze which blew through the garage. It made Abreu relax, which was not his usual style. He sat on a bench and even closed his eyes for several minutes.

An hour later a light grey Toyota Land Cruiser drove up to Abreu. On the back luggage rack of the Toyota Abreu saw half a dozen red gas cans secured by black webbing. He recognized the driver and passenger from years before. He greeted them genuinely and received a warm reception from them. As he entered the vehicle he noticed there were baskets of food and a case of drinking water. Abreu figured he was in for a long ride. The driver was a big man. He was dressed in light clothes and had a heavy black beard. He looked very mean and Abreu could see the bulge in his shirt where his weapon was hidden. The driver spoke first.

"We have been ordered to be of service to you. If there is anything you need please let us know." He then put the cruiser in gear and began their journey.

The second man smiled at Abreu and said, "It is a pleasure to meet you again. Your reputation is known to us. It is an honor to work for you. Our instructions are to transport you secretly and insure your safety, both during the trip there and the return trip. Our destination is the city of Kalat, in Pakistan. It is a long trip so please feel safe, and make yourself comfortable. Sleep if you like. There are pillows and blankets for you. We have a phone number to call when we reach Kalat. Beyond that we have no further information or instructions. It has been a long time. So in case you do not remember, my name is Jamal. Saeed is driving. For your information, just in case, there are heavy weapons under all the seats."

The trip of approximately seven hundred miles took about sixteen hours. Very few stops were made as the Toyota was well supplied with gas, good food and plenty to drink. Abreu's escorts took turns driving and sleeping. Abreu sat back and enjoyed watching the countryside go by. The rest of the time he slept comfortably.

There was one episode that awoke Abreu from a good sleep. Upon awakening he heard the sound of excited voices outside the stopped Toyota. As he sat up he saw Saeed give a large bag of money to what must have been a border guard. As the Toyota pulled away from the border station Saeed said to Abreu, "We had to pay the border guard a lot of money so there would be no record of us entering Pakistan. We could have killed him but that might have interfered with our return trip."

When they reached the outer limits of Kalat Jamal made a phone call. Abreu was half asleep as he listened to Jamal talk on the phone.

"Yes, I know the hotel," Jamal said. "I understand, we will not arrive until after midnight."

When they arrived at the hotel they were met by two men in a beat up old black sedan. They were rugged and mean looking. One of the men told Jamal and Saeed to stay and prepare for the return trip. "We will have Abreu back here in about three hours," he stated.

Abreu left in the sedan and no further conversation took place. Enroute to the unknown destination Abreu recognized that he as being escorted by two of the fiercest guards of al Qaeda's inner circle.

Abreu could see that extreme precautions were taking place to be absolutely certain they were not followed. The night was very dark. The car moved slowly and took many turns before suddenly turning off the street and entering through the huge wooden gates of a walled compound. Abreu had no idea where he had ended up. With the very dim light provided by a few street lights he could see the walls of the compound they had just entered. They were at least twelve feet high and three feet thick. Two armed men immediately closed the gates silently, as it was the middle of the night. Abreu heard the locks on the gates snap shut.

As the sedan came to a stop in front of a large three story house one of the men in the sedan finally spoke.

"You are having the meeting here. It will not take long.

We will wait for you here. When you are finished we will leave immediately."

There were no lights on in the compound. One of the armed guards led Abreu to a side entrance. He could see no windows on the finished walls of the house. Abreu experienced a sudden ominous feeling in the pit of his stomach, the light from the opening door allowed him a glimpse of at least one hundred heavily armed men in the compound. As he entered the meeting room he realized why so many armed guards were present. The entire al Qaeda leadership was there, including the Great One himself, Usama bin Ladin. Abreu's part of the meeting did not last long. Bin Ladin's instructions were simple.

An elder al Qaeda leader read them, "Instruct our astronaut to use the laser as soon as he is able to do so. Kill the astronauts aboard the space station so they cannot interfere. Do as much destruction as possible during one orbit over the United States. Set the Space Station's orbit so it deteriorates and the station falls from space. After he has done this he is to steal the shuttle. We have built a landing strip in the Iranian desert, he is to land there. The co-ordinates are on this paper." The elder handed the paper to Abreu and continued.

"Inform us immediately when the space station changes its orbit and this action is starting. This will set in motion another strike against America. Do you have any questions?"

Abreu was silent for several minutes. He thought, "This plan is so simple, yet its result is to be so devastating." Abreu responded, "I have no questions. This will be a death blow to America. I pledge my life to this plan and the jihad against America."

One of bin Laden's aides closed Abreu's part of the meeting.

"This has been a long and intricate operation. If you are successful in any part of this action you both will be greatly rewarded with money and fame. Be sure your astronaut knows this."

When leaving the meeting it was still very dark. Abreu

guessed dawn was still at least several hours away. Before the guards opened the compound gates he watched them check very carefully that no vehicles or people were near the compound. As soon as the sedan cleared the gates they were closed immediately. The sedan proceeded with its lights off for several blocks before turning them on. It took a different and round-about route back to the hotel. A great effort at stealth had been exercised both on the approach to the meeting location, and the return trip.

On the trip back to Tehran Abreu started to figure a way to contact Falcon. How could he get these orders to Falcon at NASA. It would have to be done carefully so no suspicion would be raised. He would also have to instruct Olivia Marchan in Sunnyvale to be sure and inform him when any out of the ordinary activity was taking place concerning the manned space station.

Abreu knew he had limited time to get the message to Falcon. He figured the launch date was close at hand. Upon the return to his office he called Olivia Marchan in Sunnyvale, California. It was four o'clock in the morning when the signal device buzzed indicating an incoming call on the satellite phone. It took Olivia several minutes to wake fully, pull the phone from its hiding place and answer.

"Are you alone?" Abreu asked when she answered.

She replied in the affirmative and continued to listen.

"I have instructions for you, have you given the transmitting devices to Steven Housten?"

"Yes," She replied, "He is using the pens at work. The transmitters on his watch and glasses are also functioning."

"Monitor them constantly whenever he is on duty. When you hear of any unusual activity reports concerning the manned space station notify me immediately."

Olivia acknowledged her orders and the phone went dead.

Abreu then booked a flight to Florida, USA.

James Falcon approached his apartment after a long day at

NASA. He saw a delivery slip hanging on the door knob. He read the message, entered his apartment and picked up the phone.

"This is James Falcon. You have a package for me at your office. What is your address? I want to pick it up right away."

He found the address location and entered the office. James was impressed that it actually was a private mail store. He approached the clerk and identified himself. Without saying a word the clerk pointed to a hallway. James walked down the hallway to a closed door, knocked, then entered a small office. Abreu was sitting behind the desk. James spoke first.

"I figured it was you. You're looking older my friend. Are you sure you can handle all this excitement. Is this store part of a cell?" Abreu came from behind the desk. The two close friends share a long hug.

Then Abreu speaks, "Never mind about this place. We must keep this meeting short. Here are your orders from Usama Bin Ladin himself. As soon as you are on the space station kill all the astronauts."

James tenses and listened intently to Abreu.

"Then change the orbit position and bring the station over the center of the United States. I have the co-ordinates worked out for you. They are in this envelope. Set the laser at full power and spread, and burn a path of destruction ten miles wide across the United States. This will be the death blow to America you have waited all these years to accomplish."

James looked at Abreu with a stern expression.

"This is the first time I have actually heard the plan. I am shaking inside. I feel that a great weight has been lifted from my shoulders. I pledge to make this plan work, even if it costs my life."

Abreu smiles. "My dear young friend, you have not heard the part of the plan that gives me great hope. After you have devastated America you are to steal the shuttle and land it in the

Iranian desert. Here are the co-ordinates. Usama has ordered a landing strip built there."

James considers what he just heard. "Stealing the shuttle will not be difficult if all the astronauts are dead. Flying and landing the shuttle in Iran is not as easy as you make it sound. It can be done though. Especially since it gives me a chance to survive and live out my life."

"One last thing," Abreu continues, before you leave the station, set the controls to cause the station to leave its orbit and burn up in the atmosphere or crash to Earth. Destroy any overrides so NASA cannot correct the orbit."

Abreu ends the meeting. "Al Qaeda will make you and I heroes to our world if we are successful. We will be greatly rewarded, you and I will live out our lives in luxury."

James leaves the room and begins to exit the building. The clerk calls him back and gives him a package.

"This is the package you came for sir."

James takes the package thinking, "Just in case, this package makes it a legitimate trip to the mail store."

As he heads back to his apartment with the co-ordinates both for setting up the orbit of the space station for the attack, and the location of the landing site, a thought strikes him, "I'm going to set up the laser attack so Sonya's home town is the first to get destroyed."

Chapter 23

THE WHITE HOUSE
WASHINGTON, DC, USA

Steve Arnold was a file clerk in the office of the Deputy National Security Advisor. It was Monday morning. He had been tasked with delivering files to the White House. He stopped at one of the large restrooms and entered a toilet stall at the far end of the restroom. He was the only one in the restroom until the two spies Paul Macal and Michael Heilman entered. They had just finished a two hour meeting and were returning to their office. The pair used the urinals and then washed their hands. Standing at the sinks Michael looked around the room, then turned to Paul and said, "I'll be glad when this is over. I think the al Qaeda astronaut that we got into NASA is somehow going to use that laser weapon and start burning this place up. When, and if that happens; you and I will have to get out of here fast."

Paul immediately looks around the restroom to make sure no one was there. He is very angry as he says in a seething tone to Michael, "I told you to watch your mouth, if someone ever hears you say the words al Qaeda, astronaut, and laser together we could be in deep shit, so keep your mouth shut!"

As the two spies leave the restroom and are thirty feet from the door they hear it open and turn to see Steven Arnold leave the restroom. Arnold sees them and begins walking hurriedly in the opposite direction. Paul looks at Michael and orders, "I know him, that's Steven Arnold from the National Security office. Kill him before he tells anyone what you said!"

Running in the White House was a rare sight. Steven Arnold sees Michel coming after him. He panics and begins running down the hallway. Michael pulls out his 9MM automatic and pursues. Even though he is authorized to carry a weapon in the White House he keeps it out of sight and against his body.

"I have to kill him," Michael admonishes himself. "If he tells anyone what he heard we'll be in trouble both from the U.S. and al Qaeda!"

One hundred feet into the hallway pursuit no other person has appeared. Steven Arnold sees Michael point the gun at him. No shot is taken. Steven Arnold is a middle aged man, over weight as well as out of shape. It doesn't matter. Adrenalin is pumping through his body. That, and his fear and panic, push Steven Arnold to an out of control, all out run. His pursuer is gaining. He turns a corner into a dead end hallway. At the end of the hallway there is a set of ten foot high double doors guarded by two armed Marines. The Marines are responsible to prevent intruders from penetrating the doors and entering the room beyond. The sign above the doors has one foot bold letters. It reads:

NO ADMITTANCE WITHOUT AUTHORIZED ESCORT
DEADLY FORCE AUTHORIZED
APPROACH WITH PROPER AUTHORIZATION ONLY

The Marines, standing at attention, come to full alert as Steven Arnold, panicked and out of breath, turns the corner and races down the hallway towards the doors they are responsible to protect. Without hesitation the first Marine stepped into the runner's path. When the runner did not slow down the Colt .45automatic came out along with the shouted command, STOP! Following

standing orders the first Marine discharged his weapon stopping
the running man's panicked advance. The second Marine took
a position standing against the doors in case of a second breach
attempt. Michael Heilman is twenty feet down the hallway. He
slips his silenced 9MM automatic into a specially designed coat
pocket, and slips away quietly amongst the security guards and
Secret Service agents emerging onto the scene. Before he leaves
the scene he smiles to himself because the Marine has done his
killing for him. He was sure, arrogantly sure, that no one would
ever know of the remark Steven Arnold had overheard. That remark had cost Steven Arnold his life.

The Marine who discharged his weapon kneels down next to
the mortally wounded man. The Marine is holding his head. The
dying man motions him closer. Struggling and gasping with every
word he says something to the Marine. The words are barely audible but the Marine hears them clearly. What Steven Arnold said
to the Marine was to touch off a security investigation unequaled
in the history of the United States of America.

"What did he say?" the second Marine asks.

"I can't tell you," replied the first Marine.

A dozen armed men secured the area and responding para-
medics checked the victim of the Marine's orders.

"This man is dead," was the paramedic's verbal report.

The incident was over. The result of the incident was far from
over. Marine Lance Corporal Michael Lang had followed his
standing orders in shooting Steven Arnold. The corporal was a
decorated Iraqi war veteran. The Marine Corps had just appointed
him to Annapolis. This was his last week of duty at the White
House. This duty shift he was assigned to guard a sensitive and
secure intelligence room. The standing orders were that no one
whatsoever, be allowed to penetrate the doors of the room without
authorization. Deadly force was authorized.

Both Marines came to attention as the Captain of the White

House Marine detachment approached. The Captain commanded, "At ease" and asked Corporal Lang to report.

"We have to speak in private sir." Lang responded.

The response from the corporal stunned the Marine Captain. Captain Robert H. Harrielson met the eyes of his corporal, hesitated and then said, "OK, this way."

Both Marines walked to a quiet corner.

After reporting the details of the incident up to the point where the dead man whispered his dying words into his ear, Corporal Michael Lang stated to his commanding officer, "Sir, I cannot tell you what he said to me. As he was dying he ordered me to repeat his message to the Deputy National Security Advisor and no one else."

The Captain's retort to Corporal Lang was not pleasant, "Marines don't take orders from civilians. What did he say?"

"Sir, he told me to tell the Deputy, and only her, that an al Qaeda terrorist may have infiltrated the NASA Astronaut Corps."

Captain Robert H. Harrielson was quiet for a full thirty seconds as he processed what he had just heard. Then he ordered the corporal to stand down, and report to the Deputy National Security Advisor regarding this incident.

"Corporal, you have my word," stated the Captain, "I will never repeat what you just told me. If you need any back up in any way just let me know. You can write up the report and give it to me later. Leave out what we just talked about."

Chapter 24

At 1730 hours Corporal Michael Lang, USMC, entered the National Security Administration building. As he entered through the large steel and thick glass doors he could not help but be impressed by the massive building. It was all gray stone. The corporal thought to himself that it was menacing and appropriate as the headquarters of the National Security Advisor and his staff. He especially liked the concrete and steel barriers surrounding the building.

"It would take more than a regular car bomb to get to this building." He said out loud to himself.

His thought was rudely interrupted by the security guards at the front entry. Even though he was in his dress uniform they demanded to see his identification and wanted to know his purpose in entering the building. After he was searched for weapons he informed the guards he had an appointment to see the Deputy National Security Advisor. The guards acted suspicious and skeptical. They watched Lang closely. After several phone calls an aide to the Deputy National Security Advisor appeared to escort the Marine. The security guards eased off as the aide greeted Corporal Lang and advised the Deputy was expecting him.

"Don't let those guards bother you." The aide remarked to Lang. "They all act like we are at war, it gets to be a real pain sometimes."

"We are at war, and I think the guards are OK," replied Lang.

The aide was taken aback by Lang's retort. There was no further communication as the aide escorted the corporal to the top floor and knocked on a pair of dark brown wooden doors. On one of the doors was the name:

Geraldine K. Francis
Deputy National Security Advisor

The door opened and the aide led Corporal Lang into the room. Several people were in the room and Lang figured they also were aides. He was surprised when a rather striking woman stood and approached him. He could smell her perfume. Her long blond hair and deep blue eyes made her a movie star, not the Deputy National Security Advisor. His inner thought was this woman was too young and too good looking to hold such a powerful position.

He thought; "Is she for real?"

His question was answered right away. Geraldine Francis addressed the young Marine with polite authority, "You wanted to see me corporal? There is no need to apologize to me for doing your duty and following your orders. Especially orders concerning the security of a restricted area. I am very sorry for the loss of one of my people. However, I do not hold you responsible."

Before the Deputy Security Advisor could continue, Lance Corporal Lang interrupted, "Ma'am, with all due respect, I did not come here to apologize. Although I am very sorry for having to shoot your man, especially after what he told me. I have a message for you from him. It is for you alone."

Geraldine Francis looked at the Marine, and then ordered the room cleared. The aides that were present looked at each other quizzically and departed the room.

"The room is secure Corporal. Please, relax and sit down. You don't need to be formal in this office. Now, tell me what Steven

Arnold told you as he died. Before we start, it's after work hours, I'm going to indulge myself with a glass of scotch, would you care for something? You must still be upset after having to shoot someone in the White House?"

Lang was used to Marine Corps formal protocol. He was not used to relaxing in the presence of persons in authority. He was surprised but impressed with this woman's casual but authoritative disposition. His reply brought a smile and satisfied expression to the Deputy's face as he said, "Ma'am, I am upset, and feel sick inside about the shooting, but I am a Marine. I have been in combat. So I follow my orders, do my duty loyally to the best of my ability, then deal with the results." The corporal hesitated, then said, "Yes, I will have a drink, thank you, that is; if you are having one also."

Geraldine Francis was impressed with the mature demeanor and quiet confidence of the young Marine. She poured a scotch for herself and a whiskey straight up for the Corporal.

"So, now that I have got you to relax a little, let's get to it Corporal; tell me what is so important that it is for my ears only. What is so important that it cost Arnold his life?"

The corporal took a sip of his whiskey, took a deep breath and began to speak, "Ma'am, what Steven Arnold said to me almost exactly was; 'As an officer of The National Security Advisor's office, I am ordering you to relay only to the Deputy National Security Advisor what I am about to tell you. Tell no one else. That is an order. An al Qaeda terrorist has infiltrated the NASA Astronaut Corps. The man chasing me was trying to kill me, his name is.............'

"That is all he was able to say before he died, ma'am."

The Assistant Advisor did not react for several seconds, then stated to the Corporal, "You are never to repeat this to anyone. Do you acknowledge my order and realize the importance of obeying it?"

"Ma'am, I obey orders," was all Lang, said. Then he realized and said, "My Captain also knows some of what Arnold told me. He also knows the importance of not telling anyone. And he won't."

The Geraldine Francis and corporal Lang finished their drinks in silence.

"You are dismissed Corporal." The Deputy ordered, "Tell your Captain my order to keep this information to himself. I'll read the full report of this incident later."

As Corporal Lang turned to leave the Deputy added, "I am aware of your service record Corporal. I may be calling on you again in this matter. Annapolis may have to wait."

The Corporal exited the office to report back to his commanding officer at the White House.

Geraldine Francis picked up the phone and stated bluntly to her outer office secretary, "Put me through to the President on the secure line."

After several minutes the President of the United States came on the line.

Geraldine Francis did not mince words. "Sir," She stated, "My boss is out of the country. I need to see you on an urgent security matter."

After hearing the President's reply she said, "Yes sir, I will be in your office at 9 A.M. tomorrow."

At 1900 hours, Corporal Lang entered the U.S. Marine Security Detachment Office, located in the basement of the White House. He reported to Captain Harrielson, "The Deputy National Security Advisor may want to speak to me again. She told me Annapolis may have to wait." He relayed to his Captain the order from the Deputy never to mention what Steven Arnold had said.

"The Deputy National Security Advisor does not control or give orders to U.S. Marines" said Captain Harrielson, "Pack your gear and ship out to Annapolis as your orders state. As I told you, I will never repeat what you told me concerning what the dead man said."

The Corporal saluted, and left the Marine Security Office, happy to be on his way to his next life challenge; The United States Naval Academy at Annapolis.

Chapter 25

At exactly 9 AM the following morning Geraldine Francis was in the President of the United States' outer office. She greeted the staff members pleasantly and waited to be summoned into the Oval office. Geraldine was a little nervous as this was the first time she had requested an urgent meeting. As was her usual demeanor the nervousness was held inside. She showed her usual confidence on the outside. She had worked for the President for only two years. Many people had criticized him for appointing such a young woman to be the Deputy National Security Advisor. The President had appointed her anyway. She had been recommended by several members of Congress, many considered her appointment political. The President, however, was impressed by her intelligence, demeanor, and spirit. And Robert Duncan, the National Security Advisor, wanted her as his assistant. That was enough for the President. He had been proven right in his decision, as Geraldine Francis became a formidable leader in organizing and establishing a strong team to backup and assist the National Security Advisor. Her resume` had listed, among other accomplishments, Master Degrees in both world history and political science, and four years as an officer in U.S. Army Intelligence.

The President of the United States was fifty-eight years old. As a former U.S. Marine Corps General Officer he was in excellent physical condition. Marines attached to the White House security detail received acknowledgement each time the president crossed their path.

His staff was well chosen, and all of them in line and in general agreement with the policies he established and had executed. There were no "yes" men on the staff. His personal philosophies he kept to himself and shared only with his most trusted staff and friends. This was because in most cases the President's personal philosophies would not be conducive to peace in certain regions of the world. It was well known among his staff and friends, who were sworn by oath to not publicly acknowledge that the President's personal philosophy was to bomb the shit out of America's enemies in the Middle East, sending them back to the stone age so they could never again be a threat to America.

His staff and friends knew he would like to send the Army, Navy, Marines and Air Force, the full force of America's military might, to right any evils that were taking place in the world. President John Kramer had stated his feelings to his staff often enough so they understood where he was coming from. He knew America had enough extra bombs and the capability to deliver them anywhere in the world. There were many young men and women in the armed services that were ready, willing, and able to be dispatched to kill bad people, destroy evil regimes, and right the wrongs taking place in the world.

That is what the President's staff knew he would like to do. They also knew the President was an intelligent and capable world leader who lived within the realities that his world presented.

With this knowledge of her president in mind the National Security Deputy accepted a cup of coffee and opened the conversation.

"Mr. President, I know you have been briefed and given the details of the shooting incident that took place yesterday in the secure areas."

The President interjected at this point, "I'm sorry for your loss. I did not know Arnold other than in meetings we both attended. His reputation was one of loyalty to you and the country, and that he was competent in his work."

The Deputy National Security Advisor continued, "As you know, the incident is still under investigation as we speak. The Marine who shot and killed my assistant came to my office personally with a very disturbing report. The information is only known to the Marine, his Captain, and myself."

The President, sensing he was about to hear something he may not like, put his coffee cup down on his desk, looked at Geraldine Francis eye to eye and became ramrod straight in his chair. "Go on, get to the point," He directed.

Geraldine Francis continued as she referred to her notes, "As he lay dying the Marine was holding his head. Arnold told him to come closer. Sir, Arnold whispered to him the following exact words, 'As an officer in the National Security office, I am ordering you to relay to the Deputy National Security Advisor what I am saying to you. Tell no one else, that is an order. An al Qaeda terrorist has infiltrated the NASA Astronaut Corps. The man chasing me was trying to kill me. His name is ....,' That was all he was able to say."

As she concluded she handed the note she was reading from to the President. He promptly shredded it. President John L. Kramer sat stone still for several minutes as his mind processed what he had just heard. Then he said to his Deputy Advisor, "First of all, there is nothing in the incident report about Arnold being chased. Secondly, if the information he passed to the Marine is true, then we have ourselves a very serious, and potentially dangerous situation. At this time the fewer people who know about this the better. Especially, if there is a traitor or traitors in this White House."

The President picked up the phone and issued an order to the person on the other end, "Get the Head of the Secret Service and have him report here immediately."

He then turned his attention again to Geraldine Francis.

"I will have the Secret Service find out if there is anyone who saw Arnold being chased before he was shot. I also want to know if there were any suspicious actions by anyone during the incident. Now, where is this Marine, I want to speak to him personally."

The National Security Advisor's reply brought a smile to the President's face, and allowed him to relax for the first time since the beginning of the conversation.

"Sir, I ordered that the Marine stay available, but his commanding officer told me that I do not give orders to the Marine Corps. He said Corporal Lang had orders to report to Annapolis and that is what he would be doing. I guess I'll have to go up the chain of command to see if his orders can be changed."

The President just looked at her, "Geraldine, I am the chain of command. I'll see if the Marines will accommodate me, and keep this corporal available until I can speak to him personally. Meanwhile, keep this strictly to yourself. Your boss won't be back for at least a few days, so you handle this. Report back to me face to face tomorrow morning with a tentative plan of action to deal with this situation. I'll see you then."

The meeting was over. Geraldine had her orders and left the Oval office.

The U.S. Marine Security Detachment office was located in the secure area of the White House basement. It was well lighted at 1100 hours. Captain Harrielson was sitting at his desk talking to the two Marines on duty. The Captain had been a Marine for twenty five years. During his career he served three tours in Viet Nam." He was a 'Mustang' as he had earned his commission coming up through the ranks. His assignment to command the White House Security detachment was due to his service record, and reputation as tough and highly competent Marine Corps officer.

As the conversation between the Captain and the two Marines continued the red emergency phone sounded its peculiar alert tone. The Captain thought to himself this was only the second time in his eight months of duty at this post that the phone had sounded. The first being yesterday's shooting incident. One of the on duty Marines answered the alert phone immediately.

"Marine Security Office, Sergeant Anderson speaking, what is your emergency? Yes, the Captain is here."

The Marine motioned and Captain Harrielson picked up the phone on his desk. The next words he heard on the phone caught the hard-ass Marine off guard.

"Captain, this is the President of the United States."

"Yes sir!" answered the Marine as he automatically stood up. The other two Marines in the room also stood up, not knowing what was going on and ready to react to any orders the Captain may give them. Then, realizing he was on the phone, the Captain sat back down but was on full alert. The other two Marines looked at each other and sat down also.

The President continued, "Captain, I want Corporal Lang to remain on post in your White House Detail until I can speak to him personally. This conversation is to remain between you and I. It is to go no further. No one is to ever know that this conversation and order came from me. Also, Captain, the information you received from Lang concerning what the dead man said is never to be repeated. I know you follow orders Captain, but I will stress again you are never to mention or repeat to anyone what Corporal Lang told you, Semper Fi."

The phone clicked off and Captain Harrielson did not move for a full minute. Then he picked up the standard phone and cancelled the travel orders for Corporal Michael Lang.

Chapter 26

Three mornings after the shooting, the spies Paul Macal and Michael Heilman were on the sidewalk preparing to cross Pennsylvania Avenue. Paul looked at Michael intently, and shaking his head said, "I know you assured me Arnold was killed before he could talk to anyone, but maybe we should inform Abreu of the incident just in case?

"There is no need to tell Abreu about my slip of the tongue," retorted Michael, "I saw the marine shoot and kill Arnold. It would only cause us problems with Abreu if we told him I shot off my mouth about the terrorist astronaut and someone heard me. If we don't say anything no one will ever know."

"OK, replied Paul, you're right; we'll keep your screw-up and the shooting to ourselves."

They were headed to the pedestrian gate entrance of the White House. As they stepped into the street a one ton, flat bed truck careened around the corner at a high rate of speed. The two men had no chance to avoid the truck. It struck and ran over both men. The truck sped away from the scene. Bystanders rushed to help the two downed men. Several used their phones and dialed 911. One policeman from the White House gate checked the two downed men.

"Don't worry about calling an ambulance. Both of these men are dead," He stated.

The truck that killed the two spies raced down Pennsylvania Avenue and sped several miles through back streets. The truck then pulled into a large garage. After closing the garage door the bearded truck driver took a satellite phone from a garage cabinet. He dialed the phone.

On the other end of the call Abreu answered and demanded, "Are they dead, did you escape cleanly, no police?"

"Yes," replied the bearded man, "Both are dead. I'm sure of it. I drove and Zalmi watched. We completely ran over the face and head of one of them and crushed the chest of the other. They could not have survived the violent force we struck them with. They never knew what hit them. No one chased us and we entered the garage without anyone seeing us."

"OK," said Abreu, "That's good, dismantle and destroy the truck completely. Your cell will receive the seventy-five thousand dollars in a few days. Good work and make sure your cell members keep their mouths shut about this assignment. If I hear of anyone talking you will all pay the price."

Abreu clicked the phone off exclaiming out loud to his empty office, "The secrecy of the plan remains intact."

However, Abreu would never know of the incident involving the two spies and the circumstances in the death of Steven Arnold.

Chapter 27

The second day after the shooting in the White House the President had called a secret emergency meeting. The Deputy National Security Advisor had been ordered by the President to have a tentative plan of action ready to deal with the report of a terrorist in NASA.

President John L. Kramer entered the room and the men and women he had summoned to this meeting stopped their conversations and stood. The President said to be seated and sat down himself. He called to this meeting people who he personally trusted. Each one of these people could potentially be instrumental in any investigation which would take place. Present at the meeting were Geraldine Francis; Earl Cowler, Head of the Secret Service; FBI Director Robert Fuller; George Brown Jr., Head of the CIA; Jack Prentiss, Secretary of Defense; Robert Duncan, National Security Advisor; Marine Corporal Michael Lang and his commanding officer Captain John Harrielson. The two Directors of NASA were also in the room. The President went directly to the point of the meeting without introductions of those present.

"Ladies and Gentlemen," started the President, "Geraldine and these two Marines are already aware of the reason for this meeting. Before we proceed I am giving this direct order to each one of you. Do not repeat or share any of the information we are about to discuss. That means tell no one. The information from this meeting is to be considered Top Secret."

The room grew very quiet. The President continued, "You are all aware of the shooting incident and death of Steven Arnold. The Lance Corporal here is the Marine who had the unpleasant duty of having to do the shooting." The President nodded, identifying Corporal Lang, then continued, "Before he died Arnold told the corporal, and I emphasis only the corporal, a person was chasing him and trying to kill him. He also told the corporal that an al Qaeda terrorist has infiltrated the NASA Astronaut Corps."

The President stopped talking. The room was silent as people realized what they had just heard. The faces of the two NASA Directors tightened at what the President had just said. After several moments he continued.

"Geraldine has given me a tentative plan. The purpose of this meeting is to set up and begin executing the plan in order to deal with this situation and accomplish the following. Number one, determine the validity of what Steven Arnold said to Corporal Lang. Number two, determine if spies exist in this White House, and if so search them out and identify them. Number three, and most important, investigate and find any terrorists that may be in the NASA Astronaut Program."

The President checked his notes. "Last night I had Geraldine make an assignment plan. As you may have noticed there are not many of you in this meeting. That is because I believe in and trust everyone present. If there is a traitor in the White House or in the NASA Astronaut Corps we will presume they do not know we have this information from Steven Arnold. We will hunt them down in secret, and if they do exist, they won't know they're being hunted. That's why it's imperative we keep this meeting and information secret."

The NASA director started to speak but the president held up his hand to stop him.

"I want to be involved with this because it could be a legitimate threat. Let me outline the plan and assignments, then each of you can input your initial thoughts and comments. Be assured, I want this brought to a conclusion as soon as possible."

The President looked at Geraldine, "Don't take offense, but allow me to outline the plan and assignments."

"No offense taken Sir, I appreciate your involvement."

"OK then," stated the President. "Robert, you and Geraldine use your resources at National Security. Earl, use the full impact of the Secret Service. You three work together. Choose your people carefully, keep your team as small as possible and use only those you personally trust. Review the personnel records of everyone working in the White House. Tell your people it's a vetting exercise and to look for, and report, any irregularities in the files. Do not tell them we are looking for spies. Your team members are to be sworn to secrecy in this matter. That is the best we can do. Let's take a ten minute break and have a cup of coffee"

After the break the President continued with the assignments."The Secretary of Defense will check out military personnel working at NASA. Jack, you and I know the boss at NCIS personally. Use him and his staff to help in the NASA work." Jack Prentiss, Secretary of Defense, nodded at the President to acknowledge his assignment. He was confident that between the NCIS and his excellent military staff, they could carry out any necessary steps concerning this situation.

"As for the FBI and the CIA," the President continued, "I want your heavy hitters on this situation looking at the big picture. Check any possible links to this situation. There are no jurisdictional boundaries in this. Share any information which may in any way relate to this. Back up any requests from anyone in this room with your full resources."

The President then turned to the two Marines.

"Captain, Corporal Lang will continue his duty at the White

House. Additionally you will instruct your men to keep a sharp eye out and watch for any irregular behavior, suspicious conversations, or any activity that seems out of place. They are to maintain their standard demeanor, but report to you anything they see which may not seem exactly right to them, no matter how slight. Order your Marines to keep their mouths shut about these orders. They are not to be discussed in front of anyone."

The President thought for a moment, then addressed the marine captain. "Captain, you are now authorized to station additional Marines throughout the White House. The Secret Service will put out an announcement that they requested extra Marine security until the shooting investigation is completed. Get more men for the White House detail if you need to. I'll call the Commandant if necessary. Emphasize to your men the importance of keeping a low profile and look and listen to what is happening around them."

Almost as an afterthought he addressed the Directors of NASA, "I know you have a launch coming up soon. Concentrate on that job. If Jack needs anything he will let you know."

The president ended the meeting with final orders. "National Security Advisor Duncan will have overall authority for this investigation. Everyone send him updates each morning and evening. Coordinate and request any resources and assets through him. In addition report immediately, at any time, if pertinent information is discovered. Also, nothing in writing concerning this situation, any written record will be kept by National Security Advisor Duncan. Use messengers to deliver the daily reports in sealed folders. No phone calls or faxes. I emphasize that no copies of anything to do with this investigation are to be made. One more thing, and I'm making it an executive order. No one has any right to privacy in this investigation, and if necessary no rights at all."

With that said the President closed the meeting. "We will meet back here in one week. At that time I want input from each of you on how this plan is working, and if any changes need to be made. We will determine and discuss if any conclusions have been reached.

The room cleared in silence.

Back at the Marine Security office Captain Harrielson gave Corporal Lang orders.

"OK Mike, what I want from you is a list of Marines you know who are smart and capable of carrying out our orders. We'll draw from the Washington Marine Barracks. I know Marines who have worked for me that I'm going to bring here for this temporary assignment. I want to fill out this security detachment with men you know and trust. I want men who will pay attention and notice every move in their area of responsibility, dismissed."

"Yes Sir," answered Corporal Michael Lang.

He then returned to his quarters, unlocked his locker and took out his address book. As he checked names of marines to be called to the White House detail he thought to himself and chuckled, "These guys are going to miss the Friday Night Parade," referring to the formal full dress parade put on at the Washington Marine Barracks each Friday night for people visiting Washington. The Marines always looked sharp in the parade, but it was hard work to prepare and 'maintain the proper attitude' in order to perform every Friday night. At least for a few weeks these guys won't have to worry about it as they had presidential orders to carry out.

The week went by fast. The people on the President's investigation teams had a difficult job.

They had to be casual about the knowledge known to them while they chose the people they trusted to carry out the necessary investigations. As they entered the second meeting each one of them hoped the staff members they had chosen and trusted were not the enemy. All the members of President Kramer's team were seated in the oval office as he entered to start the second meeting.

"OK, let's get to it," stated the President. Then as an

afterthought he added, "We usually would not use the Oval Office for such a meeting, however, we need to keep up the appearance of business as usual so we will meet here. As per the normal procedure my secretary and White House Security will not to let anyone enter without my permission."

Geraldine Francis stood and started the meeting.

"Sir, I have news that impacts this situation. The staff member I assigned to check into Steven Arnold's background reported this information to me. It seems that Steven had been under the care of a doctor, actually a psychiatrist. Under your order to use any means necessary, FBI agents confiscated the records from the doctor's office and brought them directly and discreetly to me. The doctor was told it was a routine matter to secure the records in Steven Arnold's case and a federal warrant would be in his hands within hours.

I contacted Robert at the National Security Council and he arranged for the warrant right away."

She paused and took a drink of water, then continued. "These records show Steven Arnold was under stress from his job and depressed due to his home life. Unknown to any of his co-workers or me, was the fact that his wife of thirty-three years was diagnosed with cancer and would die soon. The report further states he was suffering from paranoid delusions. These delusions were that unknown persons were plotting against him and his job. Just as a point of interest his last assignment was a joint study of the perimeter security of NASA facilities, and how these facilities rated in relation to a potential terrorist attack. The rest of the report includes statements and details backing up the doctor's conclusions. This information leads me to believe this whole matter may be due to a mental breakdown on the part of Steven and therefore not real."

National Security Advisor Duncan interjected immediately. "This changes the situation critically. If we continue this secretive

investigation of all the people involved, both in the White House
and at NASA, and what this Steven Arnold character said to the
Marine was a hallucination, we are risking a morale and internal
trust problem that will never be overcome in this administration."

Other people started to speak. President Kramer held up his
hand for silence and spoke.

"Geraldine, what's your take on Arnold's condition, regardless
of the doctor reports?"

The Deputy National Security Advisor thought for several
long seconds before replying, "He seemed fine at his job. His behavior indicated no problems with his work. I think he was lucid
and credible during his work hours."

Jack Prentiss, the Secretary of Defense spoke next.

"Regardless of any doctor's report, and regardless if this man
was delusional or not, we have no choice but to take what he
said seriously. We are remiss and in dereliction of our duty to do
otherwise."

At this time, Earl Cowler, Head of the Secret Service stood to
get the room's attention. He looked directly at Corporal Michael
Lang and asked, "Are you sure of what the man you killed said
to you? There was a lot of excitement and commotion at that
moment. Is there any chance you might have heard wrong or
misinterpreted what Steven Arnold said to you?"

All eyes in the room concentrated on Corporal Lang.
Especially those of the President of the United States. Captain
Robert Harrielson, in the true tradition of the Marine Corps
stiffened in his seat and started to defend his Marine. Before he
could speak the Corporal motioned to him, indicating for the
Captain to stand down. The Captain sat back and was quiet, but
his demeanor showed he was at the ready to take on these civilians in defense of his Corporal. The Captain's body language was
noticed throughout the room. The Captain's input turned out not
to be necessary.

Corporal Lang did not stand up. Instead he met the eyes upon him dead-on and stated calmly and under complete control, "What I reported to the Deputy Security Advisor, is exactly what the man I killed said to me before he died."

"That's enough," said President Kramer, "the potential is too serious to shut down this investigation based on a doctor's report of behavior that may or may not be relevant to what was said to the Corporal. And Captain Harrielson, stand easy, we are all on the same team. But I appreciate your attitude, so don't change it."

The head of the Secret Service interjected again.

"Corporal, you have answered my question. Now I have something to report that has a bearing on this matter. I questioned every agent on duty at the time of the shooting. Two of my agents did not think anything of it at the time, but during my debriefing of them concerning the incident each recalled the same thought. While they, and every other security and staff member were running toward and securing the scene, they both observed a man walking hurriedly away from the scene. These were two independent reports as neither agent had spoken to each other about this. So based on what my agents now interpret as strange behavior, gives evidence that the dead man was being chased. These two agents are looking through photographs, but the chances of identifying this individual are very small. There is nothing on the security cameras showing anyone being chased or leaving the scene of the shooting.

There was silence in the room. President Kramer asked if anyone else had anything to report. Captain Harrielson stated that additional Marines were arriving. They were being briefed and detailed as additional security throughout the White House, and the grounds surrounding the White House. A confidential memo had been issued by the Secret Service informing people that the Marines were temporary additional security until the completion of the shooting investigation.

The President stood up and stated. "Based on the information we have just heard you will continue the investigations as ordered. In ten days we will meet here to determine if we need to expand and proceed, or consider this a false alarm."

With the President's statement and order the meeting ended.

CHAPTER 28

Ten days passed quickly and the scheduled meeting was held again in the Oval office of the White House.

"OK," said President Kramer as he opened the meeting. "Let's all stay focused. The purpose of this meeting is to decide if we have enough evidence to continue our investigations."

Geraldine Francis spoke first. "The National Security office has found no information that would support what Steven Arnold told Corporal Lang."

Jack Prentiss, Secretary of Defense reported his extensive resources had found no evidence that any military personnel assigned to NASA or to the White House were traitors. He was well satisfied that his staff and the intelligence branch he employed for this mission would have found anything out of the ordinary. They went well above any normal military security investigation.

Earl Cowler spoke next, "I used the full power of the Secret Service and found no White House civilian personnel suspect. At the request of NASA I assigned a Secret Service detachment to assist them in the investigation of their people. They were assigned to Terry and reported to him."

NASA Director Terry Walsh stood up to give his report. "With the help of the Secret Service the records of every civilian employee at NASA were reviewed. Nothing suspicious was found."

Captain Robert Harrielson, USMC, nodded to Lance Corporal Lang.

"We have had extra Marines station throughout the White House," Lang reported. "There has not been any report of anything suspicious or out of the ordinary."

The FBI and CIA both reported their domestic and worldwide resources could not find anything to give credence to the allegation of terrorists in NASA or the White House.

Al Qaeda had covered its tracks well, including the killing of the White House spies Paul Macal and Michael Heilman. The unintentional result was their records had been removed from the White House active files upon their deaths. The decision by Usama bin Ladin to not attempt a second infiltrator and have the terrorist astronaut act completely alone was paying off.

National Security Advisor Robert Duncan advised that his staff reviewed all reports and had nothing to add.

President Kramer then said, "Are we as a group satisfied that we have done everything possible in determining this was a false alarm?"

Heads throughout the room nodded affirmation.

The President continued. "I am sure there are spies and traitors amongst us as there have always been. However, as far as this specific threat is concerned we will close the investigation. No word of it is ever to be mentioned. I thank you for your work in carrying out this duty."

As the room cleared, NASA Director Terry Walsh remained seated. The President noticed him hesitating to leave and motioned for him to come up to his desk and take a seat.

"I see you hesitating Terry, what's on your mind?" said the President.

"Sir," the Director of NASA replied, "As NASA is the potential source of any problem arising out of this situation I want to continue my investigation. I want to double check all the documentation on our astronauts. My problem is I do not want to disrupt our program. The chance of terrorist activity in NASA is next to zero. Any continued investigation must remain secret so the morale and trust within NASA is not compromised. I feel confident there is no problem but I feel we should continue the checking of our astronaut personnel at this time. I do not want to under estimate any enemy or take any chances that we missed something on the first investigation go around. If you concur I have worked out the details of my plan. What I need is essentially the same as before. Teams of investigators we can trust to keep a low profile and keep this investigation secret. I can outline the plan for you now if you wish."

"No," replied the President, "I don't need to know the details of your plan. If you feel you want to continue, I concur. As far as the make-up of your teams is concerned I will direct Earl Cowler and Robert Fuller to meet with you. They can assist in organizing and assigning people to your teams. The Secret Service and the FBI will have the people you need. You will have the final authority and responsibility for both your investigation and the people in your investigating teams. Inform me immediately of any evidence that may give credence to what Steven Arnold eluded to when he was killed. I will personally brief the Vice President and Robert Duncan so you can report to them if I am not available."

The President picked up the phone.

"Meet tomorrow morning at Earl Cowler's office at 0800 hours. I'll inform him and Fuller of the meeting now. I'm going to instruct them they are to use their expertise and any resources necessary to give you what you need to satisfy your investigation."

Terry nodded and started to leave. The President was not finished with him.

"One more thing Terry, we have already conducted a thorough investigation of which everyone, including you, was satisfied there is no evidence to back up Steven Arnold's dying statement.

In allowing this additional investigation we are again risking a major morale problem at NASA. However, I agree with you. I too, will not underestimate any potential enemy. Carry out you investigation until you are satisfied."

Terry Walsh left the President's office confident. With the assistance and guidance of the Head of the Secret Service and Director of the FBI, this second and very secret vetting of key people in NASA would put an end to any concerns.

Terry Walsh arrived in front of the Secret Service Building at exactly 0800 hours. He was checked in at the building entrance and escorted to the top floor. After checking his identification and confirming his identity, the outer office secretary and security guards passed him right into the secure office of the Head of the Secret Service. FBI Director Robert Fuller was already there. Earl Cowler wasted no time.

"Let's get down to it, Terry. We know the situation and reason for this meeting. Tell us your plan and what you need."

Terry Walsh also wasted no time as he began outlining his plan.

"First, no new people will be hired or assigned to NASA until we have completed this second investigation. I want two-man teams. Each team will check out one astronaut. These two man teams will follow the personnel documentation and paperwork of each active astronaut as far back as possible. What I need from you two is help in organizing and manning the teams as well as your expertise in keeping this as low key as possible. Also, keep in mind, all NASA operations are proceeding and will proceed normally. That includes the launch of the mission to the space station. Each team will be instructed that this is a top secret operation. The team assignment is to look for any discrepancy in the paperwork and back up documentation of the astronaut they are assigned. The teams have free reign and can check out any persons or organizations their subject has ever associated with."

Robert Fuller stated the Naval Criminal Investigative Service would be the best place to start in making up the teams. He would meet with the NCIS Director and start setting up teams. The remainder of the teams would come from the FBI. The three men agreed the least number of teams would be better. This would be the least disruptive to NASA and raise the least amount of questions from the NASA staff. All team leaders would report to FBI Director Robert Fuller who in turn would keep the President informed.

Terry Walsh concluded the meeting. "I will send you the roster of astronauts. Start by investigating the younger ones first and work your way through the complete list."

The next morning Robert Fuller met with NCIS Director Daniel Farmer. After hearing what Fuller wanted the NCIS Director reacted,

"The only way I will commit my resources to what just may be a wild goose chase, is that I have complete control of who is paired on the teams. The initial vetting of the astronauts in NASA by your Bureau should have found any suspicious circumstances. However, I agree that double checking the background of the astronauts is a prudent undertaking, as I also never underestimate any potential enemy. I did receive the secret memo ordering full cooperation in this matter. I will appoint my assistant to head up the teams. Tell me, what is the limit of his authority in forming the teams?"

"He can choose anyone he wants from any agency and has the authority of the President to do so," replied the FBI Director.

With that the meeting concluded. The investigation began as the NCIS Director picked up the phone and spoke to his personal secretary, "Call Joe Sulivand and have him report to me in this office immediately."

Two hours later Joe Sulivand walked into the NCIS Director's office and sat down on the big brown leather couch against the wall.

"OK Joe, this is the situation and your assignment," stated the NCIS Director sternly. "You heard about the National Security agent that was killed in the White House several weeks ago?'

Joe Sulivand nodded his acknowledgement. The Director continued.

"That agent told a Marine, actually the Marine who shot and killed him, that an al Qaeda terrorist had infiltrated the Astronaut Corps at NASA. Your assignment, in absolute secrecy, is to select two man teams and have them check all the paper work and documentation on each astronaut to see if anything was missed in the initial vetting. This investigation is under the authority of the President and top secret. You organize and pick the teams as you see fit."

Joe Sulivand, who thought this was going to be another meaningless meeting now was at full alert and paying attention. The NCIS Director continued his instructions to him.

"Choose people you trust and keep the total number of teams as small as possible. You have the President's authority to pull people from any agency. I selected you to command the teams because you've been around a long time. You know a lot of people who are loyal and can be trusted to conduct this investigation; then keep it to themselves for their entire life. Your people will report directly to Robert Fuller if they discover anything. The instructions to your teams are to completely check out the astronaut assigned to them. They are to report immediately if they find anything suspicious that could indicate in any way that the astronaut they are investigating may not be legitimate, no matter how insignificant that information may seem. The teams are not to know they are possibly looking for an al Qaeda terrorist. I wasn't suppose to tell you that, but I trust you and wanted you to know the truth, any questions?"

Joe Sulivand nodded no as he began to list in his mind the people he wanted on his two-man teams. He also began thinking of how they would start going through astronaut personnel files without a lot of unwanted questions at NASA.

Joe Sulivand had indeed been around for a long time, almost thirty years. He was a tested and tough administrator who gave no bullshit to his superiors nor took any from people under his command. In his career Joe Sulivand had conducted and resolved hundreds of serious investigations involving traitors and spying, both in the United States and in many parts of the world. These investigations were both military and civilian. Joe's thought at the moment was that if there was a traitor in the astronaut corps he knew just the people that could find him.

Daniel Farmer ended the meeting, "If you have no questions we can end this meeting. Good luck, and I hope this whole thing turns out to be nothing. But if you do uncover a terrorist or traitor, follow through until any threat to NASA or the United States is eliminated. Oh, and one more thing, all teams will be armed at all times, just in case. One last thing Joe, I was not supposed to tell you the real reason behind this. So keep the information about a possible terrorist astronaut to yourself. That part of this investigation is top secret."

Chapter 29

When the request came to Geraldine Francis from Joe Sulivand for Sam Taylor to be assigned as an investigator for a secret project, and to assign him a partner, Geraldine knew exactly what secret project he was talking about. She summoned Sam Taylor to her office.

Geraldine greeted Sam. "Sam, I have a special request for you. It is for a top secret assignment and I am granting that request. Because this could be dangerous I'm going to fill you in on what this assignment is all about. I could get in big trouble for doing so. It involves reviewing NASA astronaut records to determine if any may be fraudulent or inaccurate. This is highly secret but I will tell you, NASA is trying to be certain an al Qaeda terrorist has not infiltrated their astronaut ranks. You will be assigned one astronaut to check out. Because this is a terrorist investigation I want you to be armed at all times. I know you like to work alone but the request was for a team of two investigators. Do you have anyone you would want as a partner for this assignment?"

"No one," replied Sam, "I work alone. I have never had a partner since I've worked for you, you know that. There isn't anybody around here who I would want as a partner."

"You need someone to watch your back on this one," insisted Geraldine Francis. An idea came to her as she informed Sam calmly that he had no choice and he would have a partner on this assignment.

"I will give you a man who is not part of our agency but that you can trust with your life. He is not an investigator but he can back you up and he will definitely do what you tell him to."

Sam reluctantly agreed to have a partner but adamantly stated the partner would be under his command. "Damn," thought Sam to himself, "Another partner to watch out for and take care of."

He tried to block the memory out of his thoughts as he drove home, but could not. He remembered the young spotter on his two-man sniper team. His name was Jim Donaldson. He was nineteen years old. Sam had made a mistake by accepting the invitation from Jim's family to accompany Jim home, and visit them, during Sam and Jim's leave before being deployed to Viet Nam. After dinner at the family gathering Jim's mother had cornered Sam. She asked him to watch out for her son so he could come home safe. Sam told her he could not guarantee it but he would be next to Jim every step of the way.

Sam could see Jim's face as clear as if Jim was standing next to him now. Sam sighed as that was never going to happen. Jim Donaldson was dead. It had been thirty years or more since that day in Viet Nam. Sam and Jim were in a combat position covering an American convoy movement. As a sniper team they were well hidden on the side of a hill. The convoy had been ambushed by North Viet Nam regulars and was in full retreat. Sam and Jim were firing from their hidden position on the hillside and had taken out several enemy vehicles. Their action was slowing the North Viet Nam regulars' advance and allowing the American convoy to escape to the opposite side of the hill in order to re-group. A North Viet Nam patrol started working its way up the hill towards Sam and Jim's firing position. Mortar rounds began to fall around their position. It was time to run. If they could cover the two hundred yards to the top of the hill and get down the other side they would be safe because that was where the American convoy was re-grouping.

Sam peeled off his heavy camouflage and ordered Jim to do the same. Both men were in excellent physical condition. Sam ran as fast as he could for the top of the hill. Jim was also running, but was behind Sam. As they were nearing the crest of the hill Sam chanced a glance back to be sure his young spotter was making it ok. Jim was ten yards behind Sam.

"Come on!" Sam encouraged, "Thirty more feet and we've got it made, our guys will cover us on the way down."

Jim hollered that he was ok. Sam saw several enemy soldiers emerge from the rocks behind Jim. Sam used his sniper rifle to take the first one out. He then had to throw his rifle down and revert to his 9 millimeter Smith and Wesson automatic. He took out two more of the enemy as he took cover behind a rock. The hollow point rounds were doing their job. The enemy soldiers were hitting the dirt and taking cover from Sam's accurate fire. Sam shouted for Jim to take cover and return fire. Then he saw the panicked look on Jim's face as Jim kept running toward him.

"Get down, Jim!" Sam screamed. "I can't cover you, they're taking cover!"

It was too late. Jim went down head first as the enemy fire hit him from their covered positions. At that moment an American fire team of Marines came over the crest of the hill behind Sam and engaged the Viet Nam regulars. The North Viet Nam soldiers retreated down the hill and the engagement ended. Jim's panic running had cost him his life. If he had obeyed Sam and stopped running he would have lived through the close-in engagement. Several Marines carried Jim's body back to the regrouped convoy. Sam found a quiet spot and cried for his young spotter. One of the most difficult tasks Sam ever had to do was writing that letter to Jim's mother. Sam vowed and promised himself he would never go through that heart break again. He would never have another partner or be responsible for anyone again. Now, Geraldine had changed that. Her order was voiding his self-promised vow. "Damn!" Sam muttered vehemently.

The next day Geraldine informed Sam that he would be working for Joe Sulivand. He was to report to Joe as soon as his new partner arrived. She told him that would be within twenty four hours, she hoped. As Sam Taylor left her office she picked up the phone and instructed her secretary to call the White House and request to speak to the President of the United States. When the President came on the line Geraldine hesitated, then spoke.

"Sir, I need your help, if you approve of my idea."

"Tell me what you want, Geraldine, you are the Deputy National Security Advisor. Unless you want me to launch a nuclear attack you can have whatever you need."

"This will require a call to Annapolis, Sir," Geraldine replied.

Chapter 30

The morning after Geraldine Francis' call to the President, Corporal Michael Lang was asleep in his room at the U.S. Naval Academy at Annapolis. It was 0430 hours. Lang was suddenly awakened by the on duty fire watch. The fire watch cadet was accompanied by a Midshipman.

The Midshipman commanded Lang, "Pack your gear and report to the Office of the Commandant. Wear your dress uniform. Bring your other uniforms and utilities in your duffel bag. Be there at 0600 hours."

At 0600 Hours Corporal Lang stood at attention in front of the Commandant of the United States Naval Academy. He was mystified as to why he had been summoned.

"Lang," stated the Commandant, "Pack your gear, draw a .45 automatic and ammo from the armory and report to the main gate. A car will be waiting there to take you to the National Security Building. When you get there report to a Sam Taylor in his office. You will be working for him temporarily. I will arrange so you do not lose credits or time during your absence from the Academy. This assignment and its circumstances come from the President of the United States. They are never to be mentioned or spoken of from this time forward. Are these orders clear to you?

"Yes Sir!" responded Marine Corporal Michael Lang.

He was then dismissed and proceeded to carry out his orders.

What the hell was this all about he wondered. At the armory the on duty Midshipman looked amusingly at Lang, who was in his Marine dress uniform, and then gave him the choice of several .45 automatics. Lang chose the one with the handle inscribed with the letters "USMC."

"I figured you would pick that one," remarked the Midshipman. "Since I was ordered to issue you a weapon I assume you are qualified to use it."

"Yes Sir," Lang replied.

"The orders say to issue you a shoulder holster and two clips of ammunition. What's this all about, it's highly unusual to issue weapons and ammo like this?"

"I have no idea what's going on sir," replied Lang.

"In that case you better have this also," said the midshipman. He handed Lang a leather pouch with a shoulder strap. On the pouch a label was stamped: .45 Caliber cartridges; Hollow point, 200 Count. 4 Clips enclosed.

"Just in case you need them along with that weapon and holster, Semper Fi," said the Midshipman as the Marine took the pouch. Lang just looked at the Midshipman, saluted and departed.

When the car dropped Lang off in front of the National Security Building all he had to unload was his sea bag, it had his gear in it, and the shoulder satchel with the weapon and ammunition. The security personnel at the entrance became very tense when the alarm sounded as Corporal Lang entered the building. The three guards on duty sealed the entrance doors and no was allowed to enter while they searched the corporal and his gear. When the .45 automatic was found the guards' weapons came out and Lang was taken into an anti-room at gun point.

"I'm here under orders to report to Sam Taylor," Lang told the guards.

"We have no record of any Corporal Lang or anyone else

reporting to Sam Taylor," the guards responded. A phone call to the Deputy Security Advisor's office brought Geraldine Francis to the building entrance anti-room. She identified and cleared the Marine to enter the building. Michael Lang had been in his dress uniform but it had made no difference to the security guards.

"I'm sorry for that little episode," stated Geraldine Francis, "I didn't expect you so soon or I would have alerted the security detail to be aware of your arrival. I should have known when President gives an order there is no delay in it being carried out. Anyway, you will be working with Sam Taylor on this assignment. I chose you because you already know about the NASA situation. You'll meet Sam in a minute. No matter what you think of him, I told him you would do what says and watch his back during this assignment."

Corporal Lang met Sam in his office. Sam addressed the Marine rudely.

"You were assigned to me by my boss. I usually work alone. Since you are a Marine I accepted you as a partner on this assignment. I was ordered to. I don't like it, so you better be as good as they say you are. Your job is to assist me and watch my back."

Sam Taylor tried to be as gruff and rude as possible in their first meeting. What he did not realize was that Lang felt very comfortable meeting him. Lang was used to gunnery sergeants. He considered his first impression of Sam Taylor. Sam was older. He had light brown hair that was thinning on top. He was six feet tall and looked physically fit. He talked straight out. No bullshit. Lang decided he might like Sam and this assignment.

Sam interrupted Lang's thoughts. "Our boss on this assignment is Joe Sulivand. I spoke to him this morning. We don't have to go to his office. Our orders are to check the background documentation and history of the NASA astronaut we are assigned. We are to report any information that may be inaccurate or suspicious, no matter how insignificant."

Sam continued his instructions to Lang, "I understand from Geraldine that you are aware of what this investigation is all about. I have a folder on my desk from the Director of NASA. In it is the name of the astronaut who we have been assigned to investigate. Other teams such as us are checking the background of all the astronauts. We only have to worry about the one assigned to us. I'll get the file and find the name of our astronaut. You arrange air transport to Houston, we'll start there. Go downstairs to the security desk and get the flight details. I'll call down and tell them you are coming. Get your gear and be ready to go in thirty minutes. If you need a weapon the security desk will issue one."

"I have a weapon," Responded Lang. He did not get the chance to say another word because Sam abruptly turned and left. Lang proceeded downstairs to follow his instructions. Sam Taylor went to his desk to get the folder, which had arrived for him in the secure mail. In that folder was the name of the astronaut he was to investigate. He opened the red manila envelope. Inside, on NASA letterhead and blue paper was the name: JAMES HENRY FALCON, ASTRONAUT / NASA / USA.

"OK, James Henry Falcon," Sam thought to himself, "If you are for real that will be good. If not, I'm just the guy who will find that out."

As he considered his unwanted partner he had to admit that he made a strong first impression.

Sam spoke out loud to himself, "He's a Marine, he carried himself well and he looked physically fit. He came from Annapolis so he must be able to think, and he has been in combat so he must know how to fight. I'll trust him to start with and see what happens."

Chapter 31

On the first day of July the pre launch meeting was held at NASA Headquarters. All department heads and division chiefs were present. When the meeting was over Terry Walsh concluded and closed the meeting.

"The final readiness reports from each of you indicate all systems are go for launch. We cannot delay this mission because of its re-supply aspect. We will proceed and launch the replacement astronauts and the re-supply mission to the space station on the 25TH of July as per the previous schedule. Good luck gentlemen, ladies; Dismissed.

Sam and the Corporal arrived at NASA headquarters Thursday, August 4th at one o'clock in the afternoon. They proceeded to the administration building and went directly to the payroll and personnel records section. Sam was dressed in a United States Air Force uniform with the rank of Captain. Lang was in his Marine dress blues. Both had credentials showing them as public relations officers attached to an Armed Forces Publication. They had a letter from the Director of NASA stating they were researching information for a public relations article about NASA's astronauts.

The letter also stated both men had top secret clearances and were to be given complete access to any records and personnel files. The on duty security officer behind the desk checked the credentials and the letter.

He looked at the two men and said to them, "Please stand by for a moment." He nodded to a second security guard, "Stand by with these two gentlemen until I return."

The security officer then proceeded to a private office and placed a call to the direct line of the Assistant Director of NASA. When Jay Hart came on the line the security officer said,

"There are two armed public relation officers in my section, sir. Are they authorized access to all the records including top secret files? I have been off duty for several days. When I came on duty the off going personnel reported that other military men had been checking the personnel and payroll files. It seemed out of the ordinary to me so I am using the direct line to be sure you are aware of this activity."

Assistant Director Hart commended the security officer for his vigilance and stated, "These men are cleared for any and all files. They have the highest clearance and know what they can print for public consumption and what must remain secret or confidential. I commend you for following through and checking with me. Allow these men access to any files, and it is not necessary for them to be supervised or accompanied. Is that clear?"

"Yes sir," was the reply from the security officer.

"Well, where shall we start?" Sam Taylor remarked when he and Lang were alone in the vast records and file room. Sam was in awe as he surveyed the room. He could see Lang was also impressed. The room was a rectangle and bigger than the perimeter of a football field. The walls were concrete and painted gloss white. The floor was linoleum and buffed to a high polished shine. The ceiling was at least fifteen feet high from which hung large florescent light fixtures. The room was immaculately clean. Room temperature was maintained at sixty-eight degrees. Over fifty desk top computers lined one wall. They contained all the information that was also on paper in the file cabinets, which lined the opposite wall and were lined up military style throughout the room.

"I say we go to the file cabinets and pull all the paper files and documents on our astronaut, said Lang.

"Sounds good to me," responded Sam, "I don't want to fool around with computers. Besides that, some small piece of information may not have been transferred from the paper documents to the computers."

It took approximately an hour to find and pull all the personal records of Astronaut James Henry Falcon. The two men began reading and studying the file information together. It included personal information and application copies. Also a birth certificate copy, education records, athletic awards, commercial pilot's license copy, Air Force Academy file, and NASA astronaut training documents. All the documents had the proper Certifications and Seals. After another hour Lang looked at Sam and made the following pronouncement.

"This guy is not only a genius and a tremendous athlete but he is squeaky clean too. Not so much as a speeding ticket, and he also has one of the lowest demerit records ever at the Academy."

"It does seem to be too good to be true," stated Sam flatly, "and you know what they say when something seems too good to be true. Let's go through Mr. James Henry Falcon's life history and find out what makes him so perfect. The records here seem in order, he was born in Elko, Nevada. Ever been to Nevada Corporal? I'm thinking we should go there, shake some dice, and see what we can find, if anything, about our perfect astronaut."

Corporal Michael Lang had never been to Nevada. The flight to Elko in the NCIS Gulfstream was smooth and comfortable. Both Sam and Lang had spent many hours flying in C-51 cargo planes. Those military flights always were uncomfortable and jarring. The trip to Elko aboard the Gulf Stream turned out to be a bonus to this assignment. Sam had many trips on the Gulf Stream and anticipated a smooth trip. Lang had never been in a Gulf Stream and sat in amazement observing the lavish interior of the plane. There were plush, comfortable seats that swiveled. The entire floor was carpeted, except the bathroom, which was linoleum. The bathroom was huge compared to his experience on commercial flights. In the cabin there were two tables surrounded by built-in seats, and best of all, a full bar and a refrigerator full of food and snacks.

It took about four hours for the Gulf Stream to get from Houston, Texas to Elko, Nevada.

Upon landing Sam told the pilots to check into the Elko City Casino for a couple of days and enjoy the time off. He and Lang would find them when it was time to leave. The pilots secured their plane in the Elko County Sheriff's hangar. The hangar was locked and had twenty four hour security. The pilots left for town smiling. Sam and Lang took a taxi to the same casino and checked in separately from the pilots. The pilots were ordered not to identify themselves as NCIS pilots and to keep their mission to themselves. In the taxi ride to the casino both Sam and Lang were impressed and commented on the orderliness of the town.

After checking in Sam told Lang, "It's too late to do anything today. Let's take a walk through the casino and see what's happening."

"Sounds good to me replied Lang."

Looking around the casino they saw several women to potentially chase and have a good time with. They reluctantly passed on the good time. Instead, they blew a couple of hundred bucks playing Blackjack, then went to the steak house for dinner. It didn't bother them to pass on the women. They could have easily had a good time with them. But both men decided the gravity and importance of their assignment demanded they not get side-tracked.

"This is not Marine Corps chow," remarked Lang as they dined on thick tasty steaks, salad, baked potatoes, and a bottle of red wine.

As they discussed their work over dinner Sam told Lang, "I'm

satisfied with how we've proceeded." Sam and Lang agreed that
so far everything was in order for Astronaut James Henry Falcon.

"Since NCIS is paying for this little investigative trip, we
better call it a night and get an early start in the morning." Sam
continued, "We need to earn this little paid vacation by affirming
that Falcon is OK. Which it seems he is, or finding something
that is just not right, which is probably not going to happen. I
don't think Falcon is anything but what his documentation says
he is. That looks pretty straight forward."

Then he looked at Lang from across the table and stated,
"However, my young partner, we will not leave any detail un-
checked in this investigation. So enjoy your wine, then get a good
night's sleep. In the morning we start confirming that Falcon is
a good guy, or if there is anything out there to indicate he might
not be."

Lang smiled slyly, he raised his wine glass and made a toast,
"Here is to doing a good job, Marine Corps style."

"Huh! Marines," snorted Sam. "You're ok, but I'm Army all
the way."

Sam raised his glass and touched Lang's. Both men headed to
bed feeling good about dinner, the wine, and the fact they both
felt the same about this assignment. As they walked through the
casino towards their rooms they observed the two pilots sitting at
the bar drinking and entertaining two women. Lang commented
to Sam, "The women might look good to them right now, but
they may have a different vision waking up next to them in the
morning."

Sam looked at Lang and laughed, "I wish we could warn
them, or better yet join them. But we'll stick to business, that way
we won't have the headaches they'll have in the morning."

"Nor the rude awakening," replied Lang

At this comment they roared with laughter. Then they went
to bed thinking of the next day's work.

While Sam and Lang were in Elko the final pre-launch meeting was taking place at NASA.

"Gentlemen," NASA Director Terry Walsh said to start the meeting, "All systems remain go for launch. Announce the launch date to the press as July 25th as scheduled."

Deputy director Jay Hart added, "I'll hold a press conference and tell the press it's a standard personnel rotation and resupply mission. I'll give them the crew list and the change of pilot status from Henry Irving to James Falcon."

"Good," confirmed Terry, "Schedule the press conference for tomorrow morning."

The two days that Sam Taylor intended to be in Elko turned into four days. Sam and Lang did not find anyone who remembered James Falcon, or any family with the Falcon name.

Lang called the school district main office and made an appointment with the superintendent of the Elko School District. When Sam and Lang arrived for the meeting they saw that the school district headquarters building was obviously recently constructed. It was an up to date modern building. The meeting took place in the superintendent's office.

Sam introduced himself and Lang, and they showed their credentials. Then he got straight to the point and purpose of the meeting. "We're here looking for any information on a former student named James Falcon, have you heard or know of the family name 'Falcon'?"

"No" replied the superintendent, "I have been here all my life, but I don't know that name."

Sam continued, "Can we check the school district records for information on Falcon, he grew up here, if he was ever enrolled in any Elko schools there must be a record of it?"

"Gentlemen," The superintendent started hesitantly, "There are no school records. The building that housed the school records and archives burned to the ground several years ago. The newspaper also stored copies of their old editions in the building and they were lost too. I'm sorry to report that the only records we have date back only to the time of the fire. Since then, we have constructed this building and computerized our records. Unfortunately, the records only go back three years."

Lang remarked to Sam as they left the school building, "Well, that was another dead-end, still, no one around here has heard of Falcon."

The next stop was the police department. They identified themselves and asked if any record with the name Falcon was in the police files. The police officer behind the counter called the Chief of Police to the front counter.

"I want to make certain we get you any information we may have on the name Falcon," the Chief said. "Let's go back to the records room. The clerks there will check everything we have going back at least seventy years."

Sam and Lang spent over three hours in the Chief's office drinking coffee, and talking with police officers, while the records' clerks searched the files for any record of the name Falcon. The results did not turn up any reference to the name.

Sam thanked the Chief for the effort and the two investigators left the department building without any gain in their search.

Sam and Lang spent the rest of the day talking to every business owner on Main Street. No one recalled any family named Falcon.

The next day they spent almost a full day going through real estate records at the county courthouse. The name Falcon was not on any property titles. It was another zero in the Falcon name search.

Sam looked perplexed and said to Lang, "The population of this town is seventeen thousand. When James Falcon was born it was probably a lot less. Still, no one in this entire town so far knows the name Falcon. I find that hard to believe.

At breakfast the next morning Lang had the local newspaper. He suddenly looked across the table at Sam and said, "What's your feeling on coincidences?"

"What do you mean? Sam asked.

Lang handed Sam the paper.

As Sam read the article on the front page he looked at Lang, "It's interesting that this is happening at the same time as our investigation."

The newspaper article was reporting the announcement of the upcoming NASA mission to the Manned Space Station. The story stated that James Falcon was listed as the replacement crew member and pilot.

"That's an interesting coincidence," remarked Sam, "The guy we're checking out has just been added to the next NASA mission to the space station. I'm not sure what to think of that."

"Well," replied Lang, "So far we really haven't found any evidence that shows this guy is not anything but legitimate. His records at NASA are in order and who knows what might have happened to any records in this town from that long ago."

"You're right." Sam responded to Lang's mini summation of their investigation. "So far, there really isn't anything to discredit James Falcon. I want to do one more thing before we report that our investigation shows nothing negative about Falcon. Let's go back to the county courthouse again."

"What for?" said Lang. "We checked the real estate records, but in eight hours of searching we didn't find any record of a Falcon owning property. We asked them to search the county records and that came back 'zero' also."

"I want them to recheck the county records. Let's ask them how far back they went into their archives. There has to be a record somewhere with Falcon's name on it."

On the way out of the restaurant Sam turned to his young partner and asked, "Does it seem strange to you that not one person in this entire town remembers or recalls anyone named Falcon, and that we have not found any record with the Falcon name on it?"

"Yes." Was the one word reply from Lang.

At the courthouse they spoke to a young female clerk. They asked her to please check again and see if there were any files or records referring to a person named Falcon. The clerk was very polite and asked to see their credentials. Sam produced his badge and identification for her. She was impressed and became very professional in her demeanor. She sat at a computer and after several minutes she told them no 'Falcon' was in the computer files.

"We transferred our paper files to the computer about six or seven years ago." The clerk said. "Hold on a minute, I'm going to get my supervisor. She has been here for twenty years."

A mature and professional looking woman came to the counter. "Gentlemen, what's this all about?"

Sam once again produced his badge and National Security Identification.

"What can we do to help you?" The supervisor said. She was genuinely impressed by Sam's credentials.

The young clerk interjected. "I looked in the computer for the name they're looking for, it's not there. I know we switched the files from paper to computer. I wonder if there are old files in the archives that were never transferred to the computer files?"

"Well, there is one room of records we never transferred. We had to make a cut off and we did so leaving this room sealed. Those are old records and files. None of them were ever transferred to the computers. What name are you looking for? We'll look and see if it's in those files."

Sam told her the name and both clerks went to see if any files for James Henry Falcon existed. After fifteen minutes Sam and Lang sat down. The clerks had not returned yet.

Another forty-five minutes went by and both clerks came to the counter carrying two separate files.

"We found the file for James Henry Falcon," The young clerk said. We thought you might be interested in his twin brother so we brought that file also."

Sam and Lang looked at each other with surprised looks. They looked at the files. One was for James Henry Falcon and the second was for John William Falcon. The birth certificates indicated the births were several minutes apart. James had a twin brother!

An alarm went off in Sam's head. "Let's get back to the hotel," Sam ordered Lang formally,

"Double check the records and documents, especially the applications for the Academy and NASA. See if Falcon listed his brother anywhere on them, specifically where the forms required him to list any family. I don't think there is any listing of a twin brother. If that's the case there is definitely something amiss!"

Lang grabbed both files and birth certificates, "We're confiscating these files!" He said excitedly.

Both clerks stood fixed in place, aghast with their mouths opened, as the two men raced out of the courthouse with their files.

"What the hell?" said the younger clerk. The elder clerk couldn't speak.

"We'll take these back to Washington and give them to Joe Sulivand. He can give them to the FBI," Sam exclaimed excitedly.

Back at the hotel Sam alerted the pilots to be ready to fly direct to Washington, DC. Lang went directly to his room and began scrutinizing James Henry Falcon's application records. No mention of a brother was found. Lang thought to himself, "This might be a minor detail but why was an apparent twin brother not mentioned on any documentation?"

Lang informed Sam of the information. "Along with the fact

that no one in this town ever heard of the Falcons, let alone twin boys named Falcon, that adds up to something being strange."

Lang continued, "In a small town like Elko was, there should be someone who is a life-long resident that would remember twin boys growing up."

Sam said emphatically, "Our orders are to report any discrepancy we may find, no matter how small. Let's get back to Washington and report this to Sulivand. Then it's out of our hands, and he can make a decision on what to do with this information."

Chapter 32

"We just flew in from Elko, Nevada." Sam reported to Joe Sulivand. We came directly to you because our orders were to report any inaccuracies or discrepancies no matter how small."

Joe Sulivand interrupted. "Which astronaut were you checking out?

"James Falcon," replied Sam.

"What!" Said Joe Sulivand coming to his feet, "He's the replacement pilot on the shuttle. Tell me what you found."

"Corporal Lang and I found several things that seem strange to us. No one in Elko, Nevada has ever heard of or remembers a Falcon family. More important we found that James had a twin brother which he never revealed on any applications or documents. Even when the listing of family members and siblings was required."

This piece of information got the attention of Joe Sulivand, "It is a serious breach to give false information or omit required information on paperwork for the Air Force Academy and NASA. There could be an explanation for this. The FBI vetted this guy as they did every astronaut, so there probably is no problem."

"We brought back the birth certificates from the Elko courthouse." Lang reported.

Corporal Lang handed the plastic wrapped certificates to Joe Sulivand.

"I'm under the same orders you are," Sulivand said. "I want you to take these to FBI Headquarters." Sulivand ordered. "Give them directly to Robert Fuller. This investigation has top priority at the FBI. He can have his lab check them out. I'll call and tell him what you found, and that you're on the way to him now."

Robert Fuller was waiting at the entrance to the FBI building. When Sam and Lang arrived, he had them escorted to the lab and instructed, "I want the lab to go over these records. Wait there for any results and bring them to my office. The shuttle launch to the space station is this afternoon, but I am not going to take any action based only on the information you have presented, it proves nothing."

A FBI lab technician was waiting at the entrance counter to the lab. "Everyone in the lab will be working on these files," he said to Sam and Lang. "If we find anything, I'll let you know right away. Have a cup of coffee, sit down and relax. This may take a little while."

Sam and Lang grabbed each grabbed a cup of coffee and sat down to wait for any results from the lab.

Chapter 33

At the same time, half-way across the country, NASA was preparing to launch the shuttle on its mission to the space station. The astronaut team was strapped in tight and running through the final check list for launch. Launch site support personnel had evacuated the launch platform and the launch area was cleared for blast off. As the check lists were completed each astronaut had several minutes to reflect on their own thoughts.

Cecil Roberts and Dave Ash had been launched into space on previous missions. Roberts was mentally reviewing the manipulations necessary to dock the shuttle to the space station. He was the backup pilot in case anything happened to Falcon. His self discipline had already cleared his mind of his family and the little ranch on which they lived. This would be his last mission before retiring to that ranch and the life he had known as a young man. He was both eager to get back to the space station, and then back to Earth, so he could quietly end his career. He had a lot to live for and he had decided that he would focus all his attention on completing this mission successfully.

Dave Ash was relaxed and happy to be going back into space. His thoughts were easy. He had no responsibilities unless a fire broke out. Then he would be responsible to extinguish it. On his previous missions no emergency had arisen. Dave was single and enjoyed a carefree life. He was confident and competent. He knew every inch of the space shuttle, and though he seemed care free, he was ready to do his job. Right now though, he was sitting back waiting to enjoy the blast off and acceleration into space.

Roger Lawrence was a scientist, and the newest member of the crew. He was only mildly excited about his first ride into space. He was more concerned that the experiments he had packed away in the shuttle would survive the ride, and be useful to him in his work on the space station. As was his demeanor, thoughts of his wife and daughter were of no concern to him. Now, as in his days as a professor, they were an after-thought and only mattered when they were in his presence. He loved them, but his mind was always working to solve some scientific mystery. He worked hard at being an astronaut as this allowed him to study the scientific mysteries of man in space. He was oblivious to any potential danger because his mind was focused on the work and experiments he intended to perform.

Lisa Conrad was the only female on this deployment. As she sat buckled in, she was smiling inwardly. Since being a young girl she had excelled in sports and academics. She was a home-coming queen and cheerleader in her senior year. Her discovery in high school was that she could do anything the boys could. In her years in college she found that if she worked hard in the gym and on her athleticism she could compete with the men. She proved to be as good as most men and better than the average man. Lisa took great pride in this fact. By her senior year she had accumulated numerous athletic awards and a reputation as a tough and merciless competitor. She never worried about scholastic endeavors because her intelligence and wit put her at the top of her class. When a Navy recruiter told her she could be an officer, and choose her field of training, she was intrigued. Upon graduation she joined and became a naval weapons expert. After eight years she became well known as an expert on naval guns and was assigned to teach at the Naval Gunnery School in San Diego, California. During her time in the Navy she had taken flying lessons and became a licensed pilot. Feeling she had gone as far as she could, she applied for and was accepted into astronaut training program. As she let her mind drift in the few minutes before launch, her thoughts went to a subject which had begun to bother her in the last couple of years, thoughts of starting a family. She never had much time or desire for serious relationships. The idea of a family and children had never been part of any thought process. But now, as she sat strapped-in, waiting to be shot into space; she promised herself when she returned from this mission she would get serious about searching out a mate, and settle down to a family life. Then she laughed and said to herself, "You are a little scared, aren't you? Get serious girl, do this one time all out, then get out and have the family you have been bugging yourself about lately. Damn, you must be getting old."

Lisa looked over at James Falcon. She and James had become close friends during the months of training. "Maybe he's the one?" She said to herself. With that final thought about her life she turned her full attention to the mission which was about to start.

James Henry Falcon had a couple of reasons to be excited. As well as being confident and acutely trained for this mission, he knew that he would soon be in a position to carry out his real mission, the laser attack on the United States of America. He made sure he could use the laser weapon competently. He had coerced Lisa to give him extra training time on the weapon. He had set his mind on the fact that he was fully prepared to sacrifice his life, if necessary, in order to blaze a ten mile wide path of utter destruction across the continental United States. This would destroy and level hundreds of cities in the path of the laser. He smiled again at the thought that he set up the path so Sonya's home town would be one of the first hit by the laser. Then, in his mind, as he waited for the final countdown and launch, he reviewed the process and

procedures necessary to disengage the shuttle from the space station, and set it on the proper course for his landing in Iran. His
final thought before blastoff was that if he could successfully steal
the shuttle and land it in Iran he would survive the mission. Al
Qaeda would reward him with a grand life.

Chapter 34

While the astronauts waited for the final countdown to begin, Sam Taylor and Corporal Lang sat waiting in the entrance lobby of the FBI laboratory. They had been waiting an hour and were getting fidgety.

"What the hell are they doing? Sam asked out loud. "They just needed to look over the birth certificates and documents."

At that moment the door to the lab opened and half a dozen technicians rushed out. The one who seemed to be in charge excitedly yelled to Sam and Lang, and handed them a single page computer printout and a photograph. Sam and Lang looked at what was handed them. After quickly reading the printout Sam gave an order to the technician.

"Call the Director in his office! Tell him we're on our way up and have significant information. Tell him to be ready for us."

Sam and Lang took the elevator to the top floor. When the door opened they charged pass the outer secretary's desk towards Fuller's office. Not knowing what was going on the outer secretary hit the security alarm button. Immediately the doors to Robert Fuller's office locked shut and armed security personnel with weapons drawn begin to appear from everywhere. Sam and Lang were ordered to the floor, searched and disarmed.

"We need to see the Director right now!" Sam yelled, as he

and Lang, who were out- numbered ten to two, were pinned to the floor. Sam and Lang started to fight back but each of the ten security guards was as tough as them. Robert Fuller appeared and probably saved them from getting hurt.

"It's OK men," Fuller ordered, "These men are here to see me, there is no problem. Give them their weapons and stand down."

Sam and Lang stood up. Now both were pissed because their adrenalin was rampaging but the ex-soldier and the marine had been out-numbered and unable to fight back. Both men were shaking.

"The lab said you were on your way up, and it was important" said Director Fuller.

"Yes sir." Stated Lang, as Sam caught his breath.

"The lab found finger prints on both of the Falcon birth certificates. One print belongs to a printer in New York City who disappeared and was never found. But, more important a partial print was found that both your FBI Data Bank and Interpol's identified as belonging to a known al Qaeda terrorist named Abib Rashid. He has been on the watch list but has not been seen for at least ten years."

The Director of the FBI froze for a moment. His face drained of color. He shook his head and regained his composure. "This information changes everything, a known terrorist's fingerprint on an astronaut's birth certificate is significant evidence that something's not right! The launch is scheduled for today." He stated calmly. "What time is it?"

"It's a quarter to three," someone shouted.

Then to his secretary he ordered, "Get me the Director of NASA immediately on the direct line. We need to stop the launch!"

To Sam and Lang he said, "You guys did your job, if there is a problem, I hope we're in time to prevent it."

Robert Fuller's secretary announced from behind her desk, "We're 'on hold' at NASA."

"What!" Exclaimed Fuller. "We're on hold? Get me the President on the emergency line!"

Chapter 35

In the NASA Control Center the final countdown stage was in progress. The Launch Control Officer had the responsibility of launching or aborting the launch. He was in the process of receiving, "Go" or "No Go," from all stations. So far in the launch process all stations were reporting "Go." As the clocked ticked down, the tension in the room and among the dignitaries in attendance grew heavy in anticipation of the launch. In the final ten seconds of the countdown all systems were "Go."

The Launch Control Officer initiated the launch sequence and committed the launch. The shuttle and its rockets hesitated on the launch pad as the rockets spewed an unbelievable show of flame, smoke, and heat beneath them. Then, in an instant the hesitation was over. Without the least hint of a problem, the twin Titan rockets rode their trail of super heated expulsion upward and the space shuttle was on its way to the manned space station. Unknown to NASA at that moment in time was the problem of potential disaster in the form of the Seventh Astronaut, James Henry Falcon.

The action phone in the launch control room rang as the space shuttle cleared the launch pad. The Air Force Technical Sergeant assigned to man the action phone looked startled as he answered the phone and then addressed the NASA Director, "Sir, the phone is for you."

"I can't take calls right now son, I'm in the middle of a launch." Responded NASA Director Terry Walsh.

"It's the President, Sir. He is ordering you to the phone," Said the shaken Air Force Sergeant.

Assistant Director Jay Hart remarked to his boss. "He should hold his congratulations until we're at least docked at the station."

The color went out of the Director's face when he answered the phone.

"Stop the launch!" Ordered the President.

"It's too late Sir," The Director said shakily, "We just completed the launch, the shuttle is twenty miles into space."

"Confirm that James Falcon is the pilot." The President calmly asked.

"That is correct," came the reply.

Chapter 36

The President immediately called an emergency meeting. He ordered a conference link be set up in the situation room. NASA Directors Terry Walsh and Jay Hart were on that line. In the meeting were the Joint Chiefs of Staff of the Army, Navy, Air Force and Marines. The Commandant of the Coast Guard was also ordered to attend, since any threat may also include his jurisdiction. The heads of all the security agencies were also present. This included the FBI, CIA, the National Security Advisor and his Deputy, and the Secretary of Defense. Along with these people came their assistant commanders and necessary staff members. Everyone in the room had the highest security clearances.

"OK" said the President, "So we may have a terrorist en route to the manned space station.

If so, what are his intentions, and what are we going to do about it?"

"Well Sir," Jay Hart, the Assistant Director of NASA spoke first, "He could crash the shuttle into the space station destroying the shuttle and potentially destroying the station. That is, if Falcon is actually a terrorist."

Geraldine Francis, Deputy National Security Advisor interjected, "It must be assumed that Falcon is a terrorist. We need to make a plan to deal with him right now. The evidence now is pretty strong that what Steven Arnold told the Marine guard before he died is accurate information."

Air Force General and newly appointed Chief of Staff Cyrus Mitchell interrupted rudely. "There is a bigger threat that must be dealt with! We must make absolutely certain that if Falcon is a terrorist he does not gain access or control of the laser weapon system on the station. There is no known defense against the potential capability of this weapon."

"What exactly can this weapon do from space?" asked the President.

The answer to this question was to bring a shudder and murmurs throughout the room.

The Chairman of the Joint Chiefs nodded to an Air Force Colonel standing in the rear.

"Simply," Stated the Colonel, "This weapon, properly aimed, can destroy hundreds of square miles of Earth by burning and disintegrating whatever it is aimed at."

There were several moments of tense silence.

General Mitchell addressed the room, "For any of you, who are hearing of this laser for the first time, remember your oath. This weapon is top secret. No one outside this room knows it exists. So keep it that way!"

At that moment, the Director of NASA, Terry Walsh, was heard over the communication link.

"Jay, call in on duty astronauts and space station experts. "Set up a room, have them bring all their operational manuals so they are able to answer any questions which may arise. They are to be available every minute."

He advised Jay to instruct them to be prepared to stay in the room until relieved, and to make arrangements for food and bedding to be brought in so no one has to leave the room.

At this point the President regained the attention of the room and spoke.

"While we devise a plan to deal with this situation, I want to continue to determine if Falcon is in fact a terrorist. He looked at Robert Fuller, FBI Director and George Brown Jr., boss of the CIA.

"All other responsibilities now come second. I want a one hundred percent, all out effort, to find anything, anywhere in the world, on James Henry Falcon." The president continued sternly, "Terry, what are the tactical choices to end this threat?"

The people in the room and on the conference line, especially the military people, realized the President was getting ready to make a decision to defend against this threat. Those who knew him also knew there would be no limits in the fight to destroy this threat against America.

Terry Walsh, as the director of NASA took the lead in answering. "The simplest solution would be to order Falcon back here on the return trip with the other four returning astronauts. If he is a terrorist he might balk and try to take control or disable the shuttle. We need to prepare for that possibility. If he is not a terrorist he will just follow his orders and return on the shuttle." The Director continued with the second option. "Our other option is not going to be as easy because we never envisioned or trained for it. We could order the crew of the space station to take Falcon into custody and restrain and bind him so he cannot present a threat to them or the station. That order would have to come from you Mr. President, and it would have to come at the proper time, so the commander of the space station, along with one other crew member receives it. Falcon can then be taken into custody and returned on the shuttle in two days."

"I could authorize deadly force and order him killed if he resists or presents any threat whatsoever." This statement by the President caused a murmur throughout the room. The military staff nodded their approval. The room went silent for several minutes. Each person in the room and on the conference line was contemplating how the situation needed to be handled.

The debates went on around the table in hushed discussions. One member presented a course of action that was to wait and see. After all, Falcon had made no moves to indicate he was a terrorist. The military was adamant about protecting the laser. One thing was certain. Everyone was a virgin to this situation.

National Security Advisor Duncan brought an end to the discussions, "This could be nothing or it could lead to America's worst nightmare."

After listening to the many ideas the President stood up. Leaning on the table he announced he had reached a decision.

"Regardless of what has been said previously, here is what will be done. Terry, at the correct time you will connect me to the commander of the Space Station. I will order him and his crew to arrest Astronaut Falcon and bind him so he cannot escape. If he resists and tries to escape in any way, they are to kill him immediately. Return him on the space shuttle either way. Ladies and gentlemen, I cannot take a chance with the safety of thousands, maybe millions, of people at stake. If Falcon is a terrorist and trying for the laser I cannot let that happen. If Falcon is not a terrorist, hopefully he will not resist his arrest. If he is a terrorist plotting some kind of devastating event, then he will die resisting. In either case, if he resists he dies."

"Mr. President," spoke up the Director of NASA. "There are no weapons aboard the space station to use against Falcon."

"They will have to improvise weapons and have them ready when the time comes. Besides that, they have him outnumbered. Several of those aboard the station are military officers. They will follow orders and know what to do," the President responded,

"Now, get set up to execute my orders."

Chapter 37

225 miles in space the docking of the space shuttle to the station had been accomplished with precision. Even Lisa Conrad was impressed. Falcon had proven to a good choice as a replacement pilot. The ride to the space station had been exhilarating but without incident. The astronauts greeted each other as the new crew began coming aboard. They acknowledged the station would be crowded for the next two days.

Falcon had his plan laid out. He had realized that he had to kill the astronauts, all of them, right away before they realized what was happening. Then he would use the laser and make one pass over the United States. That would be enough to accomplish al Qaeda's goal. It would also satisfy his vengeance for the killing of his family, as he figured millions of Americans would die. Then, to what he thought was the more difficult part of the plan, fly the shuttle through the Earth's atmosphere and land in Iran. James Falcon chuckled at the idea of stealing America's shuttle and landing it in the desert of Iran. He wondered if he could pull it off.

"I am going to have to use all my ability to fly perfectly," He thought to himself. "The Americans are going to use all their power to stop me once they figure out what's going on."

When he came aboard the space station he looked at the work and sleep schedule. Several of the crew were in a sleep period right now. He determined the best way to start the killing without raising an alarm was with the small syringes he had brought aboard in his personal gear. He also had his Swiss Army knife sharpened to a fine sharp edge, he would use it also if necessary.

As the new shuttle crew was entering the space station the action in the White House situation room was heating up. The President was waiting to be connected to the commander of the space station.

Jay Hart talked to him on the conference line from NASA "Sir, we have more evidence pointing to Falcon being a traitor. It seems during his training on the laser he requested many hours of individual training. He went far and above what the instructors consider normal behavior in learning the weapon. He even took advantage of his fellow astronaut Lisa Conrad to give him insight into aiming the weapon. As you may or may not know she was a naval weapons officer for eight years before joining NASA. The consensus among the instructors here is Falcon was too enthusiastic in learning the weapon system. Of course the instructors do not know why I am asking questions about Falcon. The instructors had no reason to suspect Falcon of anything but over zealousness."

Chapter 38

Onboard the Manned Space Station:

Colonel Alex Delgado had been in command of the manned space station since his deployment six months ago. He had spent eight years in the Marines as a jet pilot and was somewhat arrogant and proud to have been a Marine aviator. He had been shot down during the Gulf war and had been rescued by a U.S. Army patrol. They had to fight their way back to American lines and he had no choice but to participate in several fire fights. In one of those fights the patrol was attacked by a group of fanatics. Some of the fight was face to face. Alex Delgado had killed several men during that fight. Although he had not hesitated in the least to do what was necessary, he was not proud of having killed men. Either face to face, or any other way. Colonel Delgado was content being an astronaut, with the knowledge he would not have to be involved with violence ever again.

Colonel Delgado was in for a surprise and it was coming right at him.

He and his second in command, Senior Astronaut Paul Stewart were on duty in the control Module. Several of the crew were in a sleep period and sound asleep. The other crew members were assisting the newly arrived astronauts.

The radio communication came suddenly and unexpectedly.

It was not a regularly scheduled transmission. Both men put on their earphones to be sure they would hear the radio traffic clearly. "To whom am I speaking? Please identify yourself," was the radio communication.

The two men gave each other a puzzled look. Usually the transmissions from NASA were informal and relaxed. This transmission sounded very formal and almost military. Colonel Delgado responded, "This is Colonel Alex Delgado, commanding officer of this station."

"Are you alone, who else can hear this transmission?" Came the reply through the communication equipment.

Colonel Delgado replied, "My second in command, Captain Paul Stewart is also listening to this communication. Who is this?"

"Can anyone else hear this transmission beside the two of you?" The voice asked.

"Only the two of us are hearing this." Delgado replied again.

"Gentlemen, this is the President of the United States. I am about to give you an order. Neither you, nor I, have the time for me to explain this order. Astronaut James Falcon is to be considered a terrorist and very dangerous. You are to use whatever means necessary to arrest and restrain him immediately. Bind him so he cannot get free and guard him at all times. I am authorizing deadly force. Arm yourselves with whatever you can use as weapons, and if he resists, kill him. He may be trying to use the laser against America. Acknowledge and execute this order immediately."

The two astronauts looked at each other in stunned disbelief.

Colonel Delgado acknowledged the order and stated, "I will execute this order, as soon as I confirm with NASA Control this transmission is authentic."

He then shut down the transmission, changed frequencies to a secure emergency channel and contacted NASA Control.

Delgado then said on the secure NASA channel, "We just received a radio transmission and need confirmation from you that it is authentic."

"Stand by," came the voice through the speaker, then;

"Colonel Delgado and Captain Stewart, this is the President of the United States. We are now on the NASA secure emergency frequency you just contacted. Acknowledge and carry out my orders. Your safety and the safety of the United States are at risk."

A pain went down Delgado's spine as he said, "Sir, we will execute your order immediately."

The two men stood up. Captain Stewart said, "We need to move fast, the new crew and Falcon are already on board."

"Grab that fire extinguisher, use it as a weapon and follow me," Delgado ordered.

The two men left the control room and headed for the docking bay where most of the astronauts should be. As they started to pass through a sleep area they saw astronaut Cecil Roberts lying on the floor. Delgado shook Cecil gently then saw the blood and the hole in Cecil's neck. Cecil was dead.

Delgado turned to Paul Stewart and exclaimed, "He's dead! We're at war!" He growled. "Let's kill that son of a bitch before he gets anyone else!"

As they entered the adjacent sleeping bay they saw Falcon standing over Dave Ash. Roger Lawrence lay on the floor at the far end of the bay. Delgado charged and flung himself at Falcon without hesitating. Falcon reacted by jumping to one side and Delgado missed him completely.

Paul Stewart discharged the CO2 extinguisher at Falcon's face. Falcon retreated beyond the discharge and fled into the next compartment. Stewart went to check Dave Ash but Dave jumped up and seemed confused and dazed at the commotion around him.

"What the HELL is going on?" exclaimed an excited female voice from behind Stewart.

Delgado was now back on his feet.

"Am I glad to see you," he yelled at Lisa. "Falcon is a traitor! He killed Roberts and Lawrence."

Steven Moore, a member of the original crew aboard the space station, stumbled into the sleeping bay. "What's all the commotion? I can't even sleep."

Delgado excitedly informed the astronauts of the situation and the presidential orders. Then he ordered them to see what weapons each had. A couple of small pocket knives and a metal flashlight emerged. Lisa had a Marine Corps issue combat knife in its scabbard, inside the leg pocket of her flight suit.

"Keep your weapons ready, Delgado ordered, "We will stay together until we capture or kill Falcon. Now let's wake the rest of the crew and warn them."

As the four astronauts stood guard outside the main sleeping bay Delgado ordered Lisa to enter and wake up the remaining crew members. The lights were off, and it was pitch black inside the bay. Lisa used her small flashlight to first check the sleep area. She wanted to be sure Falcon was not waiting in the dark to attack her. There were shadows caused by her small flashlight, and at first she could not tell if someone was standing in the darkness or not. Her pulsed rate raced and went off the scale as she almost backed out of the sleep area. She was on the verge of making a panicked exit. She suddenly could not control her fear. She was frozen in place and could not make herself move. Her throat suddenly dried up fiercely and she gasped for breath.

"You OK?" A voice whispered from behind her.

Recognizing the voice as Colonel Delgado's Lisa let out a loud breath.

"I'm OK," she managed to say shakily.

"Wake these guys up like I told you to do." Delgado ordered hotly but quietly, "We're outside watching for Falcon."

Anger raced through Lisa as she said to herself, "Delgado doesn't know me and now he thinks I'm afraid or at least hesitant in following orders."

Lisa put the thought aside. She took a deep breath and tried to regain her confidence. She moved to the first bunk and shined her light on the astronaut. She shuddered as she realized he was dead. Lisa stiffened her determination to show Delgado she could be relied on and moved to the next astronauts. Lisa's foot slipped as she stepped deeper into the darkness. She shined her small flashlight beam towards the floor. She saw she was standing in a puddle of blood. She quickly shined her light around the room to be sure Falcon wasn't lurking there. She checked the other sleeping astronauts carefully to be sure she was being accurate. Their throats were cut deeply. She almost slipped to the floor but managed to grab something in the dark to keep from falling.

Lisa poked her head out of the mid deck sleeping bay and reported in as strong a voice as she could muster, "Colonel, they are all dead sir. Only the five of us are alive."

Colonel Delgado was trying to remain calm. But his military demeanor and anger was showing. His face was contorted and red, and the veins in his neck were fully visible. His voice was now that of a military commander ready to whatever necessary to kill his enemy. He addressed Lisa first, "Stay behind us and out of the way, you'll be OK."

Lisa turned her face so the crew did not see it turn blood red. She was pissed, mostly at herself. Delgado then addressed his crew, "I don't exactly know what his plan is, but we'll start looking for him in the laser module. This is a fight to the death people. Be ready to kill Falcon. That mother fucker killed my crew! He is not going to live long enough to brag about it, and he sure as hell is not going to use that laser!"

Lisa Conrad was embarrassed. She had never before let herself down and had always been as good as the men around her. Now these men thought she had to be protected because she couldn't do the job. The anger swelled within her. She was angry at herself and vowed she would make up for her actions at the sleeping bay. Lisa grabbed her Marine Corps issue combat knife and took it out of its scabbard. She put it back in her pants pocket to be sure it was in easy reach and ready if needed. She was angry at two things, herself for being afraid, and that son of a bitch Falcon.

"He used me," she said to herself, "To make him extra proficient with the laser weapon, and now he is trying to use it against my country. How stupid of me to have considered him as a choice for a lover or husband. If I get the chance I'm going to cut his guts out!"

While the crew was gathered listening to Delgado, Falcon had made his way to the control room. In the control room he reset the computer controls for the space station orbit position and hit the execute button. He knew the longitude and latitude co-ordinates and had them already entered in the computer. The space station began to move slowly to its new orbit around the Earth, an orbit which would put it, and its laser, directly over the middle of the United States.

Chapter 39

Sunnyvale, California
Sunnyvale Air Force Base

In the Satellite Monitoring Control Center of the Sunnyvale Air Force Base, Steven Houston was on duty, and the first to see it on his computer screen. The space station was changing its orbit position around the Earth. The new orbit would bring it directly over the United States. He immediately hit the emergency red button notifying his supervisor, Sergeant Chet Daily, of the orbit change. After checking several other computer stations to confirm Airman Housten's report, Sergeant Daily picked up the phone to the command center and reported to Captain Hal Bentley, the Shift Commander, "Sir, we have a situation, the manned space station is changing its orbit without authorization."

NASA confirmed that the space station had not been authorized to change its orbit. Captain Bentley picked up the phone and advised NORAD of a potential problem developing in space. The space station was changing its orbit without authorization from NASA. NORAD, following standing orders alerted all military installations in the continental United States to upgrade their readiness status. This was NORAD protocol, even though no problem or threat had yet been identified.

Olivia Marchan was proud of the job she had done. During her affair with Airman Steven Houston she had given him enough transmitters to insure he would be wearing at least one whenever he was on duty. The miniature transmitters were sewn into his uniform coats. She had also showered him with gifts consisting of pens, watches and a ring. Each contained a transmitting device capable of sending whatever was said near it to a receiver within a one mile radius.

Olivia had the receiver. She was to inform her al Qaeda contact, Abreu, via her satellite phone, when she heard any report concerning the maneuvering of the manned space station. The plan was that the transmitting devices planted on Airmen Steven Houston would give al Qaeda the information that something was happening on the manned space station. This would trigger another al Qaeda plot. Olivia monitored the receiver constantly whenever Steven Housten was on duty. Suddenly Olivia heard voices from the transmitters on Steven Houston saying there was some kind of problem with the space station and it was changing its orbit position without authorization. The new orbit was positioning the station over the United States. Olivia pulled the satellite phone from its hiding place. She pressed the send button and spoke to her al Qaeda contact, "The space station is changing its orbit. This maneuvering by the space station is not authorized. That was all I was able to hear."

Her al Qaeda controller was Abreu. He gave her an order. "Destroy your apartment and everything in it. Use the five gallon can of gas and the half stick of dynamite you have and burn your apartment. Do it now, then report back to your cell in Los Angeles."

At this moment, in the Sunnyvale Air Base control room, Airman Steven Housten was standing next to his boss Sergeant Chet Daily. As turned from his computer station his pen fell to the floor and broke apart. The Sergeant and Housten picked up the pieces.

"What the hell is this, Housten?" Sergeant Daily questioned.

He was holding a small square device. "It looks like a transmitter. You've been transmitting from this room! Where did you get this pen?"

Steven Housten couldn't believe it as he answered, "My girlfriend gave it to me."

He couldn't believe it as he heard the next words from his boss, "Sergeant of the guard, arrest this man!"

Sergeant Daily had tears in his eyes as he watched his young Airman taken away under arrest.

He grimly remembered warning the young airman about women. Now a woman had ruined Steven Housten's career and probably sent him to prison. Captain Hal Roberts was standing next to Sergeant Daily.

"What a shame." the Captain said, "He was a real asset to us, a genuine computer expert. He had a great career ahead of him. I should have allowed myself to know him better. Maybe, if we would have reacted differently when he suddenly started being late for duty, this could have been recognized and averted. At any rate I'll put in a good word for him. Maybe it will help his situation."

"I doubt it," replied Sergeant Daily.

Steven Housten was seated in the security office. The Air Force officer in charge of base security questioned him. "Where does your girlfriend live?"

The Air Force security officers and the Sheriff's SWAT team surrounded the apartment building of Olivia Marchan. As they moved forward to bust the door to her apartment and charge in, an explosion and flames suddenly erupted from within the apartment. Several of the SWAT team received severe burns as they were thrown to the ground by the explosion. If the explosion had occurred one minute later the entire team would have already entered the apartment and been incinerated.

Firemen arrived but could not enter. The apartment and everything in it was completely engulfed in flame and destroyed. The

SWAT team members and the Air Force security team watched the fire, thinking how close they had come to death. They did not know this was an unintentional threat to them by al Qaeda.

The Fire Battalion Chief, looking at the Swat Team and the Air Force Security personnel turned to his Captain and said, "I wonder what the hell this was all about?"

After receiving the report from Olivia, Abreu informed his al Qaeda superiors the manned space station was maneuvering over the United States. This information went up the al Qaeda chain of command all the way to the top. Usama Bin Ladin and his top echelon ordered the second plot against America to proceed in anticipation of mass destruction raining down on the United States from the manned space station.

Chapter 40

On the Space Station an alarm sounded for fifteen seconds. "That's the laser alarm. Falcon must be arming the laser," Stewart said, more calmly than even he could believe.

"Son of a Bitch!" exclaimed Delgado, "We have to stop him, and right now! Stewart, you and Moore attack Falcon from the storage compartment side of the laser control room. Dave, you and I will attack him from the kitchen side. Attack as soon as you are in position."

Lisa, not receiving any orders in the attack followed Delgado and Ash.

As they hustled to follow their orders Moore said to Stewart, "I'm not sure we should have divided our forces. It would have been better to attack as one group!"

"We have our orders!" Replied Stewart, "And besides, he won't be able to defend an attack from two sides."

Usually, it took two people to efficiently work the weapon. In the laser control room it was taking Falcon several minutes longer than he anticipated to set the laser beam to its widest range and configure it so the first burst would hit Sonya's home town. He got the weapon ready to fire. The station was several minutes from being in the right position. Falcon was about two minutes from fulfilling the first part of his mission, raining terror down on the United States of America. Before he could fire the weapon he heard movement and noise in the adjacent compartment. He moved to the side of the hatch with his Swiss Army knife at the ready. He also had a three foot metal bar from a storage compartment.

The two astronauts, Stewart and Moore, arrived ahead of Delgado to attack Falcon. When they started to open the hatchway door from the storage compartment it made a scraping noise.

"So much for the element of surprise," whispered Moore.

Following their orders they opened the hatch and entered to attack Falcon upon their arrival.

Because they arrived sooner than Delgado their entrance and attack gave them only a two to one advantage against Falcon. Stewart, ahead of Moore, entered the room first. Falcon was ready for them. Stewart was met with a surprise blow to the stomach from Falcon's Swiss Army knife. He doubled over in pain and went face down on the floor. Moore was right behind Stewart and landed a blow to the back of Falcon's head. Falcon hit the floor, rolled over and came up striking at Moore with the metal bar. Moore blocked the metal bar with his forearm. His forearm broke under the strength of the blow and Moore fell backwards onto the floor. He retreated back into the compartment from which he and Stewart had started their attack. He dragged Stewart with him. Moore immediately ripped off his shirt and used it to stop the bleeding from Stewart's wound. Their non-coordinated two on one attack had been combat ineffective. Falcon let the two wounded astronauts go and returned to fire the laser.

Delgado heard the commotion and hustled forward to join the fight. As Falcon approached the laser firing mechanism, Delgado charged from the other side of the compartment and lunged at him. Falcon saw him coming in his peripheral vision and jumped clear of Delgado's lunge. The Swiss Army knife was ready and Delgado met the same fate as Stewart. As Delgado went down with the stomach wound Dave Ash charged into the room.

He was on Falcon and threw him to the floor. Falcon rolled and kicked Dave Ash's testicles and midsection. Ash fell to the floor defenseless.

Falcon now had a clear path to the laser firing console. As he jumped to his feet and started for it Lisa Conrad stepped into his path.

Falcon faced her head on, "Bitch," he hissed at her, "I'll take care of you!"

Lisa held her U.S. Marine issue combat knife hidden behind her leg. Falcon made the mistake of under estimating his enemy. As Falcon charged to put her out of commission, by head butting her square in the face, he did not anticipate the strength of the woman's determination and rage. As her nose was broken and her face flattened by Falcon's forehead slamming into it, Falcon felt the blade and the pain of her Marine combat knife as it entered his lower abdomen. He had to back away quickly as Lisa made a mad second thrust with her knife. She could not see because of the blood in her eyes from her smashed nose and face but she made a second charge anyway.

Falcon ran past her and through the next compartment. He thought to himself, the laser would have to wait. He needed to stop the bleeding and tend to the wound Lisa had inflicted with her knife.

"Damn it, I didn't see the knife," Falcon said out loud and to himself, "I should have known that bitch would be just as tough as any of those other guys."

Dave Ash recovered from his pain and started working on Delgado's bleeding wound.

Delgado sat up, and when his wound was covered he held the makeshift bandage tight on his wound. He ordered Ash to help Lisa remarking, "I'm glad Falcon's knife wasn't any bigger, or I might not be here."

Moore, assisting Stewart, dragged him into the compartment.

"Where's Falcon?" yelled Stewart, "I'm going to kill him!"

The astronauts looked at each other and knew it would be tough to carry on a fight in their condition. As Ash put a wet cold towel on Lisa's face she told them, "I got Falcon pretty good in the mid section with my knife, I don't think he will be able to fight us." Lisa then described her bout with Falcon, telling them she was able to stab him good!

Delgado commended her in front of the men, "You done good, girl," he said through his pain, "I didn't think you were worth a shit but you're the only one who did any damage. The rest of us took a dirty beating from that son of a bitch!"

Delgado put Ash on watch in case Falcon did return to attack them. The rest of the wounded group began patching themselves up so they could find and finish Falcon. As soon as Lisa was able to see and her head cleared, she and Moore shut down the laser. Delgado ordered them to disconnect the firing panel so the laser was out of commission. That way, even if Falcon did over power all five astronauts he still could not use the laser without making extensive repairs.

"Let's get ourselves patched up as good as possible," Said Delgado, "The five of us are going to have to find and kill him. We can't let him wander free in the station. Lisa put a good hurt on him, so he can't be too mobile."

In concentrating on keeping Falcon from using the laser it never occurred to them that he might try for the space shuttle. But for now Falcon was in a world of hurt. He had stopped the bleeding and had a solid bandage on the wound. The bandages had come from the first aid kit in the mechanical compartment in which he was hiding. Even though he was in extreme pain Falcon was planning his next move. He knew he was too weak to overcome five astronauts, even if four of them were wounded. The first part of the plan, to use the laser on America, would have to be abandoned.

Falcon verbalized his anger, saying disgustedly, "The laser plan failed because of a woman, shit!" James Falcon's will to survive flushed to the surface as he thought, "I have to be successful at stealing the shuttle, and at least fulfill the second part of al Qaeda's plan. If I survive, I'll get another chance for vengeance against America!

He decided he better not wait. They would soon start looking for him. Falcon began slowly and cautiously making his way to the docking bay and the space shuttle. The heavy bandages were soaked through with blood, but they had stopped the bleeding from Falcon's wound. Movement was painful but tolerable. Falcon knew for him to survive, he had no choice but to endure the pain, get to the shuttle, disengage it from the station; and land it in Iran. He figured if he waited he would not make it off the space station.

Now that the laser was disarmed Delgado decided to keep his crew together in case Falcon returned. He took his crew to the control room and reported to NASA.

"This is Colonel Alex Delgado on board the Space Station. How do you read?"

NASA answered immediately. "This is Terry Walsh, Colonel, we read you loud and clear. What's going on up there Alex?"

Colonel Delgado began to report, "Falcon has killed all but five of the crew. We have dismantled the laser weapon system so it cannot be fired at this time. Falcon is wounded and still on the loose. We are preparing to hunt him down now."

"Your first priority now that the laser is not a threat is to get the station back to its correct orbit," ordered the Director of NASA, "then you can find Falcon."

Just as Colonel Delgado was about to respond and acknowledge the order the crew felt a slight vibration. Then a mechanical noise was barely audible.

The noise was the sound of electrical motors kicking on.

Delgado looked up. "What's that?" He asked.

Dave Ash, being a secondary shuttle pilot, was the first to immediately recognize the shuttle was being unlocked from the space station. This was the first step in the procedure for undocking and separating the shuttle from the station.

"Falcon is taking the shuttle," gasped Ash.

Delgado suddenly realized he had made a fatal mistake. He had under estimated Falcon. He should have guarded the shuttle as soon as Falcon had left the fight. He looked at Ash.

"Get to the shuttle bay, see if you can stop him. Take Lisa and Moore with you!" ordered Delgado.

There was absolute silence in the NASA control room as Colonel Delgado's report was digested. The loss of life was the first aboard the Space Station. To lose six astronauts to a terrorist was devastating. The men and women on duty in the control center were stunned. Terry Walsh tried to maintain his composure in order to demonstrate his leadership. It took him several minutes to do so. Just as he regained control of his emotions, and was ready to speak to his people in the control room a radio transmission from Colonel Delgado was heard throughout the room.

"Falcon is trying to take the shuttle! We are attempting to stop him now."

Terry Walsh, now in full control of his emotions, picked up the action phone and calmly ordered the operator, "Put me through to the President."

The President was in the Oval office with the National Security Advisor when the red phone on his desk buzzed. He answered it immediately.

"Sir," Terry addressed the President, "I need to report to you concerning the space station situation."

The President put the phone on speaker so Duncan could hear the report.

Terry continued, "We have secured the laser so it cannot be fired."

"Thank God for that," interrupted Duncan.

"I'm afraid the rest of the news is very bad sir. Falcon has murdered six crew members and at this time is attempting to leave the station in the shuttle. The crew is trying to stop him now. I'll get back to you as soon as I have more information."

"Thank you Terry, keep me informed," the President replied.

The President looked at his advisor, "Well, no matter what happens now, al Qaeda and their terrorist astronaut have given us a real 'black eye,' but at least the laser is no longer a threat."

The National Security Advisor just nodded his agreement.

"I want to get ahead of this. Set up the Situation Room right now. Call in the agency heads and the military," concluded the President.

Chapter 41

On board the space station Delgado and Stewart were maneuvering it back to its proper orbit position. As Ash, Lisa and Moore approached the shuttle bay they could see the air lock doors were already sealed. Ash picked up the intercom and reported to Delgado, "We're too late."

Falcon had trouble keeping the bandage sealed tight over the wound in his abdomen. Lisa Conrad had delivered a good blow with her knife. The wound was deep but the bleeding had slowed.

"I should have known she would be dangerous" Falcon thought again, "I knew her, and her capability, and still underestimated her! I screwed up by not taking her out sooner!"

Falcon adjusted the dressing and bandage as he continued to maneuver the shuttle away from the space station, his thoughts turned away from Lisa, "Now I have to get this thing back to the ground without burning up or crashing."

The calculations for his re-entry and descent were already worked out and he entered them into the shuttle's computer. As the shuttle started its trip to Earth he hoped all the time practicing in the flight simulator was going to do him some good.

The White House Situation room was filling with the President's cabinet and staff. The secure phone whined. One of the President's aides answered, "It's the Director of NASA, Sir."

"Put him on the speaker phone so everyone gets the

information." The President's angry mood was showing even though he was trying to maintain an even demeanor.

"Mr. President," the speaker came to life as Terry Walsh reported,

"Falcon has succeeded in taking our space shuttle. He is headed back to Earth. At this point in time we cannot tell where he is going to land. That is, if he succeeds in getting through the atmosphere without burning up."

"Well, he has succeeded at almost everything else he's tried Terry, there is no reason to doubt he can land the shuttle," admonished the President.

"Yes Sir," replied the Director of NASA, realizing his boss was pissed "With your permission we will begin preparations to launch a second shuttle to the Space Station."

"Yes," replied the President. "You take care of getting a relief crew to the Space Station. Get our allies to help if you need to. We will take care of dealing with the traitor in the shuttle. Keep your emergency line manned and open in case we need your expertise." With that the President nodded to an aide, who disconnected the call. The President then addressed the room.

"OK, Ladies and gentlemen, he said evenly, take five minutes to discuss this situation amongst yourselves, and then we need to decide on and execute a plan of action."

After several minutes of discussions around the table the National Security Advisor was first to speak, "If this guy Falcon is planning on crashing into one of our cities we must destroy the space shuttle at the highest altitude possible."

For the first time since the crisis started the National Science Advisor spoke his mind, "We must destroy the space shuttle. It would be a disaster to let any of the technology fall into enemy hands. Especially terrorists, as they have the will, determination, and capability to find a way to use our technology against us. This was the last flight for this shuttle anyway. It was going to be retired to a museum, so in destroying it we're only losing a museum display."

"What capability do we have to do this?" The President addressed the question to Jack Prentiss, Secretary of Defense.

The Secretary motioned to Air Force General Mitchell, Chairman of the Joint Chiefs of Staff.

General Mitchell answered, "We can use guided missiles from our ships to reach the shuttle at high altitudes. We need to act now to make this happen."

"What if we miss with the missiles at high altitude?" Asked the President.

"The missiles will burn up as they fall through the atmosphere after expending their fuel or, if they get high enough, they will continue into space," answered the General as he continued, "We back up our missile attack with jet fighters from our carriers and land bases. They can also destroy any large pieces of the shuttle that may be left and falling to Earth. Since we do not know yet where the shuttle is headed all fighters at all U.S. installations throughout the world must be brought to battle stations in case they need to be launched against the shuttle. The shuttle could be used to attack a city by crashing into it or crash into an aircraft carrier, or another high value target. It may get out of the pilot's control. In that case there is no telling where it might hit."

"I've heard enough talk. Find out where that thing is headed. Execute a destroy order immediately. Bring all U.S. military commands to battle stations with orders to be prepared to respond and destroy the space shuttle," ordered the President.

After allowing time for the military to issue the necessary orders the President stood. "I want to be sure my position on this situation is absolutely clear. We will expend our resources and commit our military to do whatever it takes to destroy the shuttle. Then punish those responsible in the most striking way possible. This will show the world we will not let our property fall into the wrong hands, and we will find and exterminate people responsible for treachery against the United States."

Tom Belcher, Secretary of State, stood up and asked the President, "Sir, shall I notify our allies, and perhaps our enemies, that we are not going to war with anyone. How much detail do you want to give them?"

Press Secretary Norma Rosenthal interrupted.

"We have to be careful how this situation is transmitted. The media is going to have a field day with this."

President Kramer stated bluntly and rather rudely, "Tom, notify our allies and any government you feel might take advantage of the situation and react militarily against any of our forces. Tell them this is some kind of drill. We are testing our worldwide communications. Add whatever you deem necessary so no one can interpret this as a military move against anyone."

The Secretary of State left the room to carry out his orders as the President continued, "Right now our priority is to deal with the space shuttle and protect our forces from any potential military action that might be taken against them. We'll deal with the press and media later. For now, Norma, tell them you have not been briefed on what's going on and you will hold a press conference when you have information to give them."

Norma Rosenthal started to object to this plan of handling the media but a stern look from the President caused her to keep quiet and follow her orders.

Chapter 42

From deep within the pentagon the National Command Authority began the chain of command process. To every United States military installation throughout the world the order to battle stations was being transmitted.

IN THE DISTRICT OF KAISERSLAUTERN, GERMANY
UNITED STATES AIR FORCE BASE
OFFICE OF THE COMMANDING GENERAL

After a loud knock on the door the General's aide entered and announced,

"Sir, the command center just received a flash action message ordering us to battle stations with all jet fighters fully armed! The flash action states this is not a drill!"

General Charles Scott calmly placed his cup of coffee on the desk. He was an experienced combat veteran and had been through too many alerts to get excited. He issued his orders.

"Sound the general alarm and lock down the base, no one in or out. Order all aircraft to the line fully armed, manned and ready to take off."

This scenario was taking place at every land based U.S. military installation throughout the world. The same orders were sent via the secure military channels to every United States ship, submarine and aircraft carrier.

IN THE ARABIAN SEA
ABOARD THE AIRCRAFT CARRIER USS RONALD REAGAN
ON THE BRIDGE

The large American flag was whipping in the brisk wind from the highest mast of the ship. The sea was calm as the huge ship slipped through it at a speed of fifteen knots. Captain Tobin Shafer was sitting comfortably in his bridge chair. He had been in command of the carrier for over a year. The admiral in command of the USS Ronald Reagan battle group had been called to Washington along with the Marine general commanding the battle group's Marines. That left Tobin Shafer in command of the Battle Group in addition to his carrier. He was finishing his second cup of coffee as he casually watched the bridge crew go about their duties. He had let his mind wander and was thinking of the many women he had encountered in his thirty four years in the Navy. He was thinking that maybe it was time to grab one and settle down. It was getting pretty boring sailing around the world's oceans with no wars to fight. He was kind of disgusted with the lack of action on the part of the United States in not interfering to help innocent people in places such as Somalia and Cambodia, or the many other places innocent people were being hurt and killed. He had fought in three wars and had been involved in many humanitarian missions.

He remembered many years ago when he had almost disobeyed orders from then President Nixon, and his advisor. They had ordered him to return his jets to the carrier he was commanding instead of attacking North Korean gun boats, which were attacking the USS Pueblo.

Captain Shaffer's mind wandered back to that night. It was

a long time ago. The USS Pueblo had sent out an SOS that they were under attack by North Korean gun boats. The Pueblo was an unarmed United States Navy Ship.

Upon receiving the USS Pueblo SOS Tobin Shaffer immediately dispatched his combat air patrol and launched additional jet fighters. Their orders were to engage, and blow any ships attacking the Pueblo out of the water. When he reported the situation and his action to the Naval Command Authority he received direct orders from President Nixon and his advisor Robert McNamara, to recall his planes and not attack the North Korean gun boats. He reluctantly obeyed this order.

He sometimes wished he had the guts to have disobeyed that order, but he did not, and the USS Pueblo was given up to the enemy without a fight for the first time in United States military history. He was ashamed to be part of that piece of history. He was still bitter at the fact that in order to save his career he had to defend his action of initially ordering his aircraft to attack the North Koreans. Many senior military officers came to his defense, and now he was commanding one of the Navy's newest carriers. He was thinking maybe it was time to retire when his thoughts were interrupted by the phone buzzing on the console in front of him. As he picked up the phone and placed the receiver next to his ear he heard his executive officer's voice.

"Captain," exclaimed the executive officer, "We just received a flash action message, I'm sending it to the bridge now. I recommend we go to general quarters immediately."

Captain Shaffer acknowledged his executive officer and replaced the receiver on the phone.

"Officer of the deck, bring the ship to general quarters," the Captain ordered with no hesitation. His day dreaming was over.

The officer of the deck reacted by looking a little surprised at the sudden order. He hesitated to hear if it was a drill. Hearing nothing further he looked at the boatswains mate and passed on the order, "Sound general quarters."

The general quarters alarm reverberated throughout the carrier. Sailors scrambled out of bunks to man their battle stations. Water tight doors slammed shut, anti-aircraft guns were readied, fire-fighting crews manned their standby positions throughout the ship. Planes were maneuvered and moved to their launch order positions. As the huge ship came to life the Captain read the message just handed to him. It read:

> TO: Captain, USS Ronald Reagan
> FROM: National Command Authority
>
> Launch missiles under your command to destroy space shuttle. STOP
> Prepare to launch aircraft to engage and destroy shuttle. STOP
> Shuttle re-entering atmosphere, exact time unknown. STOP
> Destination on earth not determined as yet. STOP
> Be prepared to intercept and destroy shuttle. STOP
> Repeat: Destroy Space Shuttle. STOP
> Be prepared for possible hostile action against U.S. Forces. END

Captain Shaffer buzzed the commander of the air wing, "Advise the flight operations officer to arm and prepare to launch all fighter aircraft. This is not a drill."

He then ordered the communications officer to alert all missile bearing ships in the fleet to stand by to launch missiles to destroy the space shuttle. Escort vessels were ordered to general quarters to defend the fleet against any possible attack from the air, on the surface or from under water.

The same message was sent to all U.S. carrier groups. The reaction was the same as on the USS Ronald Reagan. The United States military was set up and prepared to destroy the U.S. Space Shuttle. Now they had to find it.

On board the space shuttle Falcon knew the United States would not let the shuttle fall into the hands of al Qaeda without a fight. They would do everything in their power to prevent it. Falcon had his plan though. As soon as the computer guided the shuttle to an altitude where he could manually pilot the craft he would set the lowest and most direct line to the landing in Iran.

Chapter 43

In the White House situation room the phone on the table near the Joint Chiefs of Staff buzzed its annoying alert tone.

An aide answered, "It's for you sir," he stated as he handed the phone receiver to General Snyder.

The General listened for several minutes, then looked at the President and spoke,

"NORAD has the shuttle on radar, its heading points it to somewhere in the Middle East. They are alerting the Ronald Reagan to attack now."

The General addressed a question to Jay Hart on the communications link to NASA, "Does the shuttle have any defensive capability?"

"No, the Assistant Director of NASA answered, "It can maneuver and change speeds. I'm not sure these could be termed defensive capabilities. The extent of the maneuvering capabilities in flight depends on the experience and ability of the pilot."

"Then the missiles should be able to destroy it?" The General said.

"Yes," responded Jay, "The shuttle should not be able to out maneuver the missiles, although this has never been considered or tested."

Eight missiles were launched from the platforms aboard one of the frigates in the USS Ronald Reagan Battle Group.

Upon hearing this, the President said to no one in particular, "There goes millions of dollars worth of military hardware to destroy millions of dollars worth of space shuttle."

On the shuttle Falcon saw the streaks of the approaching missiles. The computer was still controlling the re-entry as the shuttle was just entering the Earth's atmosphere. Falcon judged the trajectory and speed of the approaching missiles. He decided quickly that his only chance for survival was to kick on all the thrusters to full thrust simultaneously at the last moment and hope the shuttle would by-pass the missiles before they detonated. He only had several seconds to act. Falcon closed his eyes and prepared to live or die by his decision.

The plan worked. The sudden acceleration in the re-entry speed succeeded in getting the shuttle passed and below the missiles.

The missiles coming up at him did no harm as they passed the shuttle at 1000 miles per hour heading into space. Falcon found he was soaking wet from his own sweat. The pain from Lisa's knife wound was excruciating. He could also smell his urine. The middle of his flight suit was filled with it. But, he had survived the first attack. His mind now zeroed in on the fact that he was going faster than the design characteristics of the heat shield allowed. He shut down the thrusters hoping this would slow the shuttle enough so it would not burn up or disintegrate in the atmosphere. He was scared as the shuttle began to vibrate violently.

James Henry Falcon's thoughts went instantly to his brother, his parents and sisters. He actually felt a little comfort in the fact that if he died now, he would be joining them He relaxed a little. Then he thought of Abreu and how he was failing the mission. He had already let Abreu down in failing the first part of the mission. Now, if he failed to land the shuttle his whole life would have been a waste. Falcon shook his head and regained his determination to survive. He thought of Sonya for a brief second and was angered at the fact that he let that bitch off the hook too.

Aboard the USS Ronald Reagan Captain Schaffer was receiving the combat report from his executive officer.

"Apparently the missiles have by-passed the shuttle without detonating close enough to destroy it. The shuttle has come through the upper atmosphere moving at approximately seven hundred miles per hour. NORAD says its glide path places the landing location in the northern desert of Iran."

"Alright," said Captain Schaffer, "Launch our fighters in three groups according to the attack plan we discussed. The first two groups get ahead of the shuttle. Attack head-on and destroy the target. The third group is to take a position parallel to the attack and attack from the flank if the head-on attacks are not successful."

A sailor entered the room at that moment and handed the executive officer a message clipboard. After reading it the executive officer interrupted the Captain.

"Sir, we have new orders."

"Read them," The Captain ordered.

The executive officer read the orders, "Cease air operations. Jet fighter aircraft not able to destroy shuttle and contents completely. Shuttle will land in approximately one to two hours. Use Marines via helicopter assault. Capture pilot. Completely destroy shuttle and all contents within. Leave no parts of shuttle intact for possible use by enemy. Repeat, destroy all parts of shuttle completely. Co-ordinates of possible landing area to follow. Repeat, capture shuttle pilot alive or return body. Destroy space shuttle. That's it," Said the executive officer.

Captain Schaffer reacted, "Cancel flight operations. Have aircraft and crews stand down for now. Maintain our standard combat air patrol. Advise the Marines on board and on the helicopter assault ships to prepare to board their helicopters for a ground assault. Advise the helicopter squadrons to be ready to take off within the hour. Give them the co-ordinates of the area where the shuttle is headed. The exact co-ordinates for their assault landing will be transmitted to them in flight."

Fifteen minutes later Captain Schaffer issued a young Marine Colonel and his staff their orders.

"Take your Marines to the landing site, destroy any ground force, capture and destroy the space shuttle. Destroy the shuttle and its contents completely. Leave nothing of the shuttle for the enemy. Capture the shuttle pilot. Return him to your ship alive if possible. If he is killed return his body. Use your assault force to protect the shuttle destruction team. When the shuttle is completely destroyed your mission is complete. Return your assault force to the fleet. There is another battle group heading for us as backup. At this point in time it looks like Iran is not involved in this shuttle situation. They have not been informed by our government and may not even be aware of what is going on in their desert. However, I will have our fighter aircraft ready to support you if you need it. Good luck Marine. Semper Fi."

The colonel was handed 25 pictures of the shuttle pilot Falcon. These were to be distributed to his officers so they could identify Falcon.

"Yes sir," replied Marine Colonel Byron Comb. He then saluted, ran to the carrier deck and boarded the lead chopper.

Byron Comb was the executive officer of the Marines in this battle group. His commanding general was in Washington for meetings. That left Comb as the commanding officer of the one-thousand men in the Marine assault force. He was taking six hundred of them to this fight. He knew he had to maintain the image of a tough and confident Marine officer. In actuality he could not believe how scared he was. He had always been able to put on a good show in front of people. That is how he came to be a Colonel of Marines and the executive officer of this fleet Marine Force.

He first learned how to impress people in order to get what he wanted when he was in high school. In playing football, basketball and baseball he was well known and well liked for his athletic prowess and demeanor. His peers made him their leader and Byron Comb relished the status. His confidence and his ego grew to the point where he felt he could do whatever he wanted. He discovered that if he strutted properly and talked a good talk he could fool just about anyone into thinking Byron Comb was as good as it could be. His father had been a Marine in Korea. Byron saw how people admired Marines. Byron wanted that attention. Once in the Marine Corps his strutting and attitude got him promoted and eventually assigned to officer training school, and to the University of Maryland, where the Marine Corps provided him with a four year degree in World and American History.

Upon graduation he was commissioned a second lieutenant. Byron Comb was a peace time Marine. His show of ability and confidence, both of which exposed cockiness when not in sight of superior officers, landed him here as a colonel, and second in command of the fleet Marines attached to the USS Ronald Reagan battle group. He had slipped by and under the usual Marine Corps scrutiny of its officers. Byron Comb's mind was winding up a mile a minute. He had never been in combat. Since his commanding general was in Washington, that left Comb responsible for the mission and the lives of the marines now under his command. Now, he was approaching potential combat and his cockiness and confidence were eroding fast, he could not control it. As the assault helicopters churned toward their target with six hundred marines depending on his leadership, and his competence, Byron Combs was admitting to himself that he really didn't want to be here. Being a Marine was all for show. He never thought he would really have to fight or be in real combat. It was too late for Byron Combs. He was going wherever this mission took him.

Chapter 45

The shuttle was approaching the al Qaeda built landing strip. Abreu was waiting at the end of the runway. He had arrived at the landing strip with twelve pickup trucks. The trucks were a variety of makes and models. Each had a fifty caliber machine gun mounted on its roof and a two man crew to fire it. Each pickup also had two or three men armed with heavy automatic weapons.

The landing strip itself was packed sand mixed with cement. It had been hand built. But, the al Qaeda builders had no idea of the weight and speed the strip would have to support. They just made it six inches thick with the cement and packed sand. It was not a smooth surface.

Falcon had slowed the shuttle descent over the Iranian desert and could see the landing strip ahead, right where Abreu had told him it would be. He had lined up on the co-ordinates and was in position to make the landing strip. As he got closer to the landing strip he realized it was not asphalt or concrete. It was made of sand! Falcon's many hours of simulator practice enabled him to set the shuttle down to what should have been a near perfect landing. At touch-down the right wheel hit a weak spot in the runway and the shuttle started to veer right. It caught Falcon by surprise. He added thrust to the right engine in order to try and stay on the landing strip. He applied the brakes. The shuttle started to

skid left as the brakes had no immediate effect. This put a scare
through Falcon as he fought for control. He thought for a second
the shuttle might turn into the desert and flip over. He shut down
the engines, hit the brakes and deployed the landing chute to slow
the shuttle. This action slowed the shuttle just enough for Falcon
to maintain control. His fear of crashing in the desert sand sub-
sided as the shuttle slid sideways and came to a stop beyond the
far end of the strip. Abreu was waiting to greet him. Falcon exited
the shuttle, got out of his flight suit, and was hugged by Abreu.
Falcon looked at the landing strip and saw that the shuttle wheels
had made two six inch deep indentions the entire length of the
landing. Falcon looked at Abreu and said, "After all I have been
through to have been killed on this landing strip would have been
a joke. What idiot designed this piece of shit?"

Abreu was about to answer, but suddenly the deafening roar
of helicopters was heard.

The twenty-two helicopters broke into two distinct groups
and started landing on both sides of the landing strip. Abreu and
Falcon recognized the big bold letters on the helicopters which
read; "USMC" on several of them, and "MARINES" on the others. They knew what it meant. They were coming under attack by
United States Marines and would be killed if they didn't get the
hell out of there.

Abreu ordered his men to attack the helicopters. All the pickups in Abreu's command except one charged down the landing
strip opening fire on the Marine helicopters. Unknown to any of
the men in the pickups, Abreu and Falcon were in the remaining
pickup speeding away from the landing strip in the opposite direction; making their escape into the desert night.

The sudden jolt of the helicopter touching down rudely interrupted Colonel Byron Combs' thoughts. He was almost pushed
out of the chopper door by one of his gunnery sergeants. As
his feet hit the ground he froze as he looked around at the men

pouring out of the helicopters and running to take up their positions. He was standing in the middle of the landing strip, he tried to move but his fear overwhelmed him. He was disoriented. A gunnery sergeant ran up to him,

"What are your orders, sir!"

Byron Combs didn't react.

"Sir!" the gunnery sergeant yelled in Byron Combs face.

Colonel Byron Combs shook his head and responded as if in a daze to the sergeant, "Yes, set up my command post here and have all officers report to me. I need to give them pictures of the pilot we are supposed to capture. And, I want to know if we have the shuttle secure."

"Sir, we just landed and we're coming under attack. This is not a good place for a command post, we're in the middle of the runway!"

Byron combs shouted as loud as he could, "It's my show sergeant, get the officers now and don't question my orders again!"

"Stupid fucking officers," the sergeant said to himself as he ran to pass the word.

Without warning the contingent of eleven pickup trucks came charging down the runway from behind the parked space shuttle. Each pickup's machine gun was spewing hundreds of fifty caliber rounds. Marines disembarking from the choppers scattered for cover. The fire from the attacking pickups did not last long. The Marines did not have to wait for orders. The murderous return fire from the Marines, including grenade launchers and shoulder mounted rocket launchers turned the eleven attacking al Qaeda vehicles into burning wrecks with their crews burning or cut in half by the Marine fire power. In the after action report the only Marine casualty was the commanding officer who had been hit by enemy fire at the onset of the pickup truck attack.

The men in the pickup trucks did not live long enough to realize that Abreu and Falcon had driven off in the opposite direction from where Abreu had ordered them to attack. They had attacked with typical terrorist enthusiasm. They gave no thought to their own survival. Their leaders never told them that no one ever won any battles by being killed for their cause.

The landing strip was now secure. The job of destroying the shuttle began. The Marine force set up a defensive perimeter. The choppers remained on scene to evacuate the area when the shuttle demolition was complete.

Chapter 46

About a half an hour before the battle on the landing strip took place action was taking place at Iranian Military Headquarters in Tehran. The phone rang sharply, and loudly, on the night stand in the General's bedroom. It was the emergency phone. General Alexander Azun, Commander of Iran's military, awoke quickly and answered the phone.

"What is it," He commanded.

The on duty command officer at Iran's Air Defense Center Reported, "Sir, we have a fast moving aircraft descending across the Northern Desert, it will either crash or land there. Also, our radar picked up intermittent signals of slow and low flying aircraft headed towards the same area."

"What the hell," said the General, "There's nothing out there but desert .We need to find out what is going on. Launch the closest fighter squadron and have them check the area. It should take them less than an hour to get there. Call me back when you have information."

With that the General went back to bed.

"What was that about?" asked his wife.

"Probably nothing," He answered, "Something happened in the desert. It can't be much as there is nothing but hundreds of square miles of sand and rocks out there."

From the bridge of his carrier Captain Schaffer was monitoring the entire shuttle operation. He was astounded to learn the only casualty so far in the mission was the Marine Commander. He wondered, "Just how the hell did that happen." His thought was interrupted as his executive officer called him on the action phone.

"Satellite radar reports that six Iranian fast movers have launched and are headed for our shuttle operation. They will be there in less than an hour. We have four fighters flying air cover for the ground force now, what do you want to do?"

Captain Schaffer considered the new information for several minutes then ordered, "Launch twelve more fighters to re-enforce the air cover. Have the rest of our fighters on stand-by. I want over whelming force out there in case a fight breaks out. Ask the Marines how much longer before the shuttle is destroyed?"

Chapter 47

Lieutenant Ron Grasser had been involved in the weekly squadron poker game when the original general quarters alarm sounded along with the verbal announcement to;

"Man battle stations, this is not a drill, all pilots report to the ready room."

The day room emptied as most of the pilots and their "rears" reported to the ready room. At the poker table the game continued with half a dozen aviators. Several hundred dollars was in the pot. Ron Grasser looked at his fellow aviators at the table and said disgustedly, "This can't be for real, I've been aboard this tub for six months and every alarm has been a drill."

Grasser laughed at his fellow aviators and rudely said, "I call your fifty bucks and raise you fifty, how's that feel, pal!"

Grasser was known among his peers as a blow hard with a punk attitude, so his remark fit his reputation. Before the poker hand could be played out the hatch to the day room opened and the flight operations officer announced in a very pissed off voice, "All you prima donnas get off your asses right now and report to the ready room. This is not a drill and anybody that does not move their ass right now will be on report."

The room emptied with hundreds of dollars on the poker table. The Marine security detachment later confiscated the money, gambling was not allowed on board.

Lieutenant Ron Grasser would not be caring about the money. Ron Grasser laughed to himself as he took his seat in the squadron ready room.

"Shit," he said to himself, "A winning hand and a real general quarters sounds for the first time since I've been on this tub. Let's get whatever this is over with so I can get my money, go for a swim, and take a nap."

That was earlier. Now the fighter crews had been summoned to the ready room again. The flight operations officer grabbed Grasser's arm when he heard Grasser's name called along with several other pilots.

The "CAG" issued the pilots their orders, "You six will take off first to re-enforce the air cover over the shuttle operation. There are six Iranian planes heading for the operation now. We don't know their intentions. Your orders are to protect the ground force. Your rules of engagement are to engage the enemy aircraft if hostile moves are anticipated or made by them. Gentlemen, Captain Schaffer does not want you to start world war three, so use your best judgment and protect our Marines on the ground. Captain Schaffer's direct orders to you are to kill the enemy if you see or anticipate that he is making a hostile move against our men on the ground. The Captain does not want any Marines killed because you were hesitant to kill the enemy."

Both the flight operations officer and the CAG (Commander, Air Group) knew Lieutenant Ron Grasser was a mediocre pilot with attitude issues. They had planned to ship him off the carrier and now wished they had done so sooner. The only reason Grasser was in the lead group was that his plane happened to be on deck being checked out when the order to launch came down. There was no time for pep talks or substitutions. The flight ops officer had Grasser by the arm and pulled him aside. "Do your job son, I'm counting on you. This situation is not a game!"

Grasser did not respond as he climbed into his jet fighter. He saw his rear was already strapped in and said to him, "Hang on, the Iranians don't know who they're fucking with. If we tangle with them I'm going to be the son of a bitch everybody will remember for a long time. There's six of them, I figure I'm good to knock at least two of them down!"

Grasser's rear seater, (RIO), was a veteran aviator named Edwin Pugh. He was an African American who had flown many real combat missions, and he had the decorations to prove his service. He considered Grasser a fuck-up and had asked for a transfer many times. Edwin Pugh was told that Grasser needed a veteran 'RIO' to back him up. He did not get his transfer.

The problem was Grasser never listened to or paid attention to any advice Pugh offered. Pugh made a deal with himself that this deployment would be his last. He had fought through two wars and was ready to retire anyway. He had sent a letter to his wife of twenty five years saying she was getting her wish. He would be home permanently to enjoy his family, which included a son, a daughter, and two grandchildren. He turned in his retirement papers and was waiting for them to be processed. He didn't like Grasser and he certainly did not like flying with him. The "CAG" informed Pugh he would be relieved within the next thirty days. Pugh figured this would be his last flight so he might as well enjoy it.

Grasser was the first in line to take off. He headed straight for the landing strip to relieve the air cover returning to the carrier to refuel. He left the other five planes in his flight well behind him.

"You went to after burners a little early, don't you think?" Pugh said over the intercom, "You left the other guys behind."

"Don't worry about it Pugh," Grasser retorted, "I'm off after burners now. Just sit back and enjoy the ride. I want to be first on the scene in case the Iranians want to play."

While Grasser and the other fighters were closing the distance to the landing strip Captain Schaffer was receiving his latest orders from the Washington. The executive officer was given the written message from the ship's communications officer. He read the message, then hanging on to the duplicate copy, handed the original to the Captain. The order read:

TO: CAPTAIN, USS RONALD REAGAN
FROM: NATIONAL COMMAND
          AUTHORITY
ORDER IS AS FOLLOWS:
U.S. AIRCRAFT NOT TO ENGAGE IRANIAN AIRCRAFT UNLESS IRANIAN AIRCRAFT FIRE ON GROUND FORCES.
END

"Should I have the orders transmitted to our pilots?" the executive officer asked.

Captain Tobin Schaffer was immediately reminded of the USS Pueblo. If he issued this order Marines on the ground may be killed because U.S. planes had to wait for the enemy to fire before engaging them.

"No, replied Schaffer, do not issue this order. My original order stands."

"Yes sir," acknowledged the executive officer, as he shredded his copy of the order from the National Command Authority.

In the lead aircraft Pugh reported to Grasser,

"Iranian aircraft approaching our ground forces position"

"I'm gonna go to after-burners and hit them head on, if they so much as turn on their radar, I'm taking them out!" Grasser exclaimed.

"We should wait for our wing man and the rest of our flight, and you're burning a lot of fuel, there isn't enough for any extended dog fight," Pugh responded to no avail.

Grasser caught the Iranians by surprise as he flew directly at their formation. The Iranian flight scattered and ended up all over the sky. Grasser made a wide turn in the opposite direction of the carrier and looked for an Iranian to chase.

Grasser communicated to the other U.S fighters that he had broken up the Iranian formation and the Iranians were turning around and running for home. What Grasser did not know is the lead Iran jet had turned on his radar and saw they were outnumbered at least three to one.

Pugh urged Grasser, "Watch your fuel, that last turn with after burners used a lot."

"I'll fly this attack run, Pugh," Grasser yelled through the inter-com, "You just hang on. If I catch one of those guys I'm gonna smoke him!"

"Better cut the after-burners Ron, we've used a lot of fuel," Pugh urged.

Grasser's adrenalin was surging as he told Pugh, "Shut up 'Edwin' I'm flying this jet."

A few minutes later, when no Iranian jets were to be seen, Grasser cut his after-burners and headed back to the carrier. As he lined up he found his aircraft was eighth in the landing pattern.

Pugh advised Grasser to declare a "low fuel" emergency so they could land right away, "You better declare an emergency, our low fuel warning lights are blinking red."

"I told you I'm flying this plane. I just made some great moves against those Iranians, I'm not going to put a blemish on that action. I know when to declare an emergency," Grasser rebuked Pugh, "I know this plane and those fuel gauges tell me we have enough to land."

When Grasser and Pugh's turn to land came, Grasser put his jet on a perfect landing approach towards the stern of the carrier. It was a perfect approach until 150 feet from the carrier deck the engines flamed out and the plane stopped flying. It dropped like a rock, crashing into the stern of the carrier.

Just when he heard the engines flame out Pugh pulled the ejection handles. The canopy opened and the ejection seats fired as the plane hit the ship and exploded. The last words heard over the radio were identified as Pugh yelling, "You fucking asshole Grasser!"

On the flying bridge of the carrier the flight operations officer said to the air group commander, "I knew we should have got rid of that guy!"

"Yea, came the reply, but it's too late now. That young pilot displayed a perfect example of what we need to make sure our new pilots learn in their training. That when a pilot wants to kill the enemy so badly that it warps his judgment, he stops being a warrior and becomes a fool."

At the landing strip Marines were carrying heavy boxes of high explosives into the shuttle. The rest of the force was guarding the perimeter of the landing strip in case another attack against them materialized. None did. When the explosive charges were set in the shuttle a wide area around it was cleared. The explosion and fire that destroyed the space shuttle lit the darkness of the desert for miles. It was a hundred fourth of July fireworks shows in one! Many young Marines would have something to remember for the rest of their lives.

Once again the executive officer reported to Captain Schaffer on the bridge. "The Marines report the shuttle has been completely destroyed, including every internal component. All personnel are accounted for and the helicopters are airborne heading back to the fleet. Our air cover reports no sign of enemy aircraft. There was no sign of the shuttle pilot and the Marines think he escaped during the battle."

IRAN MILITARY HEADQUARTERS IN THE CITY OF TEHRAN, IRAN

General Alexander Azun was angry at the on duty staff. Upon

learning that American aircraft were in Iranian air space they had done nothing except launch a second flight of six fighters back to the area with orders to report on what was happening and the exact location. After the flight reported the on duty commander summoned the General from his bed.

"Bring all military commands to battle readiness. Alert the president and his staff of what is happening. We should have launched a major airstrike against the Americans and whatever they were doing in our desert," General Azun yelled angrily. It took a moment for him to calm down, "Has the second flight leader reported yet?"

"Yes sir," replied the duty shift commander.

"He states that a landing strip exists at the site and it looks like some type of battle took place there. There are destroyed vehicles scattered on the strip and a large burning mass of unidentifiable material at one end of the strip. No sign of life and no American aircraft."

"Dispatch our closest airborne brigade to secure the scene until we can determine just what the hell is going on," Commanded General Azun.

An officer brought a phone to the General. "It's the President Sir, he wants to speak to you immediately."

General Azun took the phone. He heard an angry President speaking to him, "General, what is going on? Are we being invaded?

"I don't have all the details yet, Mr. President. I don't think an invasion is occurring. It does look like some kind of incursion by the Americans occurred several hours ago."

"What!" said the President, "Are you telling me some type of military action took place in our country several hours ago and you are just now reacting to it? When this situation is over and you are sure we are secure report to my office in person."

"Yes, Sir," replied a white faced General Azun.

Chapter 48

In his office Terry Walsh looked at his Deputy Director, "How long will it take to get our second shuttle on the launch pad and ready to launch? I want to get a relief crew to the station as soon as we can."

Jay Hart was silent for several minutes as he shuffled through the notebook in front of him. He looked up from the notebook and said, "The shuttle has been in stand-by mode. I think we can be ready to launch within thirty days."

"Do it," ordered Terry, "I want Henry Irving to command this mission. Tell the medical guys to check and clear him, other than Henry, you pick the rescue crew."

Jay Hart hustled out of his boss's office to set up the work schedule and alert the ground personnel, scientists and technicians. He would consult with Henry Irving in assigning the crew of astronauts to the mission.

At his home in Florida Henry Irving was playing football with his sons when his wife called out to him that he had a phone call. Henry had been home since he was taken off flight status. Although he wanted to be at work, the time at home with his family was enjoyable and relaxing. Henry picked up the phone. "This is Henry Irving speaking."

Before he could say anything more the voice on the phone interrupted,

"This is the NASA personnel control officer, report for duty immediately to NASA Headquarters. This is not a secure line, no further verbal orders will be given."

The line went dead.

With the phone still in his hand Henry looked at his wife and said, "I have been ordered to duty. I have to leave immediately. Please call the airport and book the next flight for me while I pack."

Henry wondered why the rush, especially since he was grounded. But he hustled through his packing and hurried to the airport early the next morning to catch the next available commercial flight. To his surprise, he found two NASA pilots waiting for him at the curb. He knew both pilots. They greeted him and handed him a sealed manila envelope marked:

"EYES ONLY"
ASTRONAUT HENRY IRVING

With that they boarded a NASA airplane and departed. In the envelope Henry found his orders. They stated he was released to flight status pending a final medical exam and that he was to command a rescue mission to the Manned Space Station. He would get further details of the mission upon his arrival at NASA. Henry Irving closed his eyes and smiled during the entire short flight.

Chapter 49

WASHINGTON DC
THE WHITE HOUSE
IN THE OVAL OFFICE

It had been several days since the fight on the space station and the destruction of the shuttle in the Iranian desert. President John L. Kramer addressed his National Security Advisor, "Bob, the media is having a field day reporting the incident aboard the space station. Our partners in the space station are fuming that we let this happen. At least the laser weapon secret is still intact, let's keep it that way. The Iranians are squealing over the incident in their desert but since there was no real harm done it will blow over. There is one thing I want to do. This guy Falcon, find him and anyone else associated with him. I want to make examples of them by eliminating them in the most exploitative manner possible."

The National Security Advisor responded, "I will go to work on that right away. The way al Qaeda works I suspect we will hear about Falcon as their hero soon. From that information we will find him and figure a way to eliminate him and any associates with him. That will show the world that no one screws with us and lives long enough to brag about it."

Almost as an after-thought the Advisor added, "Oh, by the way, General Alexander Azun has been relieved of command of the Iranian military. General Snyder just found out about that piece of information. He figures Azun was relieved because there was no credible military response to our action in their desert."

"It was fortunate for them and us that they did not react more forcefully than they did," the President commented.

Before he could say anything else the Director of the CIA, George Brown Jr. was escorted into the Oval Office.

"Sir," he addressed the President: I have here a copy of an al Qaeda flyer that has been distributed throughout the Middle East. It has a picture of Falcon and some guy named Abreu. It has a detailed account of the killing of the American astronauts and the stealing of the space shuttle. It also tells of the existence of the laser weapon. It proclaims a great victory and makes Falcon and this guy Abreu heroes in their jihad against America. I brought this to you as soon as I received it."

National Security advisor Robert Duncan hurried into the room carrying his lap top. "Sir," he addressed the President, "You need to see this video. Al Qaeda has sent it out on the internet."

The video showed both Abreu and Falcon. Falcon was describing the killing of the American astronauts and the stealing of the shuttle. Falcon's real name was being used, but it was Falcon.

"This changes everything," fumed the President, forgetting about the Iran affair.

The President's face grew blood red as he scrutinized the al Qaeda flyer. He really got pissed at the bragging quote by Falcon that, "The Americans died like the cowards they are." He took a deep breath to regain his composure. After several minutes of not speaking, he quietly addressed the people in the room, "What I am about to say does not leave this room. I want these two terrorists found. Then I want them killed in the most spectacular way possible. I want the whole world to know it. George, put out the order to your people worldwide, find James Falcon."

Abreu and Falcon were back where it all began. They were

having a great time relaxing in the compound where the plot had been initiated. They each had received two million American dollars. Which was ironic since America was the country they were trying to destroy. They were enjoying their status as heroes which was being declared by the hundred thousand flyers being distributed. The flyer version of Falcon's exploits was a glorified version of the real events that took place on board the Space Station, and had little relation to the truth. It made Falcon a super hero and Abreu as the master-mind behind a great victory over America.

Little did al Qaeda and their heroes know there were forces in the United States waiting for information as to the whereabouts of the two al Qaeda heroes.

WASHINGTON DC
THE WHITE HOUSE
IN THE OVAL OFFICE

NASA Director Terry Walsh and his Deputy Director Jay Hart had been summoned to the White House for a top secret meeting with the President and National Security advisor Robert Duncan. The National Security Advisor opened the meeting addressing the two NASA Directors:

"Terry, Jay, you know by now, James Falcon, in the thousands of flyers sent out by al Qaeda, and in his video, has announced to the world the existence of our laser weapon on board the space station. Since he described in detail our laser weapon, the President decided to demonstrate it to the world with an attack on al Qaeda. This decision to use the weapon was not an easy one. It was hotly debated by my staff in the National Security Council, and the Joint Chiefs of Staff.

It was decided the use and demonstration of the power of this weapon will act as a deterrent to our enemies. It was felt that in the long term, the demonstration and use of this weapon against al Qaeda will save lives. Our enemies will know not to attack us or go to war against us, as we have the most powerful weapon known to man since the atomic bomb. A weapon for which there is no defense."

Terry, and Jay, were stunned by what they just heard. They were speechless.

Robert Duncan continued as the President looked on:

"You do not need to say anything at this meeting and you will not be here long.

We summoned you here to give you your orders. When you launch the rescue mission in the next few days be sure your crew can both repair the laser if needed and use it against an Earth target. That is all you need to know at this time. Colonel Frazer has been informed and ordered to be sure the shuttle rescue crew is well trained in the maintenance and use of the weapon. That is all gentlemen."

Terry Walsh and Jay Hart were both disheartened by the fact that the laser was actually going to be used. They took little comfort knowing it was a demonstration for deterrence and the target would be very specific.

Terry Walsh informed his assistant, "I will be retiring after the launch of the rescue shuttle. The space program is no longer civilian and I'm done with it."

Astronaut Henry Irving was not disheartened when briefed that the laser was going to be fired at a specific target on Earth. He relished the fact that the secret target was to be James Henry Falcon and any al Qaeda personnel with him. He made sure his crew was ready as the launch of the rescue mission was in two days. Along with Colonel Frazer, he made sure that every detail concerning the use of the laser weapon was reviewed by himself and his crew.

Two days later the rescue shuttle launched and docked with the Manned Space Station. The first order of business was to attend to the medical needs of the wounded crew. Then the bodies of the dead astronauts were prepared and loaded into the cargo bay of the shuttle. In several days the wounded but capable crew boarded the shuttle for the flight home.

The exception was Lisa Conrad. When she was told the laser was going to be used to kill James Falcon she insisted on staying aboard the space station and assist in firing the weapon. Her claim and reason for wanting to stay was that she was the most knowledgeable in the use of the weapon and could assist should there be a problem. Her request was reluctantly granted by Terry Walsh.

Lisa found a private space and cried when her request was approved. She vowed silently, "Now, James Falcon, I'm going to burn your ass and send it to hell!"

She was startled when Henry Irving happened upon her location and saw she was crying.

"Is there something the matter, what's wrong, I thought you wanted to stay on board. Why are you crying?" Henry asked the series of questions with sincere concern.

"I'm crying because I am very satisfied that I'm going to kill that son of a bitch James Falcon."

"So am I," replied Henry, "So am I."

Chapter 50

The al Qaeda flyers had come out very clear. They showed a picture of Falcon and a man named Abreu. Falcon's real name was used but the picture was definitely Falcon. The flyers that were distributed gave their own version of how the space crew was overcome and killed. It went into detail of how the Americans fought back weakly and died like cowards. It stated great damage had been done to the American module of the space station. It gave a glowing account of the taking of the shuttle and how much damage this had done to America's will to fight al Qaeda. The flyer erroneously stated that many American secrets were stolen from the shuttle.

It was five days after the President gave the order to the CIA to find Falcon. CIA Director George Brown was at his desk in CIA Headquarters. The secure phone sitting on the corner of the desk buzzed.

"Sir," said the CIA switchboard operator when George Brown picked up the phone,

"You have a call on the international and scrambled satellite phone. The caller gave an authentic password."

The phone was encrypted and as secure as any phone in the United States government. Less than fifty people in the world had access to this secret number. Among these people were deep-seeded American spies planted and entrenched within enemy governments and organizations throughout the world. The job of this group of spies was to live their lives in the country and within the enemy governments and organizations to which they were assigned.

Bryant Copeland was one of these American spies. That was his American name. His spy name, which he had been known by for the past twenty five years of his life in Iran, was Khali Amal. Bryant had no family. His parents had died in a spectacular fire in their home when he was fifteen years old. Bryant was trapped in that fire. Only a dangerous and heroic rescue by a group of half drunk soldiers on leave saved Bryant's life. The soldiers were celebrating the retirement of one of their sergeants and were leaving a bar when they saw a house down the street on fire. They ran to the house, entered through the heat and smoke and carried the unconscious young boy to safety. The flames of the fire kept them from searching and rescuing anyone else. The retiring soldier became close friends with Bryant. With encouragement from the soldier, and with nothing else to do, Bryant joined the Army at graduation from high school. He had been a straight 'A' student and did exceptionally well on the Army tests. He was eventually assigned to an Army intelligence unit. That's when the CIA became aware of him, and recruited him from the Army.

After five years of intense training at the CIA, including foreign languages, Bryant volunteered and was offered a long term deep spy assignment in Iran. At this point in time Bryant Copeland became Khali Amal. After his successful assimilation into Iran, the now Khali Amal attended the University of Tehran and graduated with honors. During his years attending the University he was approached and recruited by members of al Qaeda, who were also attending school. During school breaks, and after graduation, Khali went to al Qaeda training camps and after several years he was accepted as a loyal al Qaeda member.

He met his wife while in one of the camps and their marriage was still intact after twenty five years.

Khali Amal was assigned to an al Qaeda cell in Tehran. He was left in Tehran because Khali had become a successful and respected lawyer. Over the years he did many assignments for the Iranian government. Because of his work for the government he made many friends and connections. He used these many friends, and "connections" to keep al Qaeda informed of Iran information he became aware of. Information the Iranian government did not want to share with al Qaeda. He also acted as a liaison between al Qaeda operatives within the Iranian government and leaders in the upper echelon of al Qaeda.

Khali's wife, Hassa, did not seem to be aware of her husband's role in the terrorist organization. Hassa, along with al Qaeda and the Iranian government, did not know his absolute loyalty was to the United States of America.

Khali contacted his American controller only when he had important information that would be of interest to the United States. This was done very carefully and not often. Khali was extremely careful to protect his secret.

Khali genuinely loved his wife and treated her very well. At times this brought criticism and unwanted attention. The result was Khali and Hassa made a secret agreement. In public, or occasions where people were present, Hassa would be treated harshly and in line with the mores of Iranian society. In private she would be treated as the woman he loved and respected. This solved the only problem Khali had in living his life in Iran.

Khali felt very secure as an Iranian citizen. He felt safe as a spy. There was no way to connect or even suspect Khali was a spy for America. He never openly communicated with anyone remotely connected to America. His communication devices only allowed him to communicate with his al Qaeda contacts when face to face meetings were not advisable; except for one device which he kept well hidden. Even from his wife. It was a scrambled and secure satellite phone.

Khali Amal was no fool though. Known only to him, he kept two hundred and fifty thousand American dollars hidden in his car in case he had to flee.

Hassa sometimes asked him:

"Khali, why do you keep our second car always locked in the garage and never drive it. You check it, run it, and keep it full of fuel, but never take it out of the garage. And why do we have those four extra fuel cans full in the garage. Another thing I wonder about is the trunk has an extra lock and I don't have any keys?"

"Hassa," Khali would respond, "I keep the car and extra fuel in case this crazy government of ours declares fuel rationing or marshal law. We have had this discussion before. Just trust me and keep the status, and in fact, the whole issue of our second car to yourself."

What Khali did not tell his wife was that in the trunk of the car along with the two hundred-fifty thousand dollars were weapons. They included AK47's and a grenade launcher for use should they have to depart suddenly and try to escape to freedom. Khali could not tell Hassa anything about this and hoped his wife would leave with him if the time ever came. He really didn't know if she would leave her family behind. He did know he and his wife would be completely on their own should that circumstance ever come to be.

For twenty five years Bryant Copeland had lived happily and safely as Khali Amal in the midst of the Iranian government and al Qaeda. During those years he had never taken any chances of exposing himself. He had always been careful to communicate secretly and alone, taking the time to be sure the call signal to his American contact could not be traced to him.

Khali was in his office, where he learned, along with the rest of the world, of the al Qaeda flyers and their boasting concerning the

American space station and the stealing of the shuttle. Khali also had just become aware of some important al Qaeda information.

He thought to himself: "My judgment is that the information I have needs to be transmitted to the CIA right away. This is exactly why they put me here. There is no time to make sure the call won't be traced. Oh hell, It's time to leave this place anyway. Hassa will be surprised at her new life in America. Damn, I can only take the two hundred-fifty thousand with me. There isn't time to get money out of the bank, and if I were to withdraw any large amount it may cause a problem."

Khali rushed home. "Hassa," he confronted his wife. "Please do not question what I'm about to tell you. We have been together and in love for many years. I have to leave Iran tonight. It may become very dangerous. Will you come with me?"

Hassa looked at her husband in disbelief. She could not breathe or talk for several long seconds.

"What are you talking about, what are you doing?" She asked excitedly.

"I'm going to make a phone call to America. Then we must leave immediately."

Hassa was stunned and ran into another room. Khali never gave his wife's reaction a second thought. He said loudly and excitedly to her, "I'll talk to you after I make this call."

Khali picked up the hidden satellite phone and not waiting for safety features to activate dialed an international number he had not used since coming to Iran.

CIA Director George Brown took the call. After several mechanical clicks he heard a vaguely familiar voice but could not identify it.

"Hello George," Khali said in a hushed voice.

Director Brown pushed the record button on his phone which also alerted the duty staff to listen in on the call.

"You probably don't remember me George," Khali continued:

"Your agency recruited me, hired me and sent me into Iran twenty five years ago. You gave me one million dollars at that time, and this phone number, with instructions to never call it unless the security of the United States was involved.

You were not the Director at the time so congratulations on being Director now.

First I want to thank you for giving me a wonderful and rich life here in Iran. I will be fleeing for my life after this call as it may be traced back to me. I'll try for the Pakistan border. If there is any help available I could certainly use it. The traitor astronaut, Falcon, and his al Qaeda accomplice are near Tehran. Make sure you are recording this as I know their exact location."

The CIA Director heard what sounded like a gun-shot and the phone went dead.

Khali felt the burning pain as the bullet entered his back. As the phone was ripped from his hand, Khali fell to the floor from his now blood spattered easy chair. He saw Hassa looking at him with a contorted and ugly face which he had never experienced before. In a barely audible voice Khali said to his wife of twenty five years, "What are you doing Hassa?"

"I was hoping I would never have to kill you, Bryant Copeland, but that's not the way it worked out," said Hassa as she sobbed heavily and uncontrollably. "I actually liked the way you treated me."

As Bryant Copeland died he heard her last words to him.

"I hope I was in time to stop you from delivering whatever message you were trying to send to America."

Hassa dropped the gun from her hand. When she gained control of herself she called her al Qaeda controller to report she had killed the American spy. Al Qaeda would no longer be able to use him to obtain Iran government information or pass false information to Iran and the United States.

Chapter 51

George Brown still could not place or identify the voice on the phone. The secret CIA file indicated it was Bryant Copeland, AKA Khali Amal. George called the President direct.

"Mr. President, I have a possible location on James Falcon. I am taking action to confirm the information as we speak. A soon as I am certain the information is accurate, and I have the exact location, I'll call you back."

Mitch Liber and Eric Cates were among the few Americans who lived and worked in Iran. The two men operated an import and export business in Tehran named "Iran Worldwide." They were left alone by the Iranian government because they supplied military officers and government officials with arms, and other goods and valuables as part of their business. In return Mitch and Eric were well known and attended many government sponsored dinners and events. They did so as guests of their many Iranian friends and government connections. It had taken many years and a lot of hard work to establish the business and its many connections in Iran. Establishing "Iran Worldwide" was the easy part as the start up money came from the CIA, and there was plenty of it. The hard part was maintaining the secret. Especially since Mitch and Eric had many friends who kept their off-work time filled with night life and social events. Even with the strict

Iranian laws the party invitations and the supply of beautiful women never ended.

Mitch and Eric were spies for the United States of America.

"Iran Worldwide" was a legitimate business and did very well financially even though it had to work under the laws and rules of the Iranian government. Mitch and Eric were very careful in keeping finite records of the business and the money it brought in. They were also very careful in sneaking as much money as they could safely out of Iran and into secret bank accounts in Switzerland, the Cayman Islands, and several other countries where money was protected and deposits kept secret. The money was kept secret both from Iran and the United States. They considered it their retirement fund.

In their business demeanor and daily activities both men maintained a low profile. They knew that even though they had many friends in government circles the Iranian government was keeping a close eye on them. They did nothing to cause suspicion and because they ran a successful business there was no reason for anyone to suspect the two men of being anything other than what they seemed.

In addition to other monies both Mitch and Eric each had hidden $150,000.00 for get away money, in case they had to flee Iran on a moment's notice. They could not make any advance escape plans for leaving Iran as this might get back to the wrong people and raise suspicion. They had no wives or family. So if it became necessary to flee, Mitch and Eric had only themselves to worry about. The escape money should be plenty to pay their way out of Iran.

The information Mitch and Eric passed to their contacts in adjoining countries was done by using encrypted satellite phones at specific times. Usually Mitch would drive their Toyota pickup, and Eric would use the phone to talk to a contact person. The conversations were never more than one to two minutes long and never from the same location. For years now the information passed to their contacts was routine but gave the American government advanced knowledge of what was happening within the different levels of the Iranian government hierarchy. The two men lived a fairly good life by Iranian standards. Just the same they eagerly looked forward to the day they would disappear and escape Iran for the good life in America. The money they were accumulating, as well as the money the CIA owed them, would allow them to go their separate ways and live in whatever style they chose.

As part of their business activities each had a cell phone for business use. Deep within the most secret units of the CIA these two cell phone numbers were listed so the spies could be contacted if necessary. Of course, if these two cell phone numbers were ever used by CIA operatives calling Mitch or Eric, it would potentially expose them as spies. If they were ever contacted directly by the CIA on either of these phones they would have to escape Iran immediately. Mitch and Eric knew they were not trusted by many people in the Iranian government. They were pretty sure their business phones were being monitored. It was only relatively safe for them to use their satellite phone.

It was early evening. The weather was pleasant and a cool breeze was easing its way through the hedge bushes surrounding a large patio. Mitch and Eric had been invited to a dinner party. This one hosted by the deputy minister of trade. There were usually a hundred or so people invited to these events. Mitch and Eric were often seated at a table next to beautiful women, courtesy of their many friends. Some evenings these extravagant dinners turned into longer nights with the women. Not this night.

As they were enjoying the women's company Eric heard his cell phone buzz. He turned it off as it was after business hours. Mitch had heard it also and smiled when his partner turned it off. Mitch's cell phone buzzed less than a minute later. He was about to turn it off when Eric nodded to him indicating he better answer it.

"Just tell them we'll call them tomorrow morning when we open for business," said Eric.

"Excuse me please," Mitch said to the 'Persian princess' who was sitting next to him and smiling. As Mitch answered the phone and listened to what was said a surprised expression swept his face. He disconnected the call and anxiously motioned to Eric, "We have to leave, now!"

Mitch smiled at the 'Persian princess' and meaningfully said to her, "Farewell forever my dear."

Mitch looked at Eric, "You better say good bye forever to your princess too, as you and her will never meet again."

Eric gave Mitch a dirty look as they both walked out on their princesses and dinner.

Once outside Eric growled at Mitch, "What was that all about?"

Mitch got deadly serious, "Get to the truck and stand by for a call from CIA Headquarters, looks like we're out of here!"

Eric grabbed the hidden phone and turned it on. It immediately buzzed and he answered. The voice on the phone said, "Identify yourself and name your associate."

Eric responded, "This is Eric Cates and my associate is Mitch Liber."

The voice then said, "Give both CIA operatives' control numbers."

Eric gave both the numbers. The voice on the phone continued, "This is the CIA Duty Officer of the watch. I have operational orders for you. Execute immediately. The astronaut traitor James Falcon is reported to be in the Tehran area. Find his exact location and report it to CIA."

After Eric confirmed receipt of the orders the phone connection clicked off. Eric relayed the phone orders to Mitch, then added, "Let's go by the business and get our money. It looks like we'll be leaving after this assignment."

"OK" said Mitch, "While we're doing that I'll call several of our informants, maybe they have information as to where this guy Falcon can be found. Our bosses probably want us to capture him and get him out of the country into U.S. custody."

At one o'clock in the morning Eric found himself with Mitch at a hidden away bar and night club.

"I don't like this," said Eric. "Here we are in an illegal bar drinking illegal booze. The Secret Police are probably looking for us by now. If they bust in here now we're in big trouble."

"Relax, will you," retorted Mitch. "Mabar said he would meet us here and for fifty thousand American dollars he would give us the location of Falcon and an al Qaeda big shot named Abreu."

"Can we trust him?" inquired Eric.

"We shall soon find out," responded Mitch. "He has been reliable in the past and he knows we can pay."

At that moment Mabar, one of their long time informants, hurried through the rear door. He rushed up to the two American spies and said, "I have the location. It is written on this paper. Here is a picture of the two men you seek. Give me my money. We don't have much time. The police are searching for you. They are going through every bar and club in the city!"

Mitch studied the paper and the picture Mabar handed him. He then told Eric, "Give him the money and let's get the hell out of here!"

After they were clear of the city via the back streets and roads Eric pulled the truck behind several abandoned buildings. Mitch dialed the satellite phone and reported to the CIA Duty officer, "The information we have obtained is that astronaut Falcon and an al Qaeda operative named Abreu are at a compound on Mt. Damavand Road, our informant thinks Usama Bin Ladin and other high al Qaeda leaders may be there at his time. The location is about forty miles out of the city."

"Stand by," The Duty Officer ordered.

After several minutes the Duty Officer came back on the line. "Hide yourselves and observe the compound. Confirm the presence of astronaut Falcon. Report if he leaves. Identify others present if possible. Check in every two hours. Remain on scene in a stealth position. Stand by there for further orders."

"I told you," Said Eric, "They are going to want us to capture him no matter what the situation or how many people are guarding him."

"That's crazy," responded Mitch,

"Let's just get to this compound and see what's going on."

It was three o'clock in the morning when the phone next to CIA Director George Brown's bed rang. It took a minute for him to respond.

"This is George Brown speaking."

"Sir, this is Raymond Pratt, CIA Duty Officer for this watch. We have definite confirmation on the location of James Falcon. Our two operatives are on scene and have the compound under direct observation. They report having seen and identified Falcon. They had to retreat back across the road and are keeping the compound under observation from their hidden position. They also report a large number of cars and armed guards inside the compound."

It had been dangerous and not easy for the two spies to carry out their order to identify and confirm James Falcon was at the compound. There were many armed guards spread throughout the grounds inside the compound. But, like many terrorist security forces throughout the world, this force was only as good as its weakest and half-trained members. And there were no guards outside the walls. The two American CIA spies were able to scale the outside of the compound walls and lay prone on top of them.

From that position they used their night vision equipment to get a look at who was in the compound house. When they were certain they had seen Falcon they retraced their path and ran to their stealth position on the opposite side of the road. It was very dark. The guards near their position on the wall had been inattentive. Now the Americans were relatively safe in the heavy brush across the road from the compound.

George Brown instructed the duty officer, "I will be there in twenty minutes. Call the White House. Have them wake the President on my authority."

When George Brown arrived at CIA Headquarters he went immediately to the operations center.

"Are we still certain the target is at the location?"

The Duty Officer reported: We have the two American operatives with eyes on the property. The subjects are inside the home within the compound at this time. There is only one way in and out of the compound. Our men are in a hidden position across the road from the compound. They report that earlier they identified Usama Bin Ladin as being present also. There is some kind of party or celebration going on.

"Have your men maintain their position and report any changes in the situation immediately," George Brown ordered.

George Brown then called the President. "We have the location of Falcon pinpointed. The coordinates are being figured now by NASA and NORAD. Other al Qaeda terrorists are present including Usama bin Ladin."

"Execute my destroy order immediately" ordered the President.

Chapter 52

One hour later on board the Manned Space Station Henry Irving awakened Lisa Conrad.

As she opened her eyes Henry said to her, "We received a flash action message. We are maneuvering now to laser a ten square acre compound in Iran. We have the exact coordinates. It will take about two hours for us to be in position. Lisa immediately asked, "Is Falcon there?"

Falcon and some other al Qaeda creeps are there now, including Usama Bin Ladin! As soon as we are in position we are ordered to fire the laser."

Lisa jumped from her sleep, dressed, and with Henry Irving manned the laser and started the procedures necessary to fire it. Lisa's adrenalin was surging as she reported to Henry, "The weapon is ready to fire!"

The two American spies on the ground were taking turns sleeping and watching the compound. Dawn had arrived and morning sun was bright and warm. The two spies heard the following order on their satellite phone,

"Move two hundred yards away from the compound. Keep it in view and report any movements by persons in the compound. Assist arriving news crews in setting up to take film and pictures of the compound. Do this without delay. Keep news crews two hundred yards away from the compound."

To the surprise of the two American spies, a CNN News truck and camera crew arrived on the scene. Then a British News agency camera truck arrived. Next an Iran News agency camera crew arrived. Several other world news agencies with offices in Tehran joined the group. This all took place in a matter of thirty minutes.

"What are you guys doing here?" Eric confronted the news crews.

"What's going on?" asked the seemingly confused news people, "We received an anonymous call to come to this location and set up our cameras right away, and point them at the walled compound at this location because something big and spectacular was about to happen. We were also told that the two al Qaeda heroes from the brochures were at this address and there are armed guards protecting them. One of the al Qaeda heroes here is the American astronaut and traitor Henry Falcon. Usama Bin Ladin is reportedly here also for some kind of celebration. Is this a hoax or is this real?"

"This is real!" Yelled Mitch as he came rushing from his hiding place, "All of us need to be sure we are two hundred yards from the compound before you start your cameras. Point your cameras at the compound and start filming."

"What are you yelling about?" Eric said to Mitch."

Mitch answered excitedly, "I just got orders on the satellite phone to be sure we're at least two hundred yards away from the compound."

The two Americans and the news crews could now hear the guards in the compound shouting amongst themselves. Several minutes later the gates to the compound opened and six pickup trucks with heavily armed men roared out of the compound. Behind them several black cars emerged and followed the trucks. Mitch caught a glimpse of what he believed was Usama Bin Ladin in one of the cars. The trucks and cars left at extreme speeds and departed the area in the opposite direction of Tehran.

Inside the two story house located in the middle of the compound, Falcon and Abreu were laughing at how Usama and his entourage had panicked when several guards reported that there were people and news trucks across the road from the compound gates.

Abreu remarked, "They didn't even eat breakfast and left a lot of food behind. After we finish all we can eat, we'll give it to our guards."

Falcon responded, "This has been a great celebration with which to start our new lives. You are the only family I have and I love you very much."

Abreu looked at Falcon but did not respond. To himself he said, "You'll never know it was I who ordered your family killed."

A guard rushed into the room and announced, "There are news trucks outside the walls. They are filming the compound!"

Abreu said to Falcon, "It looks like the news media has found us. Let's go to the gate and let them film us. Then we can let them interview us, it will be fun."

Across the road the two American spies were becoming apprehensive. They had been there too long for their own good.

"The Iranian police, and maybe the army is going to show up here anytime, we've been exposed for too long," Eric said excitedly to Mitch.

"We're stuck here until we get orders. They still may want us to capture that guy," Mitch said, referring to Falcon. "But let's be ready to move and get the hell out of here when we do get orders."

The television and news crews were set up and filming, but were getting restless. They talked among themselves and they were about to call this a gigantic hoax and leave. Then one of the camera men saw the two men at the gate of the compound and announced, "Look, it's Falcon and the other guy on the brochure, Abreu. They're waving at us from the compound."

A crowd of people were beginning to gather around the news

crews, curious as to what was going on. This was drawing a lot of attention and both Mitch and Eric did not like it.

The bright flash caught them all completely by surprise and temporarily blinded both American spies and the news crews. When they were able to see again, after several minutes, what they saw both awed and scared them. For the American spies to be scared was an event of epic proportions because both operatives were seasoned soldiers and CIA spies. They had seen and experienced atrocities, and bombings that had crumbled buildings and killed many people. The news crews had seen disasters all over the world as well.

They had never seen anything like this.

After the smoke cleared they saw there was nothing left of the compound, only 10 square acres of black, burnt, red hot smoldering dirt. It looked like the surface of the moon. What could be seen were the disintegrated remains of the compound walls and structures mixed in with the smoking dirt. The piles of remains were pulsating like a lava flow from a volcano.

No buildings, no walls and no people existed. They had all been consumed and disappeared in the brilliant flash of light that struck the earth. The only evidence that something had existed on the 10 acre compound were flames and hot smoke.

Eric and Mitch didn't wait for orders. As soon as they recovered from witnessing the results of the laser strike they jumped in their car and got the hell out of Iran.

For many days the news agencies throughout the world reported and showed the laser strike and its horrific results. The President had accomplished his goal of demonstrating to the world both the deterrent power of the laser weapon and the fact that America would be relentless in hunting down its enemies.

Chapter 53

Four days after the laser attack the President called for a de-briefing in the White House. He wanted everyone involved in what came to be known as the '7th Astronaut Incident' to be at the meeting. One aspect of this meeting was to review security measures. Then determine how the traitor was able to penetrate the Air Force Academy and NASA, so nothing like this could ever happen again. At this meeting were the Joint Chiefs of Staff of the armed services, the Directors of NASA, Heads of the FBI, Secret Service, CIA and the National Security Advisors. The President was not at this meeting. The National Security Advisor was to preside.

The National Security Advisor stood up and opened the debriefing.

"Ladies and gentlemen," he began, "The first thing I want to say is that the President congratulates your effort in preventing what potentially was the most evil terrorist plot ever against our country. Especially, since it was to use our own weapon against us. The consequences of a laser attack upon American soil would have been devastating. Thanks to some brilliant intelligence work and a brave crew on the space station we were successful at defeating this al Qaeda plot. We can be proud and comfortable in the fact we all came together to accomplish a successful action against al Qaeda. We also demonstrated to the world, and in particular to our enemies, that we will not allow our secrets and property to be taken by anyone. The President also demonstrated our power and our resolve by using the laser to wipe out a traitor. The knowledge of the laser weapon will act as strong deterrent to our enemies."

Before he could continue the doors flew open and an Air Force Colonel charged past the Marine guards. He came to attention, caught his breath, and addressed the Joint Chiefs directly.

"Sir, NORAD has just ordered all fighter jets based in the continental United States to battle stations, fully armed. They announced this is not a drill. Jets on the eastern seaboard have been scrambled with orders to establish a combat air patrol over Washington."

The doors banged open again as a White House aide rushed in and yelled, "Turn on the televisions, quick!"

As the televisions came on the images showed New York and a tall building with huge volumes of black smoke pouring from it. As the stunned group watched they saw a large passenger jet fly into the adjacent tall building and watched as it too began yielding huge volumes of black smoke. The TV's were showing the World Trade Center on 9/11.

The people in the room knew they were the core group responsible for the security of the United States. The room emptied as the different officials headed for their posts. When the room cleared the National Security Advisor turned to his Deputy, Geraldine Francis, and stated,

"No matter what catastrophe we prevented and protected America from, it will fall to the wayside because of the events unfolding before us. Our success in preventing the laser disaster will be forgotten."

"Yes," replied the Deputy Security Advisor, "The happenings of this day will put our terrorist astronaut episode as a foot note in history."

EPILOGUE

The intercom on CIA Director George Brown's desk buzzed. His secretary advised him that one of the CIA operatives from the compound operation is requesting to speak to him on an urgent matter. He picked up the phone, "This is George Brown, go ahead." The CIA Director stiffens in his chair as he hears what is said to him.

"Sir" says the voice on the phone, "This is Mitch Liber, I need to report to you that it's possible Falcon and the other al Qaeda subject may have escaped the laser strike. We think we saw them running from the compound just before the strike. We're not sure it was them, and also not sure if they got far enough away to survive the laser strike. At any rate, we needed to be sure you were aware of this information."

THE 7TH ASTRONAUT

Our story tells of one fictional attack plan and the potential disaster to the United States that was averted by decisive action and luck. The real attack plan of 9/11 and its resulting disaster was not averted due to a lack of action and no luck.

This is the end of our story but not the end of the potential violence that will require constant severe vigilance to address and overcome.

Throughout man's history there has always existed a threat to his individual survival, as well as that of his family and the people around him. Usually, history has shown that it is the powerful that inflict terror and injustice over the not so powerful. There were the Vikings, the Romans, Pirates, Nazis, and a list that goes on for volumes. The examples are too many to list, and that is not the purpose of this short discourse. And of course, there has always been the individual outlaws, bad men and women in every culture and society. The lists of these people and threats can also fill volumes. They have been part of every society since the beginning.

In our day and in our society it's the "Terrorists" that threaten mass destruction and harm to us. We cannot bomb them into oblivion because they are among us. All we can do is watch for them, and when we find them, kill them. Without the fear of our armed forces our enemies and the terrorists in the world would be more emboldened to do us harm. Our best defense against these terrorists is make sure they know by our actions that the United States of America will use its might to find and destroy them.

I hope you enjoyed my story. It was meant to entertain and maybe provoke thoughts about a serious subject which affects us in our daily lives, whether we choose to think about it or not.

About the Author

kip Della Maggiore grew up on a pig ranch in the city of Santa Clara, California. Now, that ranch is in the center of Silicon Valley. He served twenty-two years in the fire service retiring with the rank of Captain. Skip attended two years at San Jose City College, and West Valley College, with a major in sociology. His second career of twenty years was as CEO of a ceramic tile installation company. He now resides in the city of Gilroy, California. *The 7TH Astronaut* is his first novel and he has also written a screen play for it. His second and third novels are in progress.

Printed in the United States
By Bookmasters